T0090086

We Are Where the Nightmares Go

"Cargill has a gift for haunting imagery as well as exuberant gore, and most of his horror has a beating heart, albeit a bloody one. His fans will be thrilled by this strong collection."

—*Publishers Weekly*

"Keen to get a full, and bad-dream-free, eight hours of sleep tonight? Then we recommend you *don't* start reading *We Are Where the Nightmares Go and Other Stories* . . . [the] aptly-titled collection of horror tales from C. Robert Cargill."

—*Entertainment Weekly*

Sea of Rust

"*Sea of Rust* is a forty-megaton cruise missile of a novel—it'll blow you away and lay waste to your heart. It is the most visceral, relentless, breathtaking work of SF in any medium since *Mad Max: Fury Road*."

—#1 *New York Times* bestselling author Joe Hill

"Cargill . . . effectively takes a grim look at a war-torn future where our nonhuman successors face complex moral dilemmas, exploring what it means to be alive and aware. . . . This action-packed adventure raises thought-provoking and philosophical questions."

—*Publishers Weekly* (starred review)

Queen of the Dark Things

"This is a fantasy about mythmaking, learning the uses of power, and living with the consequences of one's behavior. Recommended for readers of Lev Grossman's Magicians series and Neil Gaiman's adult contemporary fantasies."

—*Library Journal*

"Powerful. . . . Brimming with philosophical conundrums. . . . Cargill's world is abundant in detail and imagery in the service of the story."

—*Publishers Weekly* (starred review)

Dreams and Shadows

"Exceptional worldbuilding, sure-handed plotting and well-rounded characters, even the nasty ones, abound, and the whole impressive enterprise moves smartly along through a fairy culture with a structure and motivations sharply different from that of humans. A mesmerizing and highly original debut."

—*Kirkus Reviews* (starred review)

"Dark, comedic, and unsettling, *Dreams and Shadows* is everything an urban fantasy sets out to be."

—Tor.com

we are where the nightmares go

and other stories

we are where the nightmares go

and other stories

C. ROBERT CARGILL

HARPER Voyager
An Imprint of HarperCollins Publishers

"A Clean White Room" by Scott Derrickson and C. Robert Cargill was originally published in *The Blumhouse Book of Nightmares: The Haunted City*, edited by Jason Blum, published by Doubleday, 2015.

"I Am the Night You Never Speak Of" was originally published in *Midian Unmade: Tales of Clive Barker's Nightbreed*, edited by Joseph Nassise and Del Howison, published by Tor Books, 2015.

HarperCollins books may be purchased for educational, business, or sales promotional use. For information, please email the Special Markets Department at SPsales@harpercollins.com.

Harper Voyager and design are trademarks of HarperCollins Publishers LLC.

A hardcover edition of this book was published in 2018 by Harper Voyager, an imprint of HarperCollins Publishers.

FIRST HARPER VOYAGER PAPERBACK EDITION PUBLISHED 2019.

Designed by Paula Russell Szafranski
Chapter opener line art © IADA / Shutterstock

The Library of Congress has catalogued a previous edition as follows:

Names: Cargill, C. Robert, 1975–author.
Title: We are where the nightmares go : and other stories / C. Robert Cargill.
Description: First edition. | New York, NY : Harper Voyager, [2018]
Identifiers: LCCN 2018006153| ISBN 9780062405869 (Hardcover) | ISBN 9780062405876 (Trade PB) | ISBN 9780062848857 (Audio) | ISBN 9780062848949 (Audio Demand) | ISBN 9780062405883 (E-Book)
Subjects: | BISAC: FICTION / Short Stories (single author). | FICTION / Horror.
Classification: LCC PS3603.A7449 A6 2018 | DDC 813/.6—dc23 LC record available at https://lccn.loc.gov/2018006153

ISBN 978-0-06-240587-6 (pbk.)
HB 08.08.2023

For Jessica,

for all the good dreams between the nightmares.

contents

acknowledgments
······································

This book doesn't entirely feel like a book to me. It is the cul-
mination of several years of quiet nights while I was waiting for
a script to come in, or waiting for a job to start up, or simply
nights I had off in which some story or character was scratching
at the back of my brain, refusing to leave me alone until I put
them on the page. These are ideas I woke up to from dreams or
the small inspirations that arrived after a long walk. But making it from my head to the page is one thing; making it from the
page to a book is another. And once again, like all the books
before it, this came about with the help and support of a number of incredible people to whom I owe debts I feel I can never
truly repay. They are wonderful people, one and all, with whom
I hope, over the years, to find some way to settle our balance.

   Jason Murphy for the scotch, and helping me to find the
courage; Rod Paddock for all the breakfast and support; Peter
Hall for the wisdom; Will Goss for the coffee, corrections, and
keeping me in check. Their early notes all proved invaluable.

   Diana Gill, Simon Spanton, Rachel Winterbottom, and Jen
Brehl for fighting for me and this book, and for helping shape

it into what it has become. Peter McGuigan, a rock star of an agent who once showed me more swagger in two weeks than I've seen out of most people in a lifetime. David Macilvain, the man who brought me Peter, and whose advice always clears the static.

Scott Derrickson, my writing partner, my friend who held the door open for me, and who took me on a series of strange adventures. We also make movies. And, you know, wrote one of these stories together.

Jessica, who loves her writer, whose writer loves her more than breath, and who never, ever, lets me give up. You remain everything.

And for the tireless efforts of Deputy So-and-So of the local police department, without whose research this book wouldn't be possible.

we are
where the
nightmares
go

and
other
stories

The Town That Wasn't Anymore

Wilton Jacobs was a good sheriff. He had to be. Though Pine Hall Bluff was a sleepy, quiet little town, it required a certain amount of finesse to keep straight—a quality Wilton had acquired watching his father, Michael, the previous sheriff, keep the peace. He was an unassuming man, and you wouldn't think much to look at him outside of his uniform—stout, pasty, a weak hairline eroding his widow's peak a little each day. But when he put on that star and hat, you could see it in his eyes—a determination, an unflappability. He never lost his temper, never let anyone get the better of him. And if somehow you did manage to elicit a glare from him, he didn't have to say a goddamned word—his eyes did all the talking. "I'm not moving from this spot," they said. "You are."

Pine Hall Bluff was an old mining town nestled high up in the mountains of West Virginia, surrounded on all sides by trees as far as the eye could see, deep in otherwise undeveloped country that had seen its fair share of tragedy and death. The roads were mostly dirt and gravel, with only a handful of paved ones all meant for hauling ore, each winding around through hills peppered with shacks and cheap mid-century company houses. The local mine had been closed for years—not for lack of coal, but for the death of some 227 miners it had claimed in a collapse that broke the back of the town and sunk Coulson Coal, the company that owned it, into bankruptcy. There were few living in Pine Hall Bluff that didn't have kin down that mine, and fewer still that didn't lose someone in the subsequent chaos.

But that was all a long time ago. Michael had been sheriff then, and Wilton just a deputy still wet behind the ears. Most people up and left after that—said they couldn't abide living in a town cursed like it was—but those that stayed carved out what life they could. The town had started with a population of around 3,500. Now there were only a few dozen souls left.

Wilton sat in his truck at the top of Old Miller's Hill, sucking at the end of a filterless Pall Mall, ashing out the driver-side window, looking down into the valley as the sun crept closer and closer to the edge of the world. Sometimes he daydreamed that the mountains were teeth and one night they might snap shut, the mouth of the world swallowing whole the town, the valley, and all the shit that came with it. But he was never that lucky—the maw of the world gaped wide into the heavens, leaving everything just where it was. Every day the sun rose and the town was still there, a burden his father had left to him; a responsibility he couldn't bear to abandon. It was a town in name only; a smudge on the map that led to nowhere at all. And he was the law—what little that still meant out here.

With each passing moment the sun sank closer to the horizon, and with it Wilton's heart into his stomach. He hated sunset. The days in Pine Hall Bluff were quiet, easy, peaceful. It was the nights that were trouble. They were a different kind of quiet. A nervous quiet. A dead quiet. The kind where even the forest shut up lest it disturb the dead.

The truck's police radio crackled to life, a burst of garbled static like a cough drowning out distant whispers. Wilton picked up the handset, pressed the button. "Go for Jacobs."

There was no response.

He stared at the radio, waiting to see if there was another burst—turning up the volume a bit to see if there was anything behind the low hiss of the open channel.

"Go for Jacobs."

Nothing.

Looked like it was going to be a quiet night.

He stabbed out the butt of his cigarette in the ashtray before turning the key in the ignition. It was time to make the rounds. Twilight was only going to last so long.

FATHER JEREMY PADDOCK HADN'T ALWAYS WANTED TO BE A priest. The son of a North Atlantic fisherman, he spent his youth on trawlers drenched in frozen mist, the cold seeping in so deep it made his bones brittle. But when a longline went the wrong way, taking three fingers of his left hand with it, he was saddled with the choice between working belowdecks in the freezer or finding something else to do with his life. He always told people that at the end of the day he was happy he lost half a hand because it was what brought him to God, that he was the very model of the Lord working in mysterious ways, that as he sat alone in the dark of the night in that hospital staring at half a hand, he started to ask God why and God whispered back. He had a calling and it took tragedy to find it.

But now that he'd stood before his maker, stared him in the eye and saw the breadth of his creation, Father Paddock would much rather have had his hand back.

He stood in the back of the church, lighting candles that flickered weakly against the encroaching dark. Originally meant to be a dual-purpose church serving both Catholic and Protestant services, it was an odd building—very mid-century, with sharp corners, aerodynamic flourishes, and a pulley and chain up front that could swap the crucifix for a standard Christ-less cross. But that pulley hadn't been pulled in years, not since the Lutheran pastor had passed on and, lacking much of a flock anyway, was never replaced. Paddock himself had repeatedly asked for a transfer from his bishop, but every time he did the answer came back: "No, you're needed there."

He needed a sabbatical. He needed a new flock. He needed something other than a church in a dead town with a seven-member congregation, only three of whom ever bothered to attend Mass. Like everyone else, he hated Pine Hall Bluff. He just couldn't leave it.

"Sheriff," he said without looking up. He shuffled to the side, lighting another row of candles.

"Padre," said Wilton standing in the doorway, hat in hand.

"You can come in, you know."

"Doesn't feel right," he said. "What with me not being baptized and all."

"It's a nondenominational church, Wilt. Coulson Coal built it—not the parish, not God. You know that."

"Yeah, but you blessed it and all."

"I can baptize you, you know, if that'll make a difference."

"Yeah, but then I've got to take all them classes. And you don't . . . you don't really hold them anymore."

"I'll make an exception," said the priest, turning around. "You don't need the classes."

"I'm not sure God will be all right with me skipping ahead of the line like that."

"And I'm not sure God cares much about any of that, anyhow. To be honest, I'm beginning to think he doesn't care about much of anything at all."

The sheriff nodded, understanding. "Funny how the same bad thing can flip two people like us in completely different directions. Maybe there's no way to survive something like that without questioning everything."

"And maybe it's just this fucking town," said the priest. "Maybe it just exists to destroy everything it surveys. Maybe it will just hollow us out until we're nothing, like we were the day everyone went down into that mine and never came back up."

"Maybe," said Wilton.

"So how are you feeling about tonight?"

"Pretty good. I feel like it's going to be quiet."

"You sure?"

"I'm sure it feels that way," said the sheriff. "Why? You got a bad feeling or something?"

"Not as such. But I don't have a good feeling about it either."

Wilton sighed. "I'd sure feel a lot better about tonight if we had a consensus."

"A consensus has never really been a sure thing."

"No. I reckon it hasn't."

"Would you like to pray about it?"

Wilton looked around the church, still not having taken a step in past the doorway. "No, I'll say my words in the truck. But, Padre?"

"Yeah?"

"I could really use you believing again. Like, proper believing. You know, just in case."

"Yeah," said Father Paddock, "I'll put in a word with the big man and see what I can do."

"You do that."

JESSE BISH WASN'T IRISH, BUT HE FIGURED THE IRISH WEREN'T AS likely to drink in a Polack bar as the Polish were to drink in a Mick one. By the time he figured out that no one in town actually cared, the name Murphy's had stuck. Not that the bar was particularly Irish. Or particularly anything, for that matter. But it sounded better than Bish's.

Murphy's wasn't so much a bar as it was a gas station that'd had its convenience store gutted and replaced by something that approximated one. There were wobbly lacquer tables scattered about, and the wall behind the bar was nothing more than a series of mismatched glass-fronted mini fridges stuffed full of four different brands of beer—only three of which ever needed to be replenished regularly. Above those ran a shelf holding whiskeys, a handful of vodkas, and a collection of leftover schnapps that no one quite had the stomach to drink. The bar top, though, was finely crafted; hand-built and stained one weekend by a pair of regulars who were tired of drinking at a place less comfortable than their own porches.

The pumps outside still functioned, though they didn't need to be refueled nearly as often as they used to. The credit card readers didn't work anymore, but they didn't need to. Everyone paid by cash these days. Out front between the pumps and the bar was a hand-painted sign reading: GAS UP WHILE YOU WAIT.

People used to find that funny.

There were only two types of people left in Pine Hall Bluff:

landowners who were too poor to move elsewhere, and people who felt there was still a job to do in town. Both types drank at Murphy's.

By the time the sun was setting, Murphy's was almost as hopping as it got on a weeknight. Will Reilly, an old machinist best known for his thick bushy mustache and his fondness for older whiskeys—only fifteen years or older for Will—sat at the bar with his best friend. Stephen Hill, a mullet-coiffed truck driver who still made his home here, was that best friend. And in the corner sat Rocky Martinez, one of four local rent-a-cops hired to look after the several million dollars' worth of mining equipment that had been picked up at auction but had yet to be moved elsewhere. Sometimes Murphy's might see as many as six or even seven people at once. But that was usually Saturdays or sunup after a particularly rough night.

"Wait," said the 'stache. "I still don't get it."

"What's not to get?" asked the mullet.

The 'stache pointed at his glass. "How the hell is this both whiskey and not whiskey? I'm looking at it. It's fucking whiskey."

"Yeah, but for a thing to exist it also has to not exist."

"That doesn't make any sense."

"Sure it does. Look, in order for something to be hot, there must also be cold. In order for something to get wet, there must also be a state we call dry. In order for there to be light, there has to be dark. Everything has an opposite, two states of being—existing and not existing."

"Right."

"And in order for there to be whiskey, there also has to be a state of being that it is not whiskey."

"Yeah," said the 'stache. "But that's whiskey."

"That right there?"

"Yeah."

The mullet grabbed 'stache's shot glass and swallowed the contents whole. He slammed the glass on the countertop in victory, asking loudly, "Then what the fuck is that?"

"An empty glass."

"But is it whiskey?"

"That's not fucking whiskey!"

"Exactly!" he said, pointing at the 'stache.

"But it still exists. It's just in your goddamned belly."

"Being turned into something else," said the mullet. "It won't be whiskey for long. It no longer exists. But it did. So was it whiskey?"

"It *was*."

"But it won't be soon?"

"No."

"So it can be both," said the mullet. "It just matters at what point in time you're viewing it."

"This is seriously the shit you listen to in your truck?" asked the 'stache.

"Sure. Those hauls are long and there's only so many audiobooks. I mean, once you've gotten through all the Koontz and the King, what's left but the Jean-Paul Sartre?"

"Wasn't he the one who said God was dead?"

"Naw," said the rent-a-cop. "That was Nietzsche. He was the German who died of syphilis. Sartre was the Frenchman who turned down the Nobel Prize."

The bartender, the 'stache, and the mullet all turned to look at the rent-a-cop.

"What?" asked the rent-a-cop. "He's the only one who can listen to audiobooks?"

The door opened, jangling, interrupting the conversation. The sheriff strode in, hat in hand.

"Sheriff," said everyone.

"Everyone," said the sheriff. "He in yet?"

"Nope," said the bartender. "Not yet."

"It's a little late in the day, don't you think?"

"He didn't get a lot of sleep last night on account of last week. It's been pretty rough on him. Can I get you a drink?"

"Soda with lime."

"How much vodka?"

"I'm on duty."

"So only one shot, then?"

"Yeah," said Wilton. "I reckon just the one." He sat down at the last open stool at the bar. "So what are we talking about tonight?"

Will Reilly chewed on his mustache for a moment before pointing at his empty glass. "How this is supposed to be whiskey."

The sheriff peered over. "That doesn't look like whiskey."

"That's what *I'm* saying!"

"We're talking Sartre," said the mullet.

"Oh," said the sheriff. "Then it's both."

"Goddamnit!" said the 'stache, banging his head on the counter.

"You know what Sartre said Hell was, right?" asked the sheriff.

"What?" asked the 'stache.

"Other people."

The bartender paused for a moment, drinking in that thought.

"Maybe that crotchety old Frenchman was right," said the rent-a-cop.

The door tinkled, opening again. Everyone turned. Jason Manning, the town drunk, staggered in, scratching at a fresh bandage on his arm. He hadn't showered in days and you could smell yesterday's alcohol sweating out through his skin. The sheriff sipped his drink and nodded at him.

"You need a seat?" the sheriff asked.

"Nah. I'll take a table," said Jason.

"You been drinking?"

"Is that some kind of joke?"

"Do you think I'm joking?"

"I don't want to assume."

"Have you been drinking?" asked the sheriff again.

"What do you think?" answered the drunk.

"Could you use another?"

"What kind of question is that?"

"A polite one."

"Then yes. Of course I could use a drink."

"Set this man up," said the sheriff.

The bartender looked out the window into the darkening street. "You sure?"

"He deserves it. And I've got a good feeling about tonight."

"A good feeling? Or no bad feelings?"

"I'm optimistic."

"All right," said the bartender. "But I'm pouring 'em slow."

"You do that." The sheriff swallowed his drink in a single gulp, stood up, and secured his hat squarely on his head. He was all business again. "All right, I'll be at the station if anybody needs me."

WILTON SAT OUTSIDE THE BAR IN HIS TRUCK, SMOKING A CIGA-rette with the window down, watching the stars slowly poke through the black. Static screamed at him over his police radio—

garbled gibberish, angry and disaffected, if even only for a second. He picked up the handset.

"Go for Jacobs."

Nothing.

"Dad? Is that you?" he asked.

DEPUTY MILO MANNING MANNED THE DESK AT THE SILENT STAtion house. While he'd never been the brightest or the best of the old guard, he was the only remaining deputy the force had left, making him both now. He meant well, and the fact that he still manned his post, day in, day out, without a real day off, meant the world to Wilton. And Wilton meant the world to Milo.

The phone on his desk was thick, black, and heavy. It was an old phone, ancient really, the kind the phone company used to rent to you before they would let you buy your own—the receiver having enough heft to club a man unconscious. When it rang, it had a deep, wounding clang that tapered off into a chiming whimper at the end. Milo rarely let it get to a second ring. Tonight it was ringing off the hook.

"Sheriff's station. Deputy Manning."

The line crackled and popped like a fireplace, an almost imperceptible whisper clawing at the light static of the line.

"Hello?"

No answer. Milo hung up.

Wilton walked in, hung his hat on the limping, three-toed hat rack. "Milo."

"Sheriff."

"Any calls?"

"Just the usual this time of night. Awful lot, though."

Wilton sighed. "Well, the radio's quiet. Let's hope it's just the phone tonight."

The phone rang again, Milo snatching it immediately out of its cradle. "Sheriff's station. Deputy Manning." The static wobbled a bit, oscillating behind the pops and crackles. "Hello?"

Milo set the phone back down into the cradle.

"How is everybody doing tonight?" he asked.

"Welp," said Wilton, "your brother's a bit drunk already."

"He hasn't been sleeping. Not since last week."

"I heard. What's his temperament been like?"

"Cranky. Someone said something to him last week that stuck with him. I see him pacing around the yard, waving his fist in the air."

"Is it—"

"Nah. It's just a thing he does when he's arguing with himself. He kinda tells whoever he's pissed at all the things he wishes to tell them so he doesn't actually have to tell them. You know?"

"Yeah," said Wilton, "I figure I do."

The station radio crackled, squealing a long, wicked note that sounded like a scream passed through two tin cans and a piece of string. Wilton and Milo looked up at the nearly antique radio setup, then back at each other.

They threw their fists down in quick succession. One, two, three! On the third beat Wilton stuck out two fingers; Milo stuck out three. *Odds.* Milo hung his head and sighed before standing, resigned, and walking over to the radio. He pushed down the call button.

"Sheriff's station. Deputy Manning."

The static thrummed for a moment. Crackles. Pops. A tiny whistle of squelch.

"MANNING!" screamed the angry, garbled static.

"Yes," said Milo. "This is Deputy Manning."

JESSE KEPT A COT IN THE CORNER BEHIND THE BAR FOR THE nights that Jason tied one on too quickly. Tonight Jason was just tired, and the drink had finally coaxed him into a pleasant drowsiness. On the upside, no one had to deal with Jason's dour fucking grumbling; on the downside, they had to listen to him sleep. Sometimes he talked. Sometimes he said weird shit. But sometimes, sometimes, he just sang. And that was the thing he did that set everyone's teeth on edge.

Jason mumbled from his cot, alcohol practically steaming off his breath, his eyes still closed tight. Everyone in the bar looked up at once as he continued his slurring speech in his sleep, singing a song tunelessly.

"What the hell is that?" asked the bartender.

"Wu-Tang, maybe?" offered the 'stache.

"That ain't Wu-Tang," said the mullet.

"I said maybe," said the 'stache.

"Anytime he says something that sounds like *nigga* you always go to Wu-Tang."

"And sometimes I'm right."

"It's OutKast," said the rent-a-cop from the back of the bar. "'Bombs over Baghdad.'"

"What year was that?" asked the bartender.

"Oh-one or oh-two," said the rent-a-cop. "Can't remember which."

The 'stache pulled out his phone, googling the song. "December, aught-one." He looked up. "Who'd we lose back in aught-one?"

"Geraldine's boy," said the bartender. "But that was before December."

"Be at least oh-two," said the mullet. "No one died in December."

The bartender nodded. "Robbie Witherspoon had his accident down at the mill. That was spring of oh-two, wasn't it?"

"Yeah," said the 'stache. "Mrs. Gillespie had her heart attack."

"She was sixty-four," said the mullet.

"I know that."

"You know many sixty-four-year-old OutKast fans?"

"We're just listing names."

"That's not what we're doin' and you know it."

"Oh, shit," said the bartender, "the Wilkins kid. Had that car wreck in the fall after the football game."

"Oh, yeeeeeeah," said the 'stache, the mullet, and the rent-a-cop all at once.

"It's probably the kid," said the mullet.

"I liked that kid," said the rent-a-cop.

"This is bad, isn't it?" asked the 'stache.

"It's not always bad," said the bartender.

"But it's sometimes bad."

"Yeah, but not always."

"What do you reckon we should do?" asked the mullet.

"Let him sleep," said the bartender. "Maybe it's nothin'."

"But maybe it's somethin'," said the 'stache.

The bartender nodded, plucking another glass from the depths of the dishwater in the sink, and stabbing his ratty white rag into it. "And if it is, we'll know soon enough, won't we? Ain't nothin' to be done unless we get a call."

They all stared at the large black phone in the corner, wondering if at any moment it might scream with that terrible, sonorous ring it had.

Jason stirred awake with a snort, chased from sleep by terrifying dreams. The dreams were getting worse these days, guilt—even guilt he didn't deserve to take upon himself—prying open his eyelids every time he lay down. He looked around at everyone staring at him. "What the hell you assholes looking at?"

They looked at each other.

"What the hell did I say this time?"

"You were singing again," said the 'stache.

"Shit."

HARROD AND ALLISON GORSKI'S TRAILER WAS THE CLOSEST thing Pine Hall Bluff still had to a butcher. If it was meat and it was in town, either it was frozen and brought in by truck or it was hunted and trapped by the Gorskis. Either way, they sold it at the crossroads of the highway and the now-closed road to the mine. You generally never saw them out after nightfall, but sometimes, when they got caught up chasing game or it took longer to clear the traps than they thought it might, they'd find themselves in the woods after sunset, hauling ass home before the stars wheeled all the way into view.

This night, however, they got caught out far later than most. Animals had sprung a lot of traps that day, and if they left them out there too long, bobcats or foxes would set in upon them and steal a hard-earned kill. Harrod had wanted to give up whatever was left to the woods the minute the sun slipped behind the tree line, but Allison wasn't going to miss out on a cent.

Times were getting harder, paychecks thinner, and no one was ever going to buy their house. She wanted to leave, wanted nothing more of these woods. So she let greed get the best of her.

And then night fell.

Harrod was nervous as they approached the trap. The wildlife had already ceased chirping, croaking, or clicking, and the hard chill had begun to set in, mist wafting slowly over sweating earth.

His boots crunched through dead leaves, sunk into soft earth.

A small bit of fog blew over the trap, revealing the chain, the snap, and a single fox leg, gnawed off at the hip.

"Goddamnit," whispered Harrod, slowly unslinging the rifle from his back. "Ally, we got another one."

There was no answer.

"Ally?" He turned around, his wife twenty feet behind him, frozen in place, her eyes burning a hole through him. She quickly cast her gaze over to the side and he saw it as well: a three-legged fox, growling, eyes blazing unnaturally, ready to pounce.

Harrod hefted his gun.

"Whatever you do," said Allison through gritted teeth, "don't kill it."

Harrod nodded silently, leveling the rifle.

The fox stood motionless, waiting for either of them to move, the wound on his hip oozing and raw.

Harrod's finger hovered over the trigger.

The fox darted, leaping at Allison.

Harrod fired.

The fox's head exploded, its limp, headless body tumbling into the brush.

"No!" screamed Allison before stopping, frozen, arm extended, her eyes beginning to glow unnaturally. She turned and looked at Harrod, mouth curled in a snarl, eyes brewing with hate.

"No, no, no, no, no . . ." muttered Harrod, backing away slowly. "No, baby, no."

Allison held her arms out wide, her body levitating six inches off the ground, her head thrust back. She shrieked in angry horror, filling the woods with a cry like an animal being slowly slaughtered. The trees shivered and the ground trembled and the whole of the night seemed to flee at the sound.

Harrod ran. There was no way he was shooting his wife. Not unless he had to. So he ran up the steep hill blindly through woods, praying silently that his wife wasn't following close behind.

THE LARGE BLACK PHONE RANG.

"Sheriff's station. Deputy Manning." Milo cast a stern look over to the sheriff. "Yeah?" He paused. "I'll let him know, thanks." He rested the phone back in its cradle.

"What is it?" asked Wilton.

"Mrs. Chambers. Says there's fog."

"Fog or *fog*?"

"*Fog.*"

"How high?"

"About eight feet, I reckon. Said it was touching the awning of her house."

"Yeah, that's about eight feet." He muttered a few swears under his breath.

"I wouldn't worry too much, Sheriff. Could still be a quiet night."

The phone rang again. Wilton gave Milo a withering glare as if he'd somehow jinxed them both.

"It's probably just one of them," said Milo, picking up the handset. "Sheriff's station. Deputy Manning." There was a long-drawn-out silence as Milo simply nodded, expression darkening. "Right. Well, lock yourself indoors. Don't go near the windows. And we'll be up as soon as we can."

Wilton was already buckling on his holster when Milo hung up. "Who is it?"

"Allison Gorski. She's gone and run off into the woods."

"Is it—"

Milo stood up, pulling a well-worn, stained department jacket from the back of his rickety chair. "Yeah, looks like it. Says it started as a fox, but now it's got Mrs. Gorski."

"Damn it," cursed Wilton. "How many damned times have I told those assholes to clean their traps before sunset?"

"Seven. At least whiles I was around."

Wilton glared again. "I was being rhetorical."

"Sorry, boss."

"Just get the ammo. I'll make the call." He picked up the handset. "And here I had a good feeling about tonight."

Milo turned to walk to the armory, then stopped, turning back around. "Can I be honest with you?" asked Milo.

"Yeah."

"I hate your good feelings."

"They're not always wrong," said Wilton in almost a wilting whimper.

Milo gave a shake of the head, sort of nodding without fully committing.

"Just get the goddamned ammo."

JASON SIPPED AT TWO FINGERS OF BUFFALO TRACE FROM A thick-bottomed glass as he stared mindlessly at his reflection in the dark gas station window, whispers and melodies beginning to creep in through the back of his mind. While he'd sobered up a little during his nap, he was still a little hazy, nursing a buzz that a little more work would bring back up to speed. He thought about throwing back the glass in a single swallow, slamming it down on the bar top, and loudly ordering another, but it was still early yet, and getting good and proper hammered probably wasn't the best idea. But he wanted to. He really, really wanted to.

And then the phone rang.

Everyone else looked up, staring at it ominously. But not Jason; Jason took another sip and set the glass down on the counter.

The phone was large, old, heavy, and black, its plastic scuffed, chipped in places, exactly like the model at the police station, but its ring was even deeper, more sonorous, lasted a little longer, as if the clanger was pissed off at the world and wanted to wake it, screaming with each strike of the bell. Everyone knew what it meant; after all, it only ever rang for one reason.

Jesse picked up the phone. "Murphy's," he said, just in case. "Yup." Then he hung up the phone, walked over to Jason, and gently pushed his whiskey out from in front of him. Jason looked up, eyes bitter.

"I was drinking that."

"I reckon you were," said Jesse. "I'll make you some coffee."

"What is it?" asked the 'stache.

"Anyone in trouble?" asked the mullet.

"It's always someone in trouble," said the rent-a-cop. "They don't call Jason for any other reason."

"A man can hope," said the 'stache.

"Not in Pine Hall Bluff, he can't. Hope died down in that mine with all the rest of them."

"PADRE?" CALLED WILTON INTO THE CANDLELIT DARK FROM the doorway of the church. He stood there, hat in hand, refusing once more to step in any farther.

The priest slunk out from his darkened rectory, shirt untucked, clerical collar undone and splayed out at the neck like a bone sticking out of his throat. His eyes were weary, full of dread at the sight of the sheriff. He shook his head, broken. "What happened to that good feeling of yours?"

"It was only a feeling. I'm told they're not so reliable."

"Wilt, how much longer you think we can keep this up?"

"As long as we have to. Or as long as we can. Whichever comes first."

"I can't do it. Not tonight. Not again."

"You can do it."

"I'm tired, Wilt. I know you've got to stick around and play sheriff, for whatever reasons—"

"I'm not playing anything," said Wilton sternly, his eyes squinting in his patented glare.

"Wilt, you were never elected. You inherited the job, and nobody questioned it because everyone else left. Being the last man standing is admirable and all, but there comes a time when you have to admit that this isn't your fight."

"Padre—"

"For the love of God, stop it with the padre. My name is Jeremy."

"You're a man of the cloth, Padre."

"For the time being."

"Well, I ain't calling you Jeremy."

"I'm a man, not a job."

"No one in Pine Hall Bluff is anything but their job anymore. That's kinda the point of the place. It's what we've become."

Father Paddock walked forward, nodding gently, and sat down in a pew. "You know," he said, holding up his two-fingered hand, "they call us the fishers of men. But when people say that, they think of the disciples in rowboats, casting nets out into crystal-clear still water on a warm sunny day. They don't think of a small boat in the North Atlantic, being tossed around like a fucking toy, the men inside it being battered and bruised, terrified that the next wave is going to swallow them whole and cast them down into a frozen grave no one will ever find. They don't think about the man who loses half a hand to a stray fishing line, or that his shipmates are so used to such things that they react to it instinctively and expect you to finish up your shift after they stitch you up. They don't think of the men shivering, icicles streaming out of their beards, desperate for just one night in a warm bed, being held by someone who cares about them. No, they think it's all about that fucking rowboat on still fucking waters in the middle of the fucking Mediterranean. They think being a priest comes with all the answers. That we're not men anymore. That we're not normal. That we wear the armor of God against the day-to-day awfulness that tries to kill our spirit." He folded his hands in his lap, staring up at Wilton. "I'm just a man, Wilt. There's no armor left. No magic. Just a man in a boat, scared shitless, waiting for the next wave."

"Fishers of men," said Wilton. "They don't just say that. It's from the book of Matthew. Chapter four, verse nineteen."

The priest looked up, surprised. "Yeah," he said, somewhat enthusiastically. "You've been reading."

"There's only so much of this shit you can see before you have to acknowledge that there's something bigger going on."

"You won't find the answers in there. That book is only questions."

"Well, I have to try."

The priest sat back, sighing. "So how much longer can we keep that up before we crack . . . or go the way of those things?"

"One more night," said Wilton.

"It's always just one more night."

"That's the only way we'll make it. It's the only way any of us will make it." The sheriff sighed. "Look, there's a woman out there with one of those things in her. She's deep in the woods, probably headed back to the breach. She's dangerous, she's alone, and she needs our help. It takes at least three men to save her—the body, the gun, and the holy man. Now the big man might not be right with you at the moment, but you sure as shit are right with him. He still hears your prayers. He still throws those things back where they belong. So I'm only gonna ask you one more time: are you gonna get your goddamned cross and kit, or not?"

The priest nodded. "Yeah. I reckon I'll get my kit."

THE HIGH BEAMS OF THE POLICE CRUISER CUT THROUGH THE night, pancaking in a sea of white against the dense tree line. Fog trickled along the ground, slowly rising, climbing. Soon the entire mountain would be swallowed whole and the things that walked the earth with it would roam, shrieking, howling, looking for something to drag back through the breach. Jason and Milo stood along the side of the road at the top of the hill, staring down into the deep, dark woods beyond the light and the fog.

"You sober yet?" Milo asked of his brother.

"No," said Jason.

"You sober enough?"

"I'm hearing things, if that's what you mean. Not much. But I'm starting to hear them."

"You let me know if—"

"I need a drink," he said, fiddling with the bandage on his arm.

"You'll get everything you want once that sun comes up and that fog burns off. I'll even kill a bottle with you if you like."

"I need one now."

"Don't be an ass," said Milo. "Don't pretend you don't know the drill. You aren't going to impress anyone with that hard-ass routine."

"I'm not being a hard-ass," said Jason.

"No, you're not. You're pretending to be a hard-ass. So quit it."

Jason turned to look at Milo. "I'm scared."

"So am I," said Milo.

"I hate this."

"So do I."

The two stared into the night for a moment, Jason taking repeated, nervous puffs from a cigarette while doing a sort of junkie shuffle along the side of the road. He looked like he needed a fix, but really his stomach was doing a dance against his bladder and he just wanted to ball up a fist and pound the living shit out of something. Milo tried to distract him.

"What do you think Dad would make of all this?" he asked.

"You want me to ask him?"

Milo shot his brother a shocked glace. "You've seen—"

"Of course I've fucking seen him, asshole. Ain't a person who's died in this town that I haven't seen floating across the fog, or worse, screaming down in the breach."

"How is he? I mean, how does he—"

"He's like the rest of them. Dead. Pissed off. Tortured."

"I'm sorry," said Milo. "I didn't mean—"

"They aren't people anymore, Milo. Remember that. They're shades. Shadows of who they were. All that's left of them is their anger, their fear, their hunger. They're just fragments broken off from the whole. Everything else that was them died with them. It's all gone, stripped away, melted off into some ethereal slag, and they're in agony—feeling nothing but pain, and fear and hate. All they want is to take it out on the living. To find a way back into this world and get back whatever it is they lost of themselves. Yeah, Milo, I've seen Dad. And if you saw what he looks like now, you'd piss yourself. He ain't our dad, anymore. In fact, he's nothing like us at all. All that bad stuff, that's all that gets left of us."

"Maybe we have to leave all that stuff behind to move on. Maybe that's just all the stuff you can't take with you to Heaven."

Jason gave his brother a deeply bitter look. "And maybe all that stuff is really all that was there to begin with."

Headlights lit up the road as the sheriff's truck crawled around the sharp turn.

Jason looked out at the swelling fog. He could hear the whispers of the damned creeping up the hill with it. Whimpers. Cries. Growls. Screams. He could feel the pain coming, smell the rot on the wind. There was a breach in the wall of the world out there, swarming with the angry dead who all looked across the divide with jealousy and unquenchable rage. They hated the living world because they missed it and in death felt nothing but longing and pain. There was an afterlife, and it was misery. Nothing but sheer, undeniable misery. And it wanted revenge, not for some past wrong, but for everything that came after.

Jason's stomach tightened. No one else realized it yet, but tonight wasn't like most other nights; this wasn't just a search and rescue followed by another sewing shut of the breach. This was a storm; this was the afterlife coming out swinging. For the first time in a long time, Jason was genuinely worried that they weren't all going to come back. In fact, he wasn't sure any of them were coming back at all.

Wilton stepped out of his truck, pinched the cherry off his cigarette, and flung the butt out into the brush. "He sober?" he asked Milo.

"Sober enough," said his deputy.

"He tell you that?"

"Nah. He's gettin' good and pissy, and is approaching downright mean. He's good."

Jason shot his brother a wicked stare. "Don't play your brother's keeper games with me, asshole."

"Told ya."

The sheriff slid a box of shells out of his pocket, pulling a fistful out and presenting them to Father Paddock. "Padre, you mind blessing the ammo?" he asked.

"I've already blessed these."

"Yeah, but you blessed it all last time, and that was about a week ago. So . . ."

"Blessings don't wear off, Wilt," said the priest through a nasty bit of side-eye.

"Just say the damn words, Padre. I'd feel an awful lot better about all this if you would."

The sheriff held out the handful of bullets, each of them with a cross carved onto the front. Father Paddock pulled an ornate aspergillum out of his pocket and sprinkled the shells with a spritz of holy water, waving his two-fingered hand over them, speaking a mouthful of Latin before mumbling out ". . . in the name of the father, and the son, and the holy spirit. Amen." He looked Wilton square in the eye. "Now try not to kill anyone with those."

"That's the idea, Padre. That's the idea."

TIME AND SPACE ARE DIFFERENT IN THE FOG; THEY JUST DON'T mesh anymore. It rolls in and the night can last for days. Or an hour. The trees can seem both closer together and farther apart at the same time. The corners of your vision warp and bend like a trick lens on a camera. You can hear your own footsteps and you can hear someone talking to you, but you can't hear much of anything else. Not a bird, not an insect, not the rustling of leaves in the wind. Sometimes, in the distance, you can hear the dead, screaming. But that's about it. And you best not wander off alone in it; those that do rarely find their way back or are ever seen again.

The rules of the fog are simple. Tight groups. Always stay in tight groups. Always keep someone else in your line of sight. Always keep your voice low. Never panic. Never run. Just keep moving forward. And if you see one, never, ever let it touch you.

They could be anywhere. Possessing an animal. Possessing a person. Fiddling with a door or window so it bangs angrily over and over again. Sometimes they wander aimlessly; other times they are aggressive with purpose—like they can think, like they have a plan, like they are more than just the disembodied, desperate to feel what it is to be alive again.

Elsewhere, the wall of fog crawled over houses, trickled down hillsides, swallowed mostly abandoned neighborhoods. Houses shook at their foundations; windows clattered open and shut; mirrors fogged up, faces pressing against the glass from the other side, staring out at the world; trees came to life, flailing at the dark; streetlamps flickered on and off; lawn mowers wheeled around yards, engines buzzing, blades tearing to pieces anything they could find; pools of water rippled from footsteps skittering across the surface; shadows crept just outside of the light, dancing madly in the mists. And under beds or in closets or behind couches hid the last few remaining townsfolk of Pine Hall Bluffs, each and every one of them asking themselves why they hadn't just left, wondering whether they would make it through until morning.

It was pea soup as far as twenty feet out as the four men walked through the woods, flashlights lighting up the whole night, each facing another as to both look behind the person and keep them in sight. Milo also clutched a rifle, Wilton a .38, and Father Paddock a cross. Jason didn't carry anything; he simply balled his hands into fists—not to fight, but to release the stress bubbling up in his gut. He could hear the voices, the chittering, the singing, the rambling—all just out of earshot. But there was one voice that shrieked the loudest, and he could hear that one as clear as a bell.

There's no telling how long they walked—even watches and phones lied—but Jason pointed them straight through and they pressed on, never dawdling, never letting themselves get distracted by distant madness. They knew well the woman they were hunting, and they no doubt knew the name of the thing that was inside her—at least the name it'd had when they knew it. But it was best not to think about that. Sometimes they figured out who it was that they were up against; other times their attempts to stay ignorant were rewarded.

All of them had seen friends out here before; none of them liked to see what they'd become. Death was a far crueler thing than they'd ever imagined. They would weep for their friends, and then they would weep for themselves.

Jason heard a dozen different songs out here, the lyrics on repeat, the melodies fractured, the tunes all off-key. He heard one spirit drawing close, rambling the words to "Bombs Over Baghdad," and a chill ran up his spine, his mind putting together the terrible things the spirit had shown him in his sleep. He didn't want to think about it. He shoved all that awfulness to the back of his brain where he kept the hours and hours of bad dreams that didn't belong to him, and he just pressed forward, dreaming of the tall glass of whiskey waiting for him at the end of the night.

The whiskey would do its work; the whiskey would chase the voices away; the whiskey would make everything quiet again;

the whiskey would buy him peace until the next time the fog came, until the next time they had to sew the world shut. *The whiskey. The whiskey. The whiskey.*

He watched as several spirits passed, recognized their faces, their voices. He didn't want to remember them. Not like this.

And then he heard two voices at once coming from the same place. Mrs. Gorski, howling hysterically into the night while the spirit of some poor soul chanted and gibbered and hooted deep inside of her, working her like a marionette with the strings all on the inside.

"There," he said quietly, pointing into the dense fog.

Everyone cast their flashlights ahead of them, beams lighting up a white wall of fog. And there she was, her shadow dancing fifty feet away, through beams, cutting toward them at a frightening clip. The way she moved was unnatural, like her limbs were all on backward, being worked by levers and pulleys.

"Milo," said Wilton softly. "You know what to do."

Milo nodded, swallowing hard as he raised the rifle to his eye, bracing the butt on his shoulder. He had to be careful. He couldn't hit anything vital. At this distance he couldn't exactly be sure where she was. He needed her to clear the fog, get close enough to see her for real.

Of all the things he'd had to do, this was the part that made him the most nervous. That was a real person out there. If he missed, he would be the one that killed her, not the thing inside of her.

Jason reached under his shirt and pulled out two iron chains that were affixed to a girdle under his clothing—a modified straitjacket without the arms—handing a chain each to Wilton and Father Paddock. The men took the chains, nodding silently, everyone waiting for Milo to fire the first shot.

Jason closed his eyes, thinking, *I'm over here. Come to me. Find me. I'm over here.*

He held his breath. He knew that the moment he thought aloud every spirit within miles would be racing to take his body for a spin. He was *sensitive*. And with sensitives, you live again; you could feel again; you could do more than just scream and flail and look at the world through eyes again—you could speak again and tell the world why you hated it and what you wanted to do to it.

Allison Gorski barreled toward them through the fog like a charging rhino.

Milo held his breath to steady the shot.

Wilton and Father Paddock held tight their ends of the iron chains.

The rifle jumped in Milo's hands, the blessed bullet tearing a mound of flesh off the top of Allison's shoulder.

Allison Gorski shrieked as the thing leapt out of her, dropping her body limp on the ground.

It rose up in the air, a luminous shade, wailing in agony, screaming toward Jason, claws out-extending from its elongated fingers—desperate for his body. It was a negative of a man, all of the colors backward, almost indiscernible, but clearly dressed head to toe in mining gear. These were the worst, the angriest, the ones whose death tore open the veil between the living and the dead. All that was left of them was a hatred for what had happened to them, the pain and the loneliness of those who had lain broken and buried for days under all that rock and rubble.

Father Paddock held up his cross, praying under his breath, trying to keep the thing from Milo and Wilton.

Milo dropped the rifle and leapt for Jason, grabbing the third and final chain resting beneath his shirt.

The thing entered Jason and his eyes went black. He writhed

against the chains, lurched into the air, floating a foot above the ground. Milo, Wilton, and Father Paddock all heaved in unison, wrenching him back down toward the ground. He screamed like he was being flayed alive.

Allison sat upright with a shot, stricken with terror. "What the—"

"You were taken, Mrs. Gorski," said Milo.

"Get home now," said Wilton, his voice deep with bass. "Run. Don't stop for anything. And if you see anything moving, just keep running."

"Just keep running," she said.

"Just keep running."

She jumped to her feet and took off in a full sprint, the adrenaline pumping her legs much faster than she ever imagined they could go. Within seconds she had vanished up the hill into the fog.

"The power of Christ compels you," said Father Paddock, clutching his cross in his two-fingered hand, the chain gripped tightly in the other.

"Fuck the Christ!" Jason bellowed in a voice that sounded like it was speaking backward. The words were all in the right order, but they all sounded wrong. They were stretched out, clipped in the wrong places.

"I call upon God the almighty to calm this beast, to soothe it in its—"

"God? There is no God! Only pain! Only death!"

"Those are Satan's words, not yours."

"There is no Satan. Only lies. Only stories for children. Only this!" Jason yanked at the chains, trying to free himself, but each man held fast, slowly walking him down the hill. "What??? Stop it! Let me go!"

"The Lord is waiting for you on the other side," said the priest.

"You were always full of shit, Paddock. You never believed! You were right not to. It was the only thing you were ever right about."

Wilton cast a wary eye at Father Paddock. "Padre, don't listen to it."

"This isn't my first rodeo, Wilt!"

"I know, I'm just—"

"Just walk us down that hill. I really don't like this fucker, whoever he is. Or was."

"Let me go! Let me go! Let me go!"

And with that, the whole forest came alive, tree branches clawing at the men, the earth quivering beneath them, the fog whipping around them in dueling gusts of bitterly cold wind.

"What the hell is going on here?" asked Wilton.

"It's not this thing," said Father Paddock.

"How can you be so sure?"

"I've never seen one do anything like this."

"One, no," said Milo. "A couple dozen, yes."

They all looked at Jason. "He called too many," muttered Father Paddock.

"There were too many out," said Wilton. "Why didn't he tell us there were this many out here?"

Milo tugged on the chain against the fighting spirit. "All due respect, Sheriff, but I fucking hate your good feelings."

"Duly noted, Deputy."

There were so many spirits in the forest that wanted life, and yet they couldn't stand to get close to the priest. His light burned—though you couldn't see it on this side of the world, on the flip side, the dark side, the dead side of the world, he was a blinding beacon that singed the essence of the souls away. So they took to the next best living things—the trees.

The whole forest screamed at once, limbs almost snapping

off trees as they grasped at the men. Each was growing ever more battered and bruised as they inched their way down the hill toward the mine, but each held on to their chain for dear life, knowing that if one of them let his slip, they might all be doomed.

Father Paddock continued to pray under his breath, Milo swore silently to himself, and Wilton just held on, giving the thing in Jason a look that said, "I will not let you go."

The whole night was angry now, yelling, kicking, and screaming—a storm of animus roiling to a froth.

They just had to hold on a little longer.

A large branch swung down at Milo, missing him but connecting with the chain, knocking it clean out of his grip. Milo lunged to pick it up, but the tree swung back, slamming into his chest, knocking him twenty feet back.

"Milo!" shouted Wilton, making sure to keep his grip.

He and Father Paddock immediately redoubled their efforts to keep the chains steady. Already the thing was trying to wriggle away as Milo stumbled to his feet, rubbing his sore chest. Another branch swung at Milo, but this time he ducked before stepping out of the way of its backswing.

Milo sprinted back to grab the chain, positioning himself out of reach of any other trees. He picked it up, pulled it taut, and nodded to everyone else.

Wilton looked down the hill, branches swinging to and fro, the entire forest a chaotic din of creaking wood and snapping branches. "There are too many trees down that way," he said.

"This is a forest. There are nothing but trees," said Father Paddock.

"Yeah," said Milo, pointing across the hillside, "but there's fewer if we go that way and around."

Father Paddock looked down that way. "You mean down by the road?"

"Yeah."

"Well, that's gonna double the time, isn't it?"

"Yeah."

"Shit."

"Yeah."

Milo and Father Paddock looked over at the sheriff, who nodded begrudgingly. Then the three began tugging Jason and the raging thing within him the long way around, making sure not to step within twenty feet of anything living, moving or no.

Time is funny in the fog. If you asked any of those men how long it took to get down to the mine, each one would give you a different answer. For one it was an instant, another all night. There's no telling how long it took or how far they dragged Jason's body through the countryside. But the trees were behind them now, the outraged forest a quarter mile at their backs.

After the collapse that tore a hole in the universe and shat the dead out onto the land, the mine was shut up, chains were laid across all the roads, and equipment was moved away. But Wilton and his men had come back in and set it all right again, moved all the roadblocks, clearing a path through the worksite for the nights when they had to do exactly what they were about to do.

Each man knew this place like the back of his hand. Even now, in the pitch black of a moonless fog-choked night, they knew their way, inching step by step toward the main shack. It was a run-down thing, plywood and corrugated metal consolidating all the wires into one place.

The men gripped tight their chains, wheeling around so Wilton could switch on the power.

The sheriff flipped the switch on the junction box and the whole worksite lit up like a circus. Strings of lights—many of the bulbs shattered or burnt out—blazed to life, and the generator started chugging like the engine of a tractor trailer. The entrance to the mine shaft glowed like a beckoning streetlamp on a pitch-black street—two strings of lights leading in from opposite sides. The three men walked steadily toward it, dragging Jason along by his chains.

"No! No!" it wailed. "Not back in! Not back in!" The thing within Jason snarled and snapped, eyes wide and unblinking, but each man kept up his end of the chain. They'd done this more times than they'd like to count, and this was by far one of the angriest spirits. It grabbed the chain Wilton held, but Wilton didn't budge. It tried to levitate off the ground again, head held high to the heavens, letting out an unearthly howl, but the men just yanked it back down. "Not the pit! Not back in the pit!" it screamed.

But they were unfazed.

The men knew that Hell wasn't down that shaft; they didn't believe in Hell anymore. What was down there was worse. They'd seen it before, faced it before, closed it before, but not a bit of that made them any less scared. There was so much pain down there, so much despair. It was palpable. It pulsed and spat and became physical. Most of the time only Jason could see or hear or feel these things, but down there, anyone could.

No, it wasn't Hell. But it might as well have been.

They dragged Jason onto the massive elevator, once meant to take dozens of miners down at a time, holding the thing dead center. Wilton grabbed the control box with one hand and pressed the large green button. The elevator stuttered to life, descending slowly, groaning, whining, and clanking its way toward the bottom.

"I'll kill him!" yelled the thing inside of Jason. "And then I'll take each of you one by one!" He started punching himself in the face.

"The power of Christ compels you to stop!" shouted Father Paddock.

The thing writhed inside of Jason, losing its grip on him. "No!"

Wilton counted silently to himself. "Just a few more seconds. Just a fewwwww . . . more . . . seconds."

Even the air down here was offended by the living. It didn't want them there. It was oppressive, choking, spiteful. The sounds of tortured souls drifted up from the depths of the mine. The whole place was alive with the dead.

It knew what was coming. Everyone knew what was coming.

The elevator jerked to a stop with a raucous clangor and the men all lurched together at once, dragging the thing down deep into the dug-out passage. It grew colder and colder the deeper they went—unnaturally cold, the sweat on their brows freezing in place, rapidly dusting their faces with frost.

"Last chance!" shouted whatever was in Jason. "Last chance! You don't have to do this part!"

"We can do this part just fine," said Wilton.

"I don't think you can. You're weak! WEAK! Can't do it."

"'Yea, though I walk through the valley of the shadow of death,'" began Father Paddock.

"'Yea, though I walk through the valley of the shadow of death,'" repeated Wilton and Milo.

"'I will fear no evil,'" continued the priest, "'for thou art with me; thy rod and thy staff they comfort me.'"

"'I will fear no evil: for thou art with me; thy rod and thy staff they comfort me,'" the two repeated in unison.

Jason quivered, writhing against the chains harder than before.

"Just keep repeating the prayer," said Father Paddock. "We'll get through thi—"

And then came the worst part.

Down here, close to the breach, the spirits were far more powerful; down here, the darkness choked the light. They were better able to endure the harshness of the priest's aura on the other side of everything. And here, they were able to try to possess the men; to inflict upon them the very worst memories that made up these spirits—the things that made them truly, deeply, profoundly angry at the world.

Father Paddock gripped tight the chain and the entire world slipped away, the color bleeding out, the fog melting. *Trapped. Weight crushing his back. Arm pinched off, turning black. Hungry. So hungry. And thirsty. Parched, throat cracking, stomach convulsing. Alone. So alone. No one returning shouts anymore. The stench of death coming through the rocks. Father Paddock tried to move beneath several hundred tons of rock and soil, but he couldn't budge. "'Yea, though I walk through the valley of the shadow of death,'" he repeated, "'I will fear no evil: for thou art with me; thy rod and thy staff they comfort me.'"*

Wilton stood before his father, his father's belt in his hand. "Is that the belt you choose?" asked his father. "Yes, sir," he replied. Why did he say that? That's not the belt he chose. This wasn't his father. This was Old Man McCreary. But younger. That boy wasn't a kid. It was Sylvester McCreary. This wasn't Wilton's memory at all. "'Yea, though I walk through the valley of the shadow of death,'" he repeated. Old Man McCreary took the belt and Wilton bent over, pulling down his own pants. "This'll teach you to stay out of my liquor cabinet," said the Elder McCreary. "This isn't mine," repeated Wilton, and the thick leather strap beat his bare ass. "This isn't mine. This isn't mine. This isn't . . . 'I will fear no evil: for thou art with me; thy rod and thy staff they comfort me.'"

Milo stood in the center of the house, the wind howling

outside, a loose shutter banging. He took a few steps forward to a cabinet, unlocking it, pulling out a rifle. He recognized the rifle. He'd seen it before. Handled it before. The weight of it felt familiar. Then he walked slowly toward a first-floor bedroom, silently turning the doorknob. "Why was this house so familiar? Why did it—oh, no." He walked into the room, two little boys sleeping on separate beds. "No, no, no." He raised the rifle. BANG! BANGBANG! Three shots, and the two children were gone.

"Mommy!" yelled a girl. "Mommmmmmyyyyy! What was that?"

He could hear the pitter-patter of tiny feet running across the creaky wooden floor.

"Mommy?"

He turned and fired the rifle again.

"No, no, no, no, no, no, no." He'd been here before; was the first on the scene. He knew what this all looked like from the other side of it. Knew what happened next. Milo did not want to see this part.

He crept slowly across the floor, passing the tiny little clump of bloody bedclothes, and sat down in a chair in the center of the room. He was Mrs. Marszalek. This was one week after the mine. After her husband hadn't come back. After the possessed in town ran amok, taking as many of the living back with them as they could. She could live without Adam; couldn't bear to have her children endure another night in which the nightmares walked the earth; couldn't bear living in the city where Hell kept vomiting up the dead. So she did something about it.

He could taste the metal in his mouth. Could feel the smooth wood of the gun as his hand slipped across it to the trigger. "No, No, No. I can't. I just can't. Don't pull the—"

The men snapped out of it. They had reached the end of

the excavation, the farthest point from which any survivors had been dug up. Had the company dug any farther, the whole mine would have come down on them, so beyond the rubble-strewn wall ahead was the resting place of 184 men and women, none of whom would ever see the surface again.

And in front of it was a swirling, indescribable mass of clawed hands tearing at the seams of reality, climbing over one another trying desperately to push out through a pinprick in the fabric of space. The air vibrated, thrumming with malevolence, hundreds of terrified voices howling obscenities.

Milo dropped the chain. Father Paddock and Wilton snapped out of it, chasing the ghosts from the inside of their heads.

"Milo!" shouted Wilton. "Pick up the goddamned chain!"

Milo leaned his head back, held out his arms, and howled as he levitated a foot off the ground.

"Christ!" yelled Wilton.

"We can only exorcise one at a time, Wilt," shouted Father Paddock over the howling and tortured screams of the dead.

"I know!"

"Make the damn call, Wilt!"

"Jason! We start with Jason!"

Wilton pulled out a hunting knife, its blade razor sharp, its hilt a cross, and every inch of it having been submerged in holy water.

"In the name of the Lord God," yelled Father Paddock over the cacophony of the dead, "I command you to leave this body, and go back whence you came, closing the door behind you!"

"No!" shrieked the thing, its black eyes crying tears of blood.

Wilton slashed at Jason's bandaged arm, cutting a razor-thin gash across it.

"Fuck you!" the thing howled as it rocketed out of Jason's body, cast headlong into the breach.

The men both dropped their chains, jumping back from the epicenter of undulating mass.

Father Paddock raised his cross and began the first few syllables of a prayer. Jason reeled, trying to regain his bearings, stumbling away from the mass.

"Milo!" Wilton shouted.

Milo looked down and shook his head. "I'm not going back."

"Yes you are, you bastard!"

"If I go, he goes!"

"That's not the deal." Wilton steadied himself, ready to slash Milo somewhere they could patch up easily enough.

But Milo kept shaking his head. "I go, he goes." Then Milo stuck his hands into his stomach, piercing the skin, and grabbing hold of his rib cage. "I go, he goes!" Then the thing yanked with both hands, tearing the rib cage in two, Milo's chest exploding, organs spilling out.

Milo hit the ground, dead.

Father Paddock rushed forward, sprinkling holy water on the screaming mass of clawed hands and horror. "In the name of the Lord God, shut! This! Door!"

And then the whole world fell quiet.

The earth no longer quivered, the air no longer held an unnatural chill, and the fog was falling and breaking away.

The tear in the veil between the living and the dead had been stitched shut. And what once was four men was now only three. All of whom stared at each other silently, hearts broken.

JESSE STOOD BEHIND THE BAR, POURING DRINKS FOR EVERYONE. A beer for the priest, a double vodka soda with lime for the sheriff, and a tall glass of whiskey for the drunk to drown out the voices. The bar was quiet, a pained vigil for the freshly dead.

Jason tried not to think about what his brother would look like—what he might sound like—the next time he saw him, but he couldn't get it out of his head. The worst part of his brother being gone wasn't that he would never see him again; it was that he would see him constantly, no doubt until the day he died. He drank, and he drank hard, and slowly but surely the voices faded away.

Father Paddock was angry. Angry at himself. Angry at the dead. Angry for not leaving. Angry at the sheriff for dragging him into this time after time after time. But most of all, he was just angry at God for making the whole damned thing. There had to be a reason for it all, something that made everything he'd seen make sense. He wanted to pray that there were answers, pray for guidance, but deep down, he knew God wasn't listening. Not really.

Wilton stared out the window, nursing his drink faster than usual, his thoughts on all those he'd lost. The department was him and him alone now. There were no deputies left. They were gone, all of them. The ones that didn't leave after the first night, he'd gotten killed on nights just like it. He was the law without a force in a town without much left living. He had become sheriff to the dead. He could go at any moment, but where would that leave everyone else?

The priest glanced up from his beer and looked the sheriff dead in the eye. "So is that it?"

"No," said Wilton. "That's not it. Not yet."

"I can't do this anymore."

"That's what you always say."

"How much longer until we're all down there? There's just no point."

"Of course there's a point. What happens when that thing tears open and there's no one here to close it? What happens if it tears open and spills out into the whole world? Someone has to be here. *We* have to be here."

"But how many more times can we do this?" asked the priest.

"One more night," said the sheriff.

"It's always just one more night."

We Are Where the Nightmares Go

Everyone knows the story of the little girl who fell down the rabbit hole and of the children who walked through the wardrobe and of the little girl who was scooped up by the tornado and of the little boy who found the book that never ended and of the little girl who said the right words on the other side of the mirror and of the little girl who unlocked the bricked-up door in the cellar and of the little boy who had such wonderful dreams night after night. But those are the children who came back. No one talks about the other children, the children who walk through basement doors and rabbit holes never to return, or the ones who are never quite the same again once they do. The things that happen to those children are not so magical, not so delightful. Their adventures are not the things of pageant retellings and matinees. Rather, they are the things we try not to think of, the things instead we dream about when we would rather be dreaming of something else.

This is the story of just such a child, a child who awoke to find herself stiff as a board, unable to so much as move a muscle, so stiff in fact that she was able to wriggle her soul free and loose it out into the night. And as that child stepped from her body and onto the floor, she saw the faintest hint of light leaking out from beneath her bed, a light that spilled across the hardwood like errant moonbeams, beckoning her to peer into the dark, past the curtain of cascading bedspread and the clutter of discarded toys. There, as she knelt, she spied a door in the wall beneath the bed frame: a door that had not been there before—just large enough for a small child to squeeze through—a door no adult could fit through, which was fine, as no adult in their right mind would ever believe in such a thing. But this little girl did believe in such things and this little girl was just small enough to fit through it and this little girl could find no reason not to investigate where the light leaking out from the space between the door and the floor was coming from.

The light beyond the door was blinding against the midnight black, but warm, inviting. And as she squeezed her way through the tiny portal, every inch of her body scraping against the wood on its way past, she felt as if she were getting safer, inch by inch. Though the room behind her was her own and she knew it like she knew her own freckles, it was dark and the place beyond the door was bright. She imagined for a moment that when her eyes adjusted she would find herself on some white-sand beach, crystal-blue waters lapping against the shore, palm trees stretching toward the sky, the smell of salt and sea foam on the air.

But when her body was through and her eyes adjusted and the light seemed to dim all on its own, she found that it was hardly that—in fact, it wasn't like that at all. There were no beaches; there was no sun. There was only shadow and moonlight, ruin and terror.

The land was broken, overgrown—thick, ancient, gnarly trees surrounded by scrub and sharp yellow grass. Buildings with shattered windows, towering hospitals next to shut-up factories next to abandoned playgrounds peppered with gravel and disused equipment. The land was a ghost town built by recession and fear, lit only by the full moon and a handful of flickering streetlamps; a tattered city, damned and forgotten.

At once she knew she had stumbled into a place of which she wanted no part, but when she turned to go back through the door, it was gone. It had become nothing but a crumbling brick wall climbing to the heavens, no door or even window in sight. Wherever she was, she was stuck, with no way to go but forward.

Before her was a shattered cobblestone path, dead grass between each stone, weeds sprouting from the cracks. And along the sides ran a chain-link fence, clipped and torn, jagged and rusty. The little girl made her way down that path, eager to find her way home, unsure which way it was. And that's when she saw it.

The Thing on the Other Side of the Door.

At first he looked as if he were none but shadow, like a thing backlit on all sides, but as the light trickled in over his skin, the shape became a form and the form became a face and the face took its place atop arms and legs and a concave chest. It moved like a thing with all the life sucked out, left to dance at the end of a marionette's strings. He was a man without muscle, an atrophied mess of bone and skin withering beneath tatters of rotten soiled cloth. He wore a steel-wool beard beneath lifeless blue eyes, his skin gaunt, dripping over bone, sagging at the joints, ravaged by time but never the sun. His gaze seemed to focus on nothing at all, as if he was staring at something else even when he was looking right at you, his eyes having seen horrors, such horrors—things that could be witnessed but never explained. And behind those eyes the little girl could sense a terrible thing lurking, a thing she could not begin to fathom. It was a hate so foul, an anger so unrelenting, a desire so unquenchable, that it prickled her skin as he drew closer; it was a thing, such an awful thing, that she prayed silently she might never come to understand it.

He smiled through thin pale lips and pristine pearly teeth. "Hello, child," he said. "How is it that you came to be lost?"

When he spoke, he did so through the hiss of an old record, his voice like a recording played on a phonograph with a dirty needle and blown-out speakers. *ChchchchchchchchchchcPOPchch-chchchchchchchchchchchchcHISSSSSSSchchchchchchchPOPchchchch-chchchchchchchchcHISSSSSSS.*

"How do you know that I'm lost?" she asked, her eyes narrow, her hands on her hips.

"Because no one stays here who doesn't have to. You are a child in a land of lost children, wandering aimlessly, looking for a door you have no idea how to find."

"Do you know where the door is?"

"Of course I know where the door is. It's my job to know."

"So which way is the door?"

"It's every way."

"That doesn't make any sense."

"On the contrary, it makes nothing but sense. You just don't know what sense to make of it."

"You're not answering my questions."

"I'm answering everything you ask, but you're asking such terrible questions. Ask better questions, get better answers."

She pointed a stiff arm led by a stiffer finger out into the twilight ahead of her. "Is this the path to the door?" she asked.

"It's a path to the door, yes," he answered.

"Will I find the door at the end?"

"The door is at the end, but there's not only one path to it. Every way you walk is a path, and all of those paths lead to the door. Some of them just take much longer than others. Some of them are more difficult than others. There are some paths so scary, even I never wander them. This is a land of lost children, filled with children who never find the door and those who have lost themselves trying to find it. Odds are you'll end up just like them. I haven't met a child yet who could find their way. But prove me wrong, I dare you. I double-dare you. Come find me and I'll show you the way back home, the way back to the door beneath your bed."

"Why don't you show me where the door is, then?"

"I *just* told you, I am."

"No, you're not. You're *just* being confusing."

"No, you're *just* confused. I told you exactly where the door is. I can't simply lead you there because the door can't be shown; it must be found. You have to find the door, and to find it, you have to pick a direction and then you must walk in that direction until you can't walk anymore. And that's where the door will be. That's where you'll find me. And that's where I'll show you the way home."

And then The Thing on the Other Side of the Door stepped backward, his body melting into the shadows whence he came. For a few seconds, only his blue eyes were left staring out at her from the dark. Then they vanished, winking out, leaving the little girl alone on the cracked cobblestone path.

She walked along the path for what seemed like hours, the twilight hanging over her head but refusing to bear any stars. The whole world was bleak, neither light enough to see nor dark enough to produce a moon. Streetlamps flickered on and off, fading with a buzz as she neared, snapping back on after she passed.

And then, without warning, she saw the clown. He stood there in the road, back to her, staring down the path at nothing in particular.

She ran to him and tugged his sleeve to get his attention. "Excuse me," she said. "I'm lost! Can you help me?"

The clown turned around and smiled through two rows of razor-sharp shark teeth, his makeup caked and flaky, his red nose battered and dirty. His hair was stringy, greasy, matted in places; his clothing stained with dirt and blood. And every few seconds he glitched like the tracking on a videocassette, his entire body going wobbly, bending impossibly, parts of him becoming squiggly moments of static. "How can I help you?" he asked, quite excited to have her attention.

"Where am I?" asked the little girl.

"We are where the nightmares go, the nightmares go, the nightmares go. We are where the nightmares go, but not from where they come."

"What do you mean?"

"What happens when a dream ends? Where does it go?"

"I don't know," said the little girl.

"Well, it has to go somewhere, doesn't it?"

"I guess so."

"A dream is whole only as long as it's dreamt. Once that dream ends, it begins to fade, to get rough around the edges, to erode like a sand castle lapped by the waves. Most dreams fade into nothing, drifting away like wisps of smoke. But some dreams, they last. They take root in the soul and hold strong against the tide. The nightmares that survive, the ones that come from the darkest places of your heart and refuse to fade away, they have to go somewhere. So they end up here, cast out like the trash, dumped where no one knows where to look, in the dark space beneath your bed. Well, we are where the nightmares go.

That's us. That's this place. Right now you're just a dream. Be careful that you don't become a nightmare; otherwise you might never leave."

"Like you?"

"Like me," said the clown, head bobbing comically.

"You're a nightmare?"

"I am."

"Were you always a nightmare?"

"A nightmare isn't how a dream begins, but how it ends. Some of the worst nightmares I've ever known started with the best of intentions, with bright smiles and twinkling eyes. Bluebonnets and picnic baskets. I like to think that I started out that way. But that's not how I ended up. And by the time the dreamer who made me woke up, I was the awful thing you see before you. The thing that would like to eat you now. The thing that can smell how tasty you really are."

"You . . . you want to eat me?" asked the little girl, suddenly very frightened.

"Of course I do. You look delicious. I can't help it. This is how someone dreamed me, so this is how I am."

"You're going to eat me!"

"No, no, no. I won't eat you; I just want to. It can't be helped."

"How do I know you won't eat me?"

"Do you wanna know a secret?"

"Yes," said the little girl warily.

"Nightmares have rules."

"The rules are a secret?"

"Of course they are. Has anyone ever told you the rules to a nightmare before?"

The little girl thought for a moment. "No," she said, "I guess they haven't."

For a few seconds, staticky light flickered across his face

and his body squished into a horizontal line before popping back into shape. He cocked his head to the side as if nothing had happened, and continued. "Rule number one: You can't change the lighting. Flip a switch, it won't come on. Turn on a flashlight, it'll flicker before sputtering off. The light is the light and you best get used to it, because this is all the light there is. Rule number two: A nightmare can hurt you only if you let it. It can scare you only if you let it. It can get you only if you let it. A nightmare can't do anything without your permission."

"So if I don't let you eat me—"

"I can't eat you."

"And that man who was here before?"

"What man?" asked the clown. "There are no men where the nightmares go. Only boys. Only girls. We're all just children here."

"The one with the blue eyes and the bushy beard."

"Oh! You mean The Thing on the Other Side of the Door!"

"I guess."

"Oh, he's not a man at all."

"So The Thing on the Other Side of the Door is just a nightmare?"

"Oh no, he is something else entirely. Something terrifying. I dare not discuss him at all, for if he hears even a whisper about him, he'll do such awful, awful things."

"He told me if I walk in any direction, I'll find the way out."

"He never lies," said the clown. "He just doesn't always tell the truth."

"So the way out isn't in any direction?"

"Oh, it is! But you don't want to go in *any* direction. You want to go in the *best* direction."

"Which direction is that?" asked the little girl, eyes wide and hopeful.

"I don't know," the clown said, flickering.

"So you can't get out of here either?"

"Why would I get out? I belong here. I'm a nightmare, and we are—"

"Where the nightmares go."

"Exactly! So are you picking me?"

"For what?"

"To be your clown."

"My clown?"

"Every child gets a clown."

"Why does every child get a clown?"

"Probably because there are so many of us here. They have to do something with us. So we help the children find their way out."

"Oh yes!" said the little girl. "Please help me find my way out."

The clown smiled wide, all sixty-four of his shark teeth showing at once. "Okay," he said. "But no take-backsies. I'm your clown for good and for all."

"Okay," she said.

"Shake on it?" He spit in his hand and held it out. He flickered in and out.

"Shake on it," she said, spitting in her own hand and shaking his.

She looked down at their hands, disappointed. "I thought there would be a buzzer."

The clown lost his smile, shoulders drooping. "I wasn't dreamed with one."

"Were you dreamed with a name?"

The clown shook his head sadly. "No. Most clowns don't have names."

"Would you like one?"

"Yes!" he said excitedly, flickering.

"I'll trade you."

"For what? Anything. I'll do anything for a name."

"You have to tell me rule number three."

"Oh," he said, "most children don't ask about rule number three. And rule number three is the best rule of all."

"What is it?"

"What's my name?"

"You get the name after the rule."

"No take-backs?"

"No take-backs."

"Rule number three is that you don't have to do any of the boring stuff."

"What does *that* mean?" she asked.

"It means you don't have to walk the whole way. You can just skip to the next interesting bit."

"Skip?"

"It's a dream. We are in a nightmare, and a nightmare doesn't have to make sense and it doesn't have to obey any rules but its own. A nightmare can just happen. So what's my name?"

The little girl thought for a moment, hands on her hips. She looked up. "Siegfried," she said. "You look like a Siegfried."

"Oooh, I like Siegfried," he said. "I like Siegfried a lot."

"What's the fourth rule?"

"There are only three rules."

"Good. So can we skip ahead to the next part?"

"Turn around," he said with a flicker, almost completely winking out as he did.

The little girl turned, and behind her in the distance was a vast amusement park, its rides broken down and still, its lights flickering, dimming in and out. Most of the park was dark, save for a tiny strip of games, filled with kids.

She ran toward the games. "The other kids must know how to get out of here," she said.

Siegfried chased after her. "No, they don't," he said.

"How do you know?"

"Because they're all still here."

The little girl slowed down, then came to a stop. "You mean I might not get out of here?"

"Most children don't."

She looked up at her clown. "They don't?"

"Didn't The Thing on the Other Side of the Door tell you that?"

"Yeah, but I thought he was just trying to scare me."

"I told you, he doesn't lie. He never lies. A lie in a nightmare simply becomes the truth, so a lie is just another way of looking at the dream."

The little girl narrowed her eyes. "I am going to get out of here."

"You'll have to do whatever it takes."

"I can do whatever it takes."

"Whatever it takes is always harder than you think."

"I'm going home. And if I can't lie, then that must be the truth."

"Well, find your way out of here, hotshot."

She looked around. Everything but the games was draped in darkness, all seeming to shout GO AWAY! The little girl pointed to the well-lit arcade alley. "Let's try there first."

As they approached, they could hear carnival barkers hawking their amusements. "Step right up!" they yelled. "Right this way! Strike the bell!" or "Toss a ring onto the milk bottle!" or "Knock down all the cups!" or "Spin the wheel! Win a prize!"

The little girl eyed them all suspiciously. "My daddy says these games are rigged."

"Of course they are," said Siegfried. "That's the point."

"That they're rigged?"

"You have to know the trick to them. Everything's rigged. Once you figure out how, then you can learn how to win. What fun would they be if you just walked up and won them?"

The little girl looked for a carnival game she thought she could win. She didn't like the ring toss, wasn't strong enough to swing a hammer, hated that game with the gophers where they all jumped up at once. But then she saw the shooting gallery. Point and shoot. That seemed easy enough.

A carnival barker clown stood behind a counter that had half a dozen rifles sitting on it. "Step right up," he said, through a thick, well-chewed cigar. "Hit a clown, any clown, and win a prize."

"What's the prize?" she asked.

"A ticket out of the carnival," he said.

"What kind of prize is that?"

"The only prize here worth winning."

She picked up a rifle and stared down the range. Six clowns cowered atop rickety barstools twenty feet away, each shaking and frightened. Their eyes begged her not to shoot them. They were so close they were impossible to miss. "That's it?" she asked. "Just hit a clown?"

"That's it. You get three shots."

She smiled. This was too easy.

The little girl raised the rifle, aimed carefully, then squeezed the trigger. *Bang!* The bullet veered up and hit the roof. The clowns each sighed with relief.

"Wait a second! That's not where I was aiming!"

"Hit a clown, win a prize. Never said the rifles shot straight."

"But that's cheating."

"No. That's the game." The carnival barker clown pulled the gooey cigar out from his mouth and smiled with yellow teeth, blowing several lungsful of smoke into her face.

She furrowed her brow with determination, raised the rifle, aimed really low—well below the clown she wanted to hit—and pulled the trigger.

The clown winced, shivering in fear.

The shot veered to the right, missing all the clowns completely.

"This is rigged!" she yelled.

"Only one more shot," said the clown.

"What happens then?"

"Then you stay here forever. You only get three shots."

"I can't stay here forever!" she cried.

"Then you better hit a clown," he said, smiling.

She thought for a second. The first shot had gone too high. The second shot went high and to the right. She tried to do the math in her head where it would go this time. And then she figured it out.

The little girl raised her rifle and said, "I'm sorry, Siegfried."

Then she turned the rifle on her clown, pressed the muzzle against his arm, and pulled the trigger.

Siegfried jumped and cried out in pain, grabbing his bloody bicep. "Ow! You shot me!"

She looked at the carnival barker clown, who angrily stubbed out his cigar in a cheap tin ashtray. "You said *any* clown."

He tore off a ticket with a sneer and handed it to her, pointing a stern finger at the other end of the game alley. "Way out is that way."

The little girl took the ticket, smiled, and ran off, Siegfried close behind.

"I can't believe you shot me!"

She stopped for a moment, turned to Siegfried, and took him by the hand. "I'm sorry," she said. "I don't want to be trapped here forever."

"Neither do I," he said.

"Do you want to find the way out with me?"

He nodded excitedly. "I've never seen it."

"Well, we'll find it."

And together they ran off to the exit, where she turned in her ticket and was allowed out back onto the path.

The path was dark, a poorly lit street in a bad neighborhood with monsters and angels lurking in every shadow. The little girl peered into the shadows as she passed, but could never quite make anything out.

"What are those things?" she asked.

"Those? Those are the nightmares no one ever sees—the things they know are there but are afraid to see what they look like."

"I want to see them!"

"No you don't," said a frighteningly familiar voice.

From one of the shadows stepped The Thing on the Other Side of the Door, his blue eyes glaring at her. Siegfried hid behind her, shaking.

"Who's this?" asked The Thing on the Other Side of the Door.

"Siegfried," she said.

"You gave it a name?"

"Yes. Everyone deserves a name."

"Everyone, yes. But not every*thing.*"

"Well, Siegfried is helping me find the way out, so he gets a name."

"No he isn't."

"Yes he is."

"You beat the park. Few children ever beat the park. Did you tell her how to beat the park, *Siegfried*?"

"No!" said the clown. "I swear I didn't. I SWEAR!"

"Good. Because if I found out that you had . . ."

"He can't help me?" asked the little girl.

"No, he can help you. He just can't *tell you*."

"What does that mean?" she asked.

"You'll see," he said. "Maybe."

And once again The Thing on the Other Side of the Door disappeared, leaving the little girl and Siegfried alone on the dark street.

"What now?" she asked.

"Now we get to the next part."

"And where is that?"

"Turn around," Siegfried said with a razor-sharp smile.

Before them lay a wide field of towering brown bramble bushes, each with branches twenty feet high and thorns two feet long. The bushes formed a maze and the maze went on seemingly for miles.

"Do we have to go this way?" asked the little girl.

"Of course we do," said Siegfried. "This way is forward, and we always have to go forward."

An eyeless clown sat at a cheap folding card table, atop of which sat a jar of eyeballs and a card that read ADMISSION — 2 EYES. Blood trickled from his empty sockets and he scowled as he heard them approach the bramble maze.

"Admission: two eyes!" he demanded.

"Do I have to give you my eyes?" asked the little girl.

"Of course you do! It's the price of admission! If you want to go into the maze, you have to give me your eyes!"

The little girl took Siegfried by the hand and pulled him out of earshot of the eyeless clown. "I can't give him my eyes," she said. "I won't be able to find my way through the maze."

"Well, you can't get into the maze without giving him your eyes."

She thought for a second. "I can give him yours."

"No," said Siegfried. "I need my eyes."

"*I* need your eyes. Do you want to see the end or not?"

"I won't be able to see it without my eyes."

"Give me your eyes," she said. "We'll dream them back for you later."

"I don't want to."

"Then I'll have to leave you here."

Siegfried looked sadly down at the little girl. He sighed, nodding. "All right." He dug his fingers into his sockets, so far back his fingernails almost scraped against brain, and then he plucked his eyes out in a single painful tug. Blood poured down his cheeks in scarlet rivulets. Blind, he clumsily handed her both his eyes. Then she took him by the hand and they returned to the clown at the card table.

"Here are my eyes," she said.

"Give 'em here," said the eyeless clown, holding out a greedy hand.

The little girl pretended to fumble about, placing both eyes in his palm. He examined them closely with his fingers, then stuck each of them, one by one, into his mouth to make sure they were real. Then he spit them each into the jar and waved the little girl into the maze.

"You may enter," he said.

"How do you get through the maze?" the little girl asked.

"You walk!"

"Yeah, but how do you find your way out?"

"You walk!" he said again.

She thought for a second. "Are there any rules?"

The eyeless clown leaned back in his chair. "No one's thought to ask that before."

"Are there?"

"Yes!"

"What are they?"

"Only you can find your way out. No one can help you. And you're not allowed to break any other rules."

"That's it?" asked the little girl.

"Is that it?" mocked the clown. "That's everything."

"Thank you," she said.

Then he laughed. "Good luck!"

The little girl took hold of Siegfried's sleeve and led him into the bramble maze. Inside, the walls seemed higher, the bushes thicker, the thorns sharper than they appeared from without. The two hadn't walked but a few minutes before seeing a young boy, no older than seven, sitting on the ground, crying, eye sockets empty, hands stained with blood.

"I can't find my way out," he cried. "I can't find my way out!"

The boy's clown sat beside him, as lost and confused as he was.

"Can't your clown show you the way out?" she asked the boy.

"We don't know the way out," said Siegfried.

The boy wailed, but the little girl remembered the rules. *No one can help you.* She put a hand on his shoulder. "I'm sorry," she said. "Just keep going forward. I'm sure you'll find your way out."

"No! Please don't leave me here!" begged the child.

"I have to," said the little girl. "Or else I can't get out of here either."

The little girl pulled Siegfried by his sleeve and they hurried down the corridor of the maze as quickly as they could. It wasn't long before they ran across another eyeless child, sitting in the mud, also crying and lost. This one looked up, hearing them coming. "Is somebody there?" the child asked.

The little girl put a single finger over Siegfried's lips, signaling to him to keep very, very quiet. He smiled, nodding, and together they snuck past the child, the child's clown looking up sadly at them as they passed, but not saying a word.

By the time the little girl and Siegfried ran across and slipped past a third eyeless child, it was clear they were hopelessly lost. They had walked for what felt like hours and the gargantuan brambles seemed to go on forever in every direction.

"How are we supposed to get out of here?" she asked, stamping her foot in the dirt.

"I told you, we don't know," said Siegfried.

The little girl thought for a moment, then pointed a finger at her clown. "Wait a minute," she said. "He said I couldn't break any of the rules."

"That's right," said Siegfried. "You can't."

"But the rules aren't for me."

"Yes they are. They're for everyone."

"No. The rules are that no one can change the light, nothing can hurt me if I don't let it, and I don't have to do the boring parts."

"Right."

"This maze is boring. I want to skip to the end."

Siegfried smiled. "Turn around," he said.

She turned and saw the exit to the maze, quickly making her way out of it, dragging Siegfried along by the hand.

"You got through the maze," said the frightfully familiar voice from out of the shadows.

The little girl turned to face The Thing on the Other Side of the Door. "I'm not afraid of you!" she said.

"Who said you should be afraid of me?"

She turned and pointed to the clown cowering behind her.

The Thing on the Other Side of the Door shook its head. "He's nothing but a nightmare. He has everything to fear because he is made of nothing but. But not you. You still have your eyes."

She smiled wickedly with her hands on her hips. "Yes I do. And I'm going to find the door out."

"We'll see," The Thing said, slowly fading away. "Your clown may not be able to, but you and I shall see."

The little girl looked around and saw nothing but darkness. "Where are we?" she asked.

"I don't know," said Siegfried. "You took my eyes."

"I can't see anything."

"Neither can I!"

No, I mean—" She stopped and listened close. She could hear sloshing water and the rhythmic breaking of waves. "Water!" As she focused, she could delineate between the inky black waves and a velvety starless sky. Then she saw it, a few hundred yards out in the water, a square concrete building rising out of the surf. "Can you swim?" she asked Siegfried.

"Yes, I think so," he said nervously.

"I'll be your eyes," she said. "There's a building out there. We have to get to it."

Siegfried swallowed hard. "Okay," he said. "Anything to get to the end." He knelt down and the little girl climbed onto his back. Then he waded out into the tide and began to swim.

His clothing grew heavy, weighing him down, but he swam hard, struggling to keep his head above water with the extra weight of the little girl on his back. "How much farther?" he asked.

"Not much," she said. "Just keep swimming."

His legs pumped, his arms splashed, and his clothing grew

even heavier. "How much farther?" he asked again, choking on salty seawater.

"Not much," she said again, seeing the lights of the concrete box growing closer by the second.

So he swam harder, giving it everything he had, swallowing mouthful after mouthful of seawater, taking care to keep the little girl above water. "How much farther?" he asked one last time.

"We're almost there. Swim. Swim!"

And Siegfried slipped below the waves.

The little girl let go, pumping her own legs, dogpaddling the last few feet. She reached out, grabbing a ladder at the base of the building, and held on for dear life. She looked out into the water, but saw nothing but black. "Siegfried!" she shouted. "Siegfried?"

There was no answer but the sound of waves slapping against the building.

"Goodbye, Siegfried," she said. "I'd have liked you to see what the end looked like." Then she slowly climbed the ladder, the weight of the water in her clothes like a sack of rocks strapped to her back. She climbed and she climbed and she climbed some more for what seemed like days, until she reached the top of the ladder and found there a metal door, covered in rust.

The little girl turned the handle, pushed open the door, and fell inside.

The Thing on the Other Side of the Door stood in the center of a windowless room, arms behind his back, head cocked, eyes trained on the little girl. "You're here," he said.

"Yes," said the little girl, terrified.

"Where's your clown?"

She looked down at the ground, scuffing her feet. "He didn't . . . he didn't make it."

"You used him to get all the way through, didn't you?"

She nodded, ashamed.

"Good. Good!" He smiled. "Loathsome creatures. He would have eaten you, given the chance." He began to pace around, excited. "I had hopes for you. I really did. I could see it in your eyes. You weren't going to let this place beat you. Some children you can tell right away won't make it. Others I'm not so sure. But you figured it out, didn't you?"

"Why did you bring me here?" she demanded.

"I didn't bring you here," he said. "No one brought you here. You *came* here."

"You tricked me."

"Into what?"

"Into going through the door beneath my bed!"

He shook his head. "On nights when there is no moon and the stars are the only light to see by, a door appears beneath the bed of a child—always a child, one just old enough to still believe in such things, and never beneath the same child twice. That child is roused by a clatter that makes no sound at all and tempted by a light that streams from a crack beneath the door. Only the bravest and most adventurous open the door and crawl through. The rest go back to sleep, think it nothing but a dream, and spend the rest of their lives fearing what might lurk under their bed. You *chose* to go through the door. Just as I did."

"You came through the door?"

"A long time ago, when I was your age."

"But you're old!"

"Very," he said. "It took a long time for another child to make it through. Like I said, I've never seen a child get here. Now I have." He smiled big and broad. "Finally I get to go home."

"We're going home together?"

He laughed. "No. There always has to be someone here to care for the nightmares. They have nowhere else to go. And it has to be someone who understands what they are. They are things to overcome, to be destroyed, to be sacrificed. They're what make us brave; they're what help us face the world. We trap them here so they can't infect the rest of the world. The rest of who we are. That clown wasn't your friend. He didn't want to help you. He used you to try and find his way out, to try and become a dream again. But he would only have gotten worse, would only have terrified other children. He was a nightmare that needed to be relegated to the dustbin of the universe.

"We are where the nightmares go. And where they were meant to stay. Not just anyone can look after them; it has to be someone capable of being as awful as a nightmare, someone unafraid to do terrible things, someone who can dream up such awful challenges to keep those damned clowns stuck in here forever."

"This is about the clowns?" asked the little girl.

"And all the other awfulness you saw. And all the awfulness you haven't yet seen. But you'll have time. There are so many nightmares and only one child a month to pin your hopes on. Maybe you'll get lucky. Maybe one of the first ones will find their way through; maybe they'll figure out what the clowns are for. But look at me. Look at how long it took this time."

"But you said you'd show me the way out!"

"Yes!" he said, shaking his head. "And I did! I told you how to find the door. You were my door. I get to go home now. Through you. And if you want to leave, then you have to find your door."

"But this is the end! You said the door was at the end!"

"Who said this was the end? We are where the nightmares go, and where they go, there is no end."

"So I'm stuck here forever?"

"No. All those children out there are stuck here forever. Their bodies are at home or in institutions, staring into space, no one around them aware of the nightmares they see. You get to leave. Eventually. When the right child shows up."

"What do I do until then?"

The Thing on the Other Side of the Door smiled. "Skip the boring bits. And don't let the clowns out." Then he hugged her, and he began to glow and expand until he popped out of existence. He returned to a body that had lain asleep for longer than he cared to think about.

And the little girl was a little girl no longer.

She had done whatever it took.

She had killed her clown.

She had become a thing worse than a nightmare.

She had become The Thing on the Other Side of the Door.

As They Continue to Fall

Author's note: The following story was written almost twenty years ago and was only ever published briefly online. Proud as I was of it at the time, it would most likely still be languishing on my hard drive along with dozens of others were it not for a young filmmaker named Nikhil Bhagat. As a college student, Nikhil approached me on the website reddit and asked if I would be willing to write a short thesis film for him to direct. As I always try to help out young artists and students when I can, and I had a spare week on my hands and this old story kicking around I was never going to do anything with, I agreed. The result was a short film turned viral video that earned Nikhil his first couple of professional gigs, and I've been asked about it repeatedly ever since.

I've included the story in this collection, warts and all, as a curiosity, for those of you interested in the origins of this small corner of my career.

Although the roof provided a spectacular vantage point from which to experience the breadth and scale of the city—what with its twinkling arrays of indoor lighting and aerial beacons showering a Technicolor wonderland through the midnight black—westerly winds carrying the fetid stench of rotting garbage from the dump just two miles away ensured that no one could mistake the city's beauty as anything but skin deep.

The Walker had, in fact, begun to think of the city quite like a dance-hall lover: alluring, mysterious, and enchanting; that was, until the sun came up and the cruel daylight illuminated every imperfection and dispelled every illusion that the dim lighting and three-martini buzz had ever fostered. It was strange then the night that the Walker found himself in that twenty-four-hour Chapel of Love, a cheap ring on the finger of the city, ready to wed himself to it for richer or poorer, for better or worse, in sickness and in health, till sobriety did they part. The minister had said all of the words correctly and the Walker had carried through the motions just fine, but somewhere deep in his heart he knew that the city had never really meant it. Not a word of it.

And oddly enough, neither had the Walker.

It just so happened that he never found his way out of the haze, and the two had never been properly annulled. This night, however, his wife was quite the belle; she'd put on her best face and stepped out into the evening ready for romance, and perhaps a little spin beneath the night sky.

He, on the other hand, had a rather different agenda; he had, after all, found himself an angel.

And thus he crouched atop the tallest tower on the Lower East Side, cradling in his arms a weathered thirty-aught-six and breathing patiently into the crisp night air. The rank smell of refuse burned unpleasantness into his nostrils, barely masking his own unwashed pungency. His thoughts, for the moment, briefly turned to hygiene. It had been, what, seven, maybe eight days since his last shower? After this kill he was surely off to the YMCA for a long session with a hot shower. There was no doubt about that.

He imagined it for a moment, the scalding hot water across his back, the steam kissing his skin. If only he had a pair of clean clothes to toss on afterward, it would be perfect.

There was a flicker, a brief spark of light as his target lit a cigarette from atop its perch. Sharp features and pristine skin flashed against the flare of a wooden match. And in that instant the Walker could almost make out the shadowy form of its wings. But now all he could spy was the distant floating orange dot that hovered two inches from the invisible face.

The cigarette was a blessing; the laser sight always seemed to tip them off.

The Walker rolled over onto his back and drew a deep lungful of the rancid breath of the stale night. There he lay for a moment, a mound of greasy, tattered rags, a battered wife-beater cowering beneath two ragged button-ups, and a patched-up pair of jeans hidden under crusted, worn-out sweat pants. It was summer, of course, so he'd dressed light. Yet nigh unnoticeable was his limber, athletic frame, worked passionately to a taut musculature and fed upon unheated cans of soup and missionary ham on wheat. He gazed out into the starless city night and huffed nervously in anticipation.

From his front breast pocket he withdrew one copper round, intricately etched with various symbols and designs— mostly warnings and runes, a single ankh drawing attention away from the other, more esoteric carvings. He brought it to his lips and kissed it deeply, a look of true reverence pasted upon his face. He didn't put much faith in the gods, after all, but he knew they would frown upon his actions without the proper ceremonies. Damned if they weren't as fickle as the angels themselves.

For a moment he thought back and felt the kiss once more.

Schoolyard. Fragmented memories of gravel stretching as far as the eye could see; swing sets, slides, and teeter-totters forming a bastard child's lonely megalopolis. Angels perched on the jungle gym. Daemons in the rafters of the equipment shed. Strange faeries shadowing the playing children. A granite and iron city beside a tired brick schoolhouse, three stories monolithic to the young.

They waited for him. Spat curses with wry, mocking grins and cast phantom stones with unseen alacrity. Called him "bones." "Flesh puppet." "Toy." The children on the playground cursed him too, called him "weirdo" and "freak"; made fun of the kid staring off at nothing. But the children's words weren't as creepy as those from the voices out of nowhere. No. The children who beat him black and blue were a blessing; the teachers could see their taunts, occasionally punishing the juvenile offenders who wronged him. At least for a while they did, until he just became known as the troublemaker and the altercations were shrugged off with the best of elementary school indifference.

Every day at recess the otherworldly torturers waited for him. Soon they came to know him by name, or at least by the names the children called him. Oh, how they delighted in his misery; seemed to lap it up with waiting lips, every breath that of anticipation for the coming tears. He cried. A lot, really.

Then the pretty one came, fluttered down with the aura of kindness from Heaven's parting embrace, the clouds separating into two soft banks of velvety pillow plush. She landed before him and smiled the way his mother had before she took to the bottle and beat him as badly as the schoolyard savages. Leaning close, she peered at him with inquisitive eyes.

This was the most beautiful woman he'd ever laid eyes upon, with the curves of the models that splayed out in the pages of his father's magazines and eyes of deep azure like the sky. Her teeth glimmered ivory beneath a quartz veneer, and her hair was flaxen silk, spun upon the looms of some distant dream.

She leaned closer and puckered two delicate lips, a quiet hush to her virtuous kiss. Instinctively he leaned in to return it, his heart thundering like a kettledrum, mouth dry and throat closed taut in mid-swallow. As fearful as he was, a strange rush of adrenaline thumped his foot feverishly upon the gravel below him. His leg spasmed and jerked. For a brief, wonderful second, he found Heaven, pressed between the lips of a tender, resplendent angel.

Then the rock hit him square in the back of his skull. "Look!" one of his classmates shouted. "Freak's kissin' the air!"

"It kiss good, freak?" another quickly followed. "You pretending to kiss your mommy?" Laughter, always the pervasive laughter. Then they beat him. Within an inch of his life. He could have sworn the whole time his angel was laughing the loudest, cackling harshly out of her sweet mouth.

It was his fault. Again. It was always his fault. That made it easier on the teachers and on the principal. Blame the bad kid, the one whose parents won't kick up a fuss.

THE WALKER PULLED THE BULLET AWAY FROM HIS LIPS LIKE A piece of rancorous meat, scowling as he shook the memories from his head. As long ago as it was, the sting of the rock still pained him, and the laughter echoed in his ears.

He sat up ever so slowly, keeping his head low so as not to alert the angel. Angels could sit upon a perch for hours, so there wasn't much worry of his prey flying off before he turned around to tag it—as long as it didn't see him. From his waist pocket he withdrew a small leather pouch and opened it. Dipping his fingers inside he pulled out a pinch of earth, taken from his shelter beneath Quixote Bridge, which he sprinkled over the bullet, whispering, "Walk not in the eyes of man, then fly not out of his sight. Bless this round that it indeed fly true and find its home this night. Not to an angel of god, but of one that's been cast down, lest he continue out into darkness and haunt this sacred town. Amen." Then he kissed the bullet once more before quietly loading it into the chamber of his rifle.

Rolling back over, the Walker took his position, rifle raised, his eye to the lens of the scope. The orange tip of the cigarette, now nearly to the filter, blazed from the shadowy roost like a tower beacon. He focused the crosshairs a foot below the embers and clenched tight the trigger.

The shot sounded very much like the first shots he'd taken, when he first dared strike out against his phantoms. Then he'd held the .45 caliber tight and squeezed off six shots at the taunting cherub. Each bullet should have found the angel's chest, yet they passed through unhindered and instead took out chunks of the plaster in his bedroom. That, of course, was just before his parents threw him out for good, leaving him in the streets for the angels to taunt some more.

This time, however, his aim held true. From the distance he could see the burning remains of the cigarette topple end over end toward the street. There was a brief flutter, as if a thousand pigeons were trying to escape God's wrath, and then a lonely shadow spun out from the darkness, racing the cigarette to the flickering lamplight below.

The angel won with a swift, face-first belly flop into the unforgiving pavement. It made no sound. Not to scream or cry or wail or beg. Not even as it met the sidewalk; just one hollow, silent fall into eternity. And no one wept; not a tear. Not even God.

Angels fell all the time, especially on the more hellish nights when the Walker would see two or three of them cascade down from the heavens, stripped of their status and grace, to wail for hours in the darkness. He had taken to putting these out of their misery as soon as they arrived. It was quite simple, really; they almost always fell to their knees and begged for hours before giving up, never paying attention to who might be standing behind them and not yet adept enough to know the sound of a rifle chambering a round.

One less child tormented. That was his motto; and he spoke it quietly on hushed breath the moment he saw the angel bite the pavement. It was part of his ritual. But not the end.

With a flurry of movement, the Walker was up and wrapping his rifle in the blanket he'd lain upon, crouching as he scrambled across the rooftop to the staircase back down. With his rifle concealed beneath the blanket, he secured it to his back in a makeshift leather and twine holster before quietly tiptoeing through the door and back down the steps to the street.

This always seemed to be the longest, most torturous part. He'd had angels who'd survived before, who waited patiently below to strike. He never showed any pity for those wounded creatures, but beat them mercilessly until the job was done.

The street teemed with shadows, as if they were watching him, a lynching party ready to feast on human flesh, to gorge themselves on a hunter's pride. The Walker steadied himself, feeling the reassuring heft of the sacred dagger he kept strapped to the back of his leg. He rounded the corner to find the body twisted up in itself, a postmodern sculpture of flesh and ink-black fluids, no breath on its lips, no life in its eyes. He nodded to himself in grim satisfaction. This was a good, clean kill.

There it lay peacefully, draped in dirtied white robes, a small black bloodstain in the center of its back and its hair pinned into a roguish ponytail. Its skin was fragile porcelain, delicate and spider-webbed with bluish cracks just beneath the surface. The angel's lifeless eyes peered into the dark abyss, wondering why his Lord had forsaken him.

Eager to finish the ritual, the Walker leapt upon the back of the corpse, placing his heavy black boot upon the small of its back and grabbing firm in each hand a large, feathery wing. He cried out, pulling as hard as he could, the sound of slowly tearing flesh whispering before there came the powerful snap of bone and rip of tendons. The Walker raised the wings in victory, a black blood oozing down the feathers toward his hands as he offered them up into the light of the streetlamp.

In that moment of triumph, the Walker knew for certain that God was watching.

Then he cast the wings aside, flinging them in opposite directions. In his right hand he still held a single plucked feather, the edges ratty and tattered. He smiled, slid it carefully into his jacket, and walked slowly north along the street, leaving the corpse to dissolve into a milky black muck from which the morning pigeons would feed.

There was a quiet peace to the night, and his lover, the city, spun lazily beneath the orange haze of a pollution-shrouded sky, holding him in her cold arms once more. The traffic was light and he knew that the sun would soon peek over the horizon to once again illuminate his wife's glaring imperfections. But there was no sadness, no regret in his long walk home. He had triumphed once more for the sake of the children, for childhood, for his childhood. One by one he would rid the night of its monsters. This purging had become his destiny, his life's work, and there was no sorrow in that. Only the satisfaction of a job well done.

Then, a few blocks beyond the kill, came the familiar flutter of a host of mighty angels' wings, beating in anger against the crosswinds of the skyscrapers. The Walker looked up with little trepidation, smiling a cynical, confident grin. The angels cried out in despondent voices of ire, thick bass to their tone and sharp wit to their words, but the Walker only shook his head and turned to meet them, not a trace of fear looming in his bloodshot eyes. "Not tonight, boys," he said with a hint of arrogance. Then he flung open his coat to reveal a plush white lining—hundreds, maybe thousands of feathers neatly tucked together into a velvet bosom within the jacket. "My coat's warm enough. But don't fret, your time will come. There are millions of children that need saving. Millions."

And if ever those angels felt fear it was at that moment, before with distant looks of apprehension, they stormed off back into the night, weeping bitter tears for their fallen brother. "Fucking angels," he muttered to himself as he tied his coat back in place.

Then he continued his long slow trek back to his quiet little box beneath Quixote Bridge to sleep off another day's dreams, waiting once more to make love to his city at night and keep safe another child's dreams from the silent tyranny of fallen angels.

Hell Creek

Sixty-five million years ago the creeping death came like ghosts in the night sky. Comets like stars with smears for tails. Thousands of them appearing all at once, the spirits of some ancient brontosaurus herd migrating from one side of the sky to the other. For weeks they loomed, every night growing ever larger, the smears swelling into brushstrokes, the brushstrokes swelling into rivers, until at last they arrived. And when the creeping death came down to earth, it came with the fire and the fury and the thunder and the anger and the might and the wind and the lightning and the rumble and the roar of a hundred thousand storms at once. The spirits were angry. They streaked down, their tails glowing as bright as the sun, growing puffy and black and as long as the sky itself. And when they slammed headlong into the sea, they glowed brighter still, raining hell from the other side of the world.

Chaos. The whole world fell into chaos. Heat blasted the

land, so that beasts boiled inside their skins. Dust storms rent flesh from bones. Molten rock pelted down from the heavens. The earth shook so violently that every upright living thing was knocked clean on its side. Tsunamis three hundred meters high carved new mountains, then dragged millions of limp, broken creatures back out to sea. But that wasn't the worst of it. That was just the announcement, the preamble, a brutal wiping out of generations before settling in to wipe out the rest.

Shards of a forgotten world—long since spun out of its orbit, frozen and fractured—slammed into the ocean, vaporizing instantly, with millions of tons of water, vast eruptions of steam thrust into the atmosphere, the sea boiling, belching out a million tons of angry hate. While the days that followed were a nightmare only a handful of beasts would survive, it would be neither the heat nor the fire nor the stone nor the quakes nor the poison gas nor the volcanic eruptions that would ultimately do them in. It would be something far, far worse. Because once the earth had settled and the seas receded and the skies stopped spewing fire, the rains came. And those rains brought with them the end of the world. *The creeping death.*

TRICERATOPS WAS HUNGRY. STARVING. BUT SHE DARED NOT leave the safety of her cave. Not yet. She could still hear the crackling of the searing forest fires burning away acres of food just outside. The air was cooler in here, fresher in here. And she wouldn't be burned alive. Not like the others. She tried not to think about them. Her herd had been small but kind, and she didn't want to think about how she last saw them, their eyes wide, their legs scrambling for footing before the side of the hill shifted, sending them plummeting down into the fires below.

The sound of their screams still lingered in her thoughts. They deserved better than that.

She'd seen quetzalcoatlus—the giant pterodactyl scavengers of the sky—fall from the air, flailing their charred black wings pockmarked by burning debris. Their shrill screams were mighty, but at least they died instantly, splattering against the ground. They weren't roasted, writhing, begging her to help them up. That was the truly awful part.

At first the thunder was far off, sporadic rumbles trailing into the cave. But the sound grew. The tremors sharpened. The bellows deepened. And it was clear that this wasn't a storm of the earth, but an even more terrible one of the sky.

By the time the rains reached the cave, the thunder shook its walls, reverberated through the ground, blasted and cracked with a tumultuous echo. It had never rained so hard in all her life. The skies were scrubbing clean the earth of all the hate that had preceded it. It wanted to wash away the fires, smooth out the hillsides, fill in the rough new gaps with rivers and ponds. The sound was deafening, the rain's abrasive static almost as loud as its thunder. Water pooled at the base of the upward slope into the yawning maw of the cave, growing at a rate that worried Triceratops, who feared she might soon become trapped in its narrow throat.

She poked her head down the passage, out toward the light, sniffing. Nothing coming. She shuffled closer, nearing the opening. It was dark out. Not night dark, but darker than she'd ever seen a storm. The clouds above swelled black and pendulous, the rain so thick it softened into a fog and she could see little past the mouth of the cave.

There was only one thing of which she could be certain—the fires were out.

Now she waited again, this time for the storm to pass. There was no telling how long it would take. So she settled down, curling into a ball in the far back corner of her shelter, falling into a shallow, troubled, nightmare-ridden sleep.

Horns thrashing, orange and purple flesh broiling a deep black in the smoky pits below—the smell of cooking meat wafting upward. Hollow, shrill screams. Help! Help! Help! *The kinds of cries heard only from unfortunate prey, still breathing, braying, feasted upon by larger beasts.*

Herds walking through fire, millions of them, flesh dripping from their corpses, their bellies hollowed out, carbonized skeletons shambling through smoke. Trees burned like matches, smoldering slowly from the tops down.

Thunder cracked so loud that everything shook, knocking loose dirt and rock from the ceiling, walls. Triceratops shivered, still trembling from the dream, wrestling to sleep against the crisp images that lingered. No sooner had her eyes closed than she was . . .

. . . *once again in the fields, grazing on tall grasses and sweet, minty leaves. Her herd surrounded her, back from the dead, delighting in the fruit and greenery of the wide-open expanse. It was safe here. Could see for a mile out. Nowhere to sneak up from. Always a place to run; several more places to hold your ground, standing with the herd. Safety was a rarity out here, but they'd found it.*

The flash. Brightening the sky, blinding to look at, lighting the whole world like it had emerged from the blackest cave into the noonday sun. Couldn't see anything more than a smudge of green and white, but she could hear the herd flailing and stamping, feel the fear washing over them. A second flash.

Lightning, so close that it lit the inside of the cave. There hadn't been a second flash. It was only the storm, the cave still snarling with the sound of its thunder. The rain still pounded, lightning flickering through the insides of the clouds. It seemed that this would never end.

She listened. And waited.

And then the rain thinned. The static became a staccato; then the staccato became a patter. Soon it stopped entirely, ending with a faint, listless drizzle evaporating into nothing.

The storm had finally rained itself out.

She staggered to the mouth of the cave, dropping her head into the largest puddle, lapping up the fresh rainwater. It was sweet, refreshing. But her stomach groaned, sloshing, empty, aching for something solid.

The rain had chased away the fires, but not the smoky, charred odor of ruin. There was no food on the air. She daydreamed of blossoming trees, their honeyed leaves calling to her, her stomach growling vociferously now, loud enough that other animals, had any been nearby, could hear it.

She took a tender, careful step out of the cave, pawing at the earth a few times to make sure it wasn't too slick to bear her weight. Then another awkward step. Then another. Soon she was completely out of the cave, treading on soft, muddy, but stable ground.

Triceratops made her way down the hill, then moved quickly to the smoldering tree line, the forest so thick with lingering smoke that she couldn't see more than a few lengths in front of her. But she didn't stop, her feet still carrying her forward, pressing on through the forest, her ravenous hunger drawing her ever deeper in search of something to eat.

She walked for nearly a mile before finally arriving at a large, blooming copse of ripe fern trees, their leaves glistening, drooping low with the weight of rainwater. While patches of forest around them had burned, this little thicket remained untouched, a feast that could last her days if nothing else found them.

She bit off the lowest leaf, chewing and swallowing quickly, barely able to savor it. There was little doubt in her mind that this was the greatest meal of her life. Hungrily she attacked the tree, tearing away leaf after leaf until her stomach finally began to relax, her pace becoming more leisurely.

This was a *meal*. Triceratops thought of the others and wished she could share it with them, and it was only then that it really began to sink in that they were gone. She would never see them again. She had no herd. She was alone.

She missed them. She would never again be swarmed by the spring calves, never again huddle in a pile for warmth against a sudden chill, never again bray or prance for the attention of the bulls. Never again . . .

Then another thought tiptoed slowly through the sad ones, creeping in through the back of her mind. She *was* alone; there was no one else to protect her. No one to look out while she ate. No one to call warning. What if something was watching her now? Watching her eat? Waiting to pounce?

She stopped chewing and listened to the forest, her eyes now wide with fear, mouth agape mid-chew.

The earth was silent, dead, devoid of all life. Nothing chirped or hummed or cried or gnawed. Not insects, nor the tiny mammals burrowing below. And after a day of roars and quakes, the quiet seemed all the more eerie and dreamlike. It wasn't supposed to be this way. It was never this way. As Triceratops thought back, she couldn't recall a single minute of silence amid the teeming life of the forest. Even during moments of sheer panic, when beasts several times her size crashed through nearby hills, she could still hear the hot breath of her companions and the flapping wings of quetzalcoatlus taking to the air.

This was different. This was wrong.

And then she heard something. Distant at first. The sound of rustling foliage being crushed underfoot, branches and saplings snapping against lumbering weight.

Then came the scraping of flesh upon earth, the grinding of a dragging limb, and the thump of its overworked sibling. *Draaaaag, THUMP. Draaaaaag, THUMP. Draaaaag, THUMP.* Whatever it was, it was still a ways off, slow, wounded. As long as she kept a safe distance, it couldn't cover that ground fast enough to catch her.

Triceratops sniffed. Death. Something reeked of rot, of boiled insides and meat smoked in bubbling tar. The scent wafted in with the sound, the air now drenched with it. For a moment she wondered if she'd stumbled downwind of her own herd's demise. But there were no corpses, no layers of bodies liquefying in the sopping earth. If something had died here, something else had since dragged it away, but not so long enough ago that its death didn't still linger.

Draaaaaag, THUMP. Draaaaaag, THUMP. Draaaaaag, THUMP.

It was getting closer. She looked around and saw nothing nearby. So cautiously, with as light a step as possible, she shuffled into a patch of bushes, forcing her head through the leaves to peek out the other side.

There it was, emerging through the smoke, thirty yards away, a tyrannosaur, its left leg broken, its reddish-brown side torn apart, gouged out with tremendous bite marks, its insides spilling from the wound, intestines trailing on the ground behind it. Its tail was fractured in three places, twitching and jerking stiffly as it moved, bones protruding in places. His eyes were already glazed over, milky white. It was a mystery how it even managed to stay erect, its leg mangled as it was. This king of the beasts, this mighty monster of its day, would soon fall over dead. In fact, it appeared mere footsteps away from doing so.

And yet nothing deterred its pace; its one good leg thumping forward, its broken limb shuffling bloodily behind. Its wounds were great, but no longer oozed or bled. Stranger still, it did not cry out or wince at its injuries. This tyrannosaur pressed onward, recognizing neither fear nor pain.

Until it stopped. And it sniffed. And its head turned toward Triceratops.

Then it let out a dull moan, half a growl concealed under exhaled breath. And it began to limp once more, this time straight toward her.

Triceratops bolted, her large bony neck frill tearing leaves from their branches as she turned, the forest shuddering as she galloped through it, the *thump, drag, thump, drag, thump, drag* speedily pursuing behind her. She needed to get back to the cave. The entrance was narrow; tight enough to have a fair fight in—perhaps even constrictive enough to keep the giant tyrannosaur out.

But it was a ways off still. She had to run, harder than she ever had, uphill, through the slick mud left behind after the rain. If she was lucky, the beast would die from its wounds long before it reached her.

But it pursued her still, though the sound of thumping and dragging grew weaker with each passing second, drifting behind her as she gained a substantial lead.

There it was. The path up the hill. She galloped faster, giving it her last few ounces of reserve strength, buying her the time she needed to make it up the slope. Then her feet hit the mud of the hill and she slid, slamming face-first into the dirt, her chin digging six inches in.

She scrambled to her feet, but her legs kept pumping, slipping in the mud. For a moment she thought of her herd, losing their footing before falling into the fire. This was how they had died. She would die screaming. Just like them.

Triceratops breathed deep, closing her eyes, tightening her muscles. She took a single measured step, finding her footing, then followed with another. Her feet sank into the mud, giving her just enough traction to continue.

Step. Step. Step.

Deadfall snapped in the forest behind her, leaves rustling, a broken limb and fractured tail dragged limply through them.

Step. Step. Step. She trudged solemnly up the hill, heart racing, sure she was moments away from death. But she couldn't move faster. Any more quickly up the hill and she would lose her footing, belly-sliding back down into the waiting maw of a broken beast.

It was almost on her. And she was but halfway up the hill.

She could hear it.

But she didn't have the time to turn around and look.

Trees splintered, one cracking in half, slapping down in the mud no more than twenty feet beside her.

It was here.

Step. Step. Step.

The beast moaned once more. Its jaw snapped open and shut. The smell of death flooded the air. Triceratops had only seconds left to make it to the top.

She struggled, her legs caked in mud, her muscles rigid and tense, her balance fading.

Just a few. More. Steps.

Then came the wet smack of several tons of tyrannosaur flopping into the mud. Triceratops turned. She couldn't keep herself from looking away any longer. There, several lengths behind her at the base of the hill, flailed the angry, half-dead creature, its jaw snapping futilely, its short, stubby arms clawing in vain to set itself upright. It would never stand again. Its leg was now not only broken but twisted nearly off, the other buried a foot deep in mire.

And yet the thing would not die. It didn't seem to notice its grievous wounds or inability to stand on its own two feet. It knew only hunger and continued to shift its mass back and forth through the muck, never gaining an inch up the hill it didn't immediately cede back.

Triceratops sighed, relieved, turning back toward the hilltop and her steady, methodical climb, ever the more aware that a single slip could mean the end of her. She took another step. And then another. Soon she reached the crest of the hill, where it leveled off and led to the mouth of the cave.

She sniffed. There was something in the air. Something *else*. Looking back over her shoulder, she watched as the upended tyrannosaur writhed on its back, batting at the air. It wasn't going anywhere anytime soon. But now there was another threat. Something was on the hilltop with her.

She gazed at the ground. Fresh tracks. Something not so large as her—but still big enough to be dangerous—had climbed up in her absence and made its way into the cave. Now she suffered a terrible choice.

The hill offered no other way in, up or down. Along its sides were steep stone walls—she would never survive the drop-off. If what had claimed her cave was a threat, she had nowhere to run. Her only choice now was either to face the narrow base of the hill, and the dying tyrannosaur waiting there, or enter the cave, taking her chances.

She stared at the cave's yawning entrance, hoping the interloper might show itself.

It did not.

Cautiously she sniffed the tracks, but the strong smell of wet earth overpowered whatever it left behind.

Then from her right, over the cliffside from the timberland below, came a terrible howl. Another tyrannosaur, upright, angry, and very much unhurt, staring up at her. He too had survived the day unscathed and appeared to be starving.

He gazed up, drooling, teeth bared, trying to figure out how best to scale the hill. From his vantage point he could see neither the path up nor the flopping mess of a cousin lying at its foot. Pacing back and forth, he shifted his weight from one leg to the other in a strange dance, trying to find a way up without losing sight of his prey.

It let out another shrill cry, this one sounding more frustrated than angry.

Triceratops stood her ground, trying her best not to look terrified. If the tyrannosaur sensed her fear, it would only try harder to get to her. But if she could stare it down long enough, the advantage of being on high ground might convince it to find dinner elsewhere.

Then something caught her eye. The rustling of treetops well beyond him, perhaps a hundred yards off. While many of the trees in the forest were redwoods hundreds of feet tall, the canopy of conifers in this section mostly rested below the threshold of the hilltop, and few had been spared the full wrath of the firestorm. She was looking out over miles of black patches, dipping into a valley where the redwoods once thrived and shot into the heavens, their canopy hundreds of feet high. Now most stood like black thorns poking through a choking miasma, smoke still billowing in places.

But something tore beneath it with alarming speed, swaying branches and boughs, skimming just below the surface of the fog, a rippling wake trailing behind.

The tyrannosaur wobbled, swaying with menace, unaware of the threat looming behind him.

Triceratops's heart raced.

Twenty yards out, the tyrannosaur heard it. He perked up, looked around, slowly spinning himself to face whatever was behind him, no longer interested in Triceratops. Rearing up on his hind legs, flicking his tail menacingly, he leaned forward, roaring into the soot and mist.

She'd never been this close to a tyrannosaur before. Not a live one. Not one that wasn't already twisted and broken and waiting to die. Triceratops pissed herself standing there, the roar freezing her in place. If something was to emerge from the mouth of the cave or make its way up the hillside behind her, there was little chance of her noticing it. The tyrannosaur and its mysterious pursuer had her undivided attention.

Trees splintered, branches snapped, and three tyrannosaurs emerged from the trees, the earth trembling with the sound of their stampeding feet. Each was mauled, broken, wounded in their own way, and all three descended upon their lone brethren, caring not a whit that they were in any way related.

The biggest, One Eye, towered a full head over the others, a large, jagged scar running from the top of his crimson head through an empty, gouged-out eye socket—healed over years ago—down to his chin. His claws and teeth were huge, chipped from countless fights, his mouth swimming in nicks and scars from eating things that had still struggled while he chewed. His hide was the color of fresh blood, his talons coal-black, his single milky eye standing out in the dark palette.

The other two, Stump and Cavity, clearly brothers, were smaller, squat and brown, their frames hulking, shoulders broad, making them slightly wider than One Eye despite being nowhere near as tall. Stump was armless, both tiny appendages having been chewed off all the way to the ball joints, while Cavity was covered in small bites, his entire lower abdomen hollowed out, devoured whole by an army of smaller creatures.

They surged forward, eyes dead, mouths wide and snarling.

The lone tyrannosaur managed a single bite on an attacker, his open jaw clamping down on Cavity's neck, his teeth digging in deep before tearing out its throat. It would be his last and only act of defiance, as three powerful jaws rent him to pieces where he stood. His legs hit the ground, but his torso remained aloft, being torn asunder in a tug of war between three desperate mouths, before splattering apart in a shower of gore.

Cavity managed to claim a large chunk of his own, whipping his head back and swallowing the mass whole. But it slid right out the gaping hole in his throat—the wound not bothering him at all—and he turned back to the remaining bits of his prey only to see the piece that had just slipped out, attacking it again as if it were new. It continued this sad ballet, swallowing and losing the hunk of meat before snapping it back up again, whilst One Eye and Stump consumed the remainder of their meal in an orgiastic feast of gushing blood, each of them unaware they were being watched.

The smell hit her. Triceratops breathed in the sour scent of day-old dead. And she began to understand.

She turned around slowly and looked down at the foot of the hill. Mauled and broken though it was, the first tyrannosaur still thrashed in the mud, no farther up the hill than it was when last she looked. These things would not die. They would not succumb to their wounds. And they would not stop coming for her.

She needed to get into that cave before they saw her—no matter what waited for her there. It had no smell of death. Whatever was inside was still alive. And that meant she at least had a chance to kill it.

Triceratops steadied her nerve and strode boldly into the cave, her expression stoic, her head low, horns pointed down to scare anything that might think about coming at her.

Inside the cave it was dark, her immense body blocking most of the light streaming in through the narrow mouth behind her. Whatever was in there would know she was coming. It was dank, shadowy. What had only moments before been a warm comfort now seemed black, cold, terrifying. Slowly she made her way down the passage, creeping with as light a foot as she could.

Then, reaching the opening into the wider cavern, she saw it. A shadow. Smaller than her, but still threatening enough. It was more like a moving mound of bristling darkness than anything else, shuffling against the back wall of the cave. She moved her bulk from the light, letting in just enough to illuminate the silhouette.

It was an ankylosaurus, his tiny triangular head sporting two devil spurs from his temples above its black, whiteless eyes, with two more spurs farther back, jutting from behind the hinge in his jaw. From its neck backward he was armored, covered in a rippling mass of brown bony plates, each terminating in large, dull, tan pyramidal spurs that danced when the creature moved. He waddled as he walked, slow, lumbering, its yellow-brown legs just strong enough to support its own weight. And behind him dragged his tail—also armored as well—ending in a massive white club of bone that could split a skull in two with a single powerful swing.

The ankylosaurus shuffled about, his tail raised up behind him like a scorpion, the bone both broad and menacing, ready to come down. He stamped his feet, snorting, then struck the cave floor twice with his tail. The strikes were fast, almost too fast to see, sand erupting, showering Triceratops.

This beast meant business. But it was an herbivore. Its teeth were as dull as hers, its mouth too small to even get a grip of her flesh. Triceratops knew that this ankylosaurus was every bit as scared as she. So she stepped lightly, pointing her horns at the ceiling. Then she sniffed the air, checking to see if he was alive or dead, more for show than anything else.

Ankylosaurus narrowed his eyes a little, lowering his head, easing back his tail, but keeping it raised at an angle, just in case.

He took a cautious step toward her and sniffed as well.

Then he took another step, smelling deeper and harder this time. They crept slowly toward each other, investigating, each hoping their company was no real threat at all. In the wild, before the thunder and the fire and the rain and the quakes, these beasts wouldn't have given the other a second thought. They'd eat from the same tree, chewing off adjacent leaves and never doing more than shoving the other out of the way. But here, now, things were different. Something had changed.

For a moment, each held out hope.

Then Ankylosaurus stepped back, tossing his head with a snort, padding a little dance with its feet. He quickly shuffled the sand around, dropping onto it, making himself a cozy nest, curling his tail around to touch his nose.

He didn't care about Triceratops being in the cave at all, as long as she left him alone.

Triceratops snorted as well, chuffing under her breath before making her way past him, deeper into the cave to the spot where she'd nested before, leaving Ankylosaurus between her and the cave mouth. She curled up on the floor, her head, and more important, her horns, facing the mouth of the cave. She lay there, eyes trained on the mouth of the cave, waiting.

Waiting.

Waiting.

Eyelids fluttering, consciousness faded so slowly she barely noticed.

THE ROAR WAS A HURRICANE GALE OF ROTTEN, FETID WIND belched out from the maggot-swollen belly of a barely standing beast. Their sanctuary was a secret no more. The passage out had darkened, light trickling in through the few narrow spaces not blocked by the approaching predator. Triceratops had no idea how long she'd been out, but it was clearly long enough for the monsters to have tracked them down. She was groggy, tried to shake the sleep from her head, whipping her snout back and forth.

The beast roared again, its stench beginning to fill the cave.

Ankylosaurus anxiously looked back at Triceratops, his eyes narrow, body trembling, tail swinging combatively back and forth. He had the room to engage the tyrannosaur if he had to, but just barely. Stepping back a few paces, he hunched his body forward, tail raised in the air. Then he nodded toward the far corner of the cave, eyes still trained on her. She knew what he meant.

She skulked quietly to the far side of the cave, a dark corner that put her squarely in line of anything that might emerge from the passage. There she set the charge, her muscles tense, head down, horns pointing at the corridor. Her breathing became fevered, short, tight breaths like whipcracks driving her heartbeat ever faster.

The thing roared again, clearly stuck in the passage, scraping against the rock walls. It howled, but not in pain. Only anger. This was something that knew no pity, felt no fear. It had to be one of the shambling, broken dead. No other creature would push so hard through so narrow a cave, bellowing angrily all the while.

Its head emerged, freeing its bulk from the tight enclosure, its massive fatty body stumbling as its distended stomach was finally pulled through the tunnel and into the cavern. It was Stump, the armless tyrannosaur, or what was left of him. The torturous passage along the rock walls had scraped off layers of his clammy, festering skin. His hide was shredded—an oozing, pus-drenched mess.

Stump staggered farther in, teetering to regain his balance before falling face-first onto the ground. He hit the sand with a titanic *whump,* his jaw shattering against the rock floor. The hit shook loose any connection between his brain and body, and he stared, milky eyed, at the wall, confused. And then he snorted, sniffing the air, smelling the fresh herbivore just meters away, at once coming back to life. Scrambling to his feet, he burst upright. His mangled jaw dangled limply, jagged teeth dripping blood, his exposed muscles now covered in coarse sand.

And he roared again, this time mightier and hungrier than he had roared before.

Ankylosaurus swung his colossal clublike tail, his body swiveling around on four stubby little legs.

The blow struck Stump square in the chest, the sound of splattering meat and splintering bone like a crack of thunder in the tiny, echoing chamber. Stump reeled from the force of the hit, but was otherwise entirely unfazed. Stump took a single, measured step toward Ankylosaurus, ignoring the dented cavity in his chest pooling with blood.

Then he took another. And another.

Ankylosaurus shuffled backward until he could shuffle no more, the bone spurs of his back pressing up against the cave wall, his tail left with just enough room to take one more shallow stroke.

He looked over at Triceratops, eyes pleading.

Triceratops, frozen in fear, stared agape at the monstrosity before her. There it was, flesh peeled away, chest caved in from a terrible blow, arms gnawed completely off, jaw destroyed, and still it hungered, still it stood, still it moved, refusing to give up, lurching toward Ankylosaurus.

There was only one thing left for her to do.

She charged, head down, muscles pushing harder than they ever had.

She slammed into Stump at full speed, horns goring him in the side, picking him up off his feet, battering him into the wall. The creature shattered and spattered between Triceratops and the solid rock. She flicked her head to the side, her horns tearing their way out through the predator's stomach.

Stump groaned, trying to work his legs. He flailed, lashing out at Triceratops with his upper jaw, his lower jaw dangling uselessly.

Triceratops bucked away, taking a dozen steps backward all at once in a terrified shuffle. She'd given it everything she had; she felt like she could have knocked a brontosaurus on its side with that hit. And yet Stump still moved, still snapped, still shambled toward her.

Ankylosaurus brought down his tail with a terrible *thwack,* the bone mallet crushing Stump's skull into powder, following through, driving the tyrannosaur right into the dirt. Brains and bone splashed, spraying the cave.

Stump lay belly down on the earth, its beaten, ravaged body finally still, a crater of pulpy slop where its head used to be.

Triceratops and Ankylosaurus shared a bewildered look of relief, both leaning in to sniff the crater. This thing was dead. And it wasn't getting back up. They shared another look.

The head. You had to aim for the head.

Ankylosaurus approached Triceratops slowly, head down,

tail dragging. He nuzzled her lightly with his head along her gore-spattered neck frill and under her chin. She knew what he meant and nuzzled back—friendly, but not too friendly. They weren't out of danger yet.

Stump's stomach burst, spilling out its half-digested contents— chunks of flesh, bone, teeth, talons, feathers, and the chewed-off heads of smaller dinosaurs—all pasted together in a molten slag oozing out onto the cave floor. The slurry emitted a stench so foul that it blistered the chalk off the cave walls, wilting both Triceratops and Ankylosaurus.

Every instinct told Triceratops that leaving the cave meant certain death, but her eyes watered, her insides heaved, her head swam from the rotten scent. She had to get out. Ankylosaurus had to get out. Together they bolted for the fresh air, no longer caring what waited with it.

Outside, the fresh air was intoxicating. Deliriously fresh. Triceratops and Ankylosaurus cleared their nostrils, breathed in lungsful of clean, clear air. The refreshment was so overwhelming that it took a few seconds for them to register the shuddering earth and the gurgling mess of another monster stampeding straight for them.

Cavity. His festering innards dangled from the gnawed hole in his abdomen, one end of his intestines dragged on the ground behind him. He thundered across the top of the hill, pinwheeling arms clawing at them.

Ankylosaurus reacted without thinking, swinging his mighty tail. But his body skidded in the mud and he missed Cavity's head entirely, instead sweeping his legs right out from under him. The bones in Cavity's legs shattered, and he dropped with a tremendous slap to the fresh wet earth.

Now Triceratops's instincts kicked in. She pounced, throwing all of her body weight into a single head butt. Her horn struck true, sinking right through Cavity's eye socket on into the brain, its force so great that it pierced through the skull on the other side. Cavity seized up, every muscle spasming at once. Then the beast went limp, its struggling limbs flopping to its sides.

Triceratops backed away, easing her horn out of the skull, thick, viscous, gore dripping off it. She'd never killed before. She'd charged; she'd hit things; she'd wounded a handful of predators, convincing them to seek dinner elsewhere. But she'd never killed anything. Never delivered a blow from which a thing couldn't stand back up.

It felt good. Powerful. A great sense of relief overtook her.

This could work. She and Ankylosaurus didn't have to hide from these things or run from them on sight. Sure, that might still be the best idea. But they didn't have to be afraid. Not of the dead. The dead they could kill again; they just had to be careful about it.

Ankylosaurus looked at her proudly. They'd brought it down together. He felt safer now as well. He took a few steps boldly forward, following the trail down into the forest.

Triceratops chuffed, stamping her feet.

Ankylosaurus looked back, his whole body turning to see past his bulky dome of a back.

She stamped her feet again and shook her head back and forth. Then she squatted, creeping low, making her way slowly toward the edge of the slope.

Ankylosaurus squawked, deferring to her. He crept as low as he could as well, sensing her caution, following behind, wondering what she knew was down there.

Triceratops peeked over the hilltop.

Below, still writhing in the mud, was most of a tyrannosaur. Ankylosaurus's eyes went wide, his tiny brain trying to work out a way past this mud-covered heap. He'd seen tyrannosaurs before, but he'd never seen so many in one day. As bad as things were, they were steadily getting worse.

The one-legged tyrannosaur flopped back and forth like a beached fish. Occasionally it would work its one leg into position and would slide up the hill a few feet, but no matter how hard he tried, he couldn't make any headway up the mud-slicked path.

But Triceratops knew there was one remaining standing tyrannosaur out there in the woods—One Eye—and that the light would not be with them much longer. She also knew that there was no way off this hill other than past the mangled wreckage below. For despite its injuries, the one-legged tyrannosaur could still destroy them, given the chance. There was no other choice. It was time to be daring.

Ankylosaurus eyed her curiously, wondering what was on her mind.

She padded back as quietly as she could, stood up, steadying herself, then took a running charge down the trail.

Ankylosaurus scurried out of the way, whimpering, eyes wide, wondering if she'd gone sick or crazy.

Triceratops launched herself into the air over the side of the hill. Pulled her legs in close. Belly-flopped onto the slick downhill slope. Then she roared down the hill at an incredible speed, shifting her mass as she went, horns pointed directly toward the head of the tyrannosaur.

The tyrannosaur looked up, for a moment giving up on its struggle, cocking its head, confused to see a meal running right toward its mouth. It opened wide, hunger getting the best of it.

The horn tore through its skull, popping it like an exploding dandelion, the shower of goo spraying Triceratops head to toe. Her momentum carried her forward, pushing the horn deeper, tearing what remained of the head off the neck, plunging her farther into its rotting chest. The beast's torso erupted, spraying rancid guts down the hillside

Triceratops broke free of the shredded corpse, and came to a rest a few yards away. Stench covered every inch of Triceratops's body. Her nostrils burned, tears flooded her eyes.

Water. She needed water.

Ankylosaurus bounded down the hill as carefully as he could, excited. He'd never seen anything like Triceratops before. She was amazing. Indestructible. A tyrannosaur-killing machine. He'd been very lucky to happen upon her and wasn't letting her go anytime soon. He nuzzled her again with his snout, thanking her.

Triceratops nuzzled back, carefully trying not to smear tyrannosaur goo on him.

She pulled away, sniffing the air, searching for water but smelling nothing but fetid fluids. Casting an inquiring eye at her companion, she bowed her head, as if she were drinking, then sniffed the air again. Ankylosaurus thought for a moment, then turned, walking into the charred woods.

He turned back around to see if she would follow. She hesitated a moment, wondering if he really knew where he was going, then relented, plodding behind him, eyes cautiously scanning for any signs of life. There was nothing. The forest was as dead and quiet as it had been before. No footsteps, no insect hum, no birdsong, no rustle of leaves. Nothing that sounded like the world they had once known.

BY THE TIME THEY REACHED THE LAKE, THE SUN HAD LONG SET and the stars had wheeled out from the darkness. The sky was at war with itself, stars continuing to streak down, some flaring as bright as daylight as they fell. Sometimes as many as half a dozen would fall at the same time. Meanwhile, the long tails of the brontosaurus spirits still hung in the sky—though they were smaller now, dwindling as they wandered away, having lost a handful on their way past.

Across the crystal sheen of the still lake, the mirrored display was twice as amazing. The water was fresh here, though the surrounding forest had been burned away, leaving a charred hellscape peppered with soot, the lake a yawning jaw with smoldering, splintered timber for teeth.

Triceratops dunked her head beneath the surface, but only for a second. She couldn't hold her breath and had to time her dives with each exhale. The water grew pink around her, ichor sliding off her skin. Ankylosaurus drank deep, standing away to avoid the runoff from Triceratops.

They hadn't seen anything else on their way here save for the charred husks of those caught in the fires. Blackened, crisp, they hadn't budged at all. Only the freshly dead, the still corpulent, seemed able to rise and walk. But the two kept their distance anyway.

Ankylosaurus brayed, calling to his herd. He'd lost them as the flaming forest exploded around them. He'd been stranded with his mate on the other side of a raging wall of fire, but she'd been crushed beneath the weight of a falling tree soon after. He hadn't had time to mourn, only to run. Now he needed to find his herd again. So he called. But there was no answer.

He brayed again.

No answer.

He brayed once more.

And the smoldering forest began to chitter.

And it began to rustle. And scuffle. And patter.

Ankylosaurus and Triceratops looked at each other, frightened. *What had he done?* But as they traded glances, Ankylosaurus began to shuffle and stamp, eyes wide, waving his tail defensively in the air. He splashed through the water, running to shore, braying.

Triceratops turned to see ripples of water headed right toward her—something submerged in the shallows, the black eyes and head ridges of an alligatoroid skimming the surface. She jumped with a start, bolting for shore. Behind her the wide jaw of a brachychampsa opened, its razor-sharp teeth glistening, its tail thrashing.

The smoldering forest grew louder with chitters and trills, Ankylosaurus now backing away up the shoreline, terrified of the things coming from both directions. Triceratops made it to shore, tearing after Ankylosaurus in full gallop just as the brachychampsa made landfall, its jaws snapping shut.

Triceratops spun, pressing her mass against Ankylosaurus, standing side by side, her head down, his tail up.

The brachychampsa stopped, staring at them, wondering if they were worth the fight. He stamped a little, flicking his tail menacingly, sizing up their moxie. Alone, it was an even fight; maybe he would eat, maybe he would have his skull crushed. Against them together he wouldn't make it. And these two were standing together.

Ankylosaurus smashed his giant bone club of a tail into the sand twice, positioning himself a bit closer to the brachychampsa, nudging Triceratops slightly behind him. The message was clear. He was not going to let anything near Triceratops.

Best to find a meal elsewhere, thought the brachychampsa.

And then, just as he was turning to return to the water, the forest erupted with a pack of a dozen leptoceratops screaming wild, hungry caws as they charged the brachychampsa. The alligatoroid thrashed, snapping his powerful jaws at the easy meal. Leptoceratops were, after all, herbivores; small enough that he could swallow one whole without terrible effort. But when a dozen beaks meant for tearing plants set upon snapping at his flesh, he recoiled, immediately overtaken, the pain of each bite surprisingly awful.

The beaks dug into his flesh, tearing off small chunks. He snapped his jaw, cleaving one in half, its rancid, sunbaked innards slopping out. These things weren't alive; they tasted dead. He thrashed, casting as many off of him as he could, charging immediately back into the lake, a trail of blood spilling out into the water from his wounds.

But the eleven remaining leptoceratops kept on after him, chasing him into the water, refusing to let up, swarming him from all sides. The fight was a violent, thrashing dance; the brachychampsa clearly losing on all counts.

Triceratops and Ankylosaurus exchanged looks and simultaneously bolted off along the shoreline, headed for the nearest green they could see. They stamped in the damp sand, kicking up a trail as they went. And then behind them the thrashing stopped, and they heard only the rending of flesh and the shrill chitters of the leptoceratops.

Leptoceratops didn't eat meat. And they were small compared to Triceratops and Ankylosaurus. They were essentially giant hundred-pound lizards with parrot heads—they weren't bold enough to attack something their own size, let alone have any reason to. Something had driven them to it.

The whole forest had gone mad, and everything in it. This wasn't the way things were supposed to be. Before the firestorm, there were very specific threats. Once you knew what they were, you and your herd would work together, watch and listen for the signs, and you would be safe. But not now—now it seemed everything was lethal, everything wanted to eat you.

The pair made their way into the green on the farthest edge of the lake, digging themselves deep into the brush, hiding as much of themselves as they could. Together they watched the crimson pool spread across the lake around the leptoceratops. The things ate, well past what could possibly be their fill, then, without warning, stopped all at once. The brachychampsa thrashed to life in the water, tail twitching.

Triceratops and Ankylosaurus watched as the thing that was dead came back again.

And all of a sudden, everything became much, much scarier.

Triceratops and Ankylosaurus stared at each other, jaws unhinged in surprise. If they died, they too would continue to walk; they too might hunger for flesh; they too would be predators.

The spirits that had come from the sky hadn't brought only death with them; they had brought the end of all things.

The two turned together and pawed as silently as they could through the brush, hoping that the brachychampsa and the leptoceratops pack had forgotten about them. Deadly though these things might be, they didn't seem exceptionally bright. Perhaps they only reacted to stimuli and didn't otherwise think at all.

Triceratops was frightened, but felt safer with Ankylosaurus by her side. She had never spent time around one before, but found their behavior, particularly the behavior of this ankylosaurus, to be remarkably familiar. He felt like a member of her own herd; like they'd been keeping each other safe for years rather than hours.

They trudged through the forest together, looking for food, looking for a place to hole up for the night. Occasionally, Ankylosaurus would bray, calling out to his herd, each time Triceratops giving him a pained *keep quiet* look. She was terrified of the things lurking out there, and he clearly hadn't yet learned his lesson. That time they had been lucky; the next time maybe not so much.

Twigs snapped in the distance and both stopped.

There was a patter of feet padding through the muddy woods, stepping on branches, rustling through greenery.

This day, it seemed, was not going to let up, was not going to let them have a moment of rest.

It came from all sides. Whatever this was, it was coordinated. They were being surrounded.

Triceratops peered deep into the forest, trying to make out what was lurking just out of sight. She listened close for the sounds. Whatever they were, they were running, the patter of their feet much faster than the larger, cyclopean beasts. But they weren't small. No, these were decent-sized hunters.

Dakotaraptors.

Pack hunters. On their own a manageable threat; together, murderous devils with hooks for feet that could strip a large sauroid in an hour. They were smaller than Triceratops and had less mass than Ankylosaurus, but that could be made up in numbers of three or four. Triceratops knew this could get really, really bad, really, really quick.

Triceratops spun around, pressing her side against her companion to cover their flank. Ankylosaurus swung his tail high above them, signaling that he was ready to smash anything that got close. As he swayed, tail flicking, she stamped her front foot, horns pointed dead ahead, hind legs crouched and ready to charge.

A dakotaraptor slunk out from behind a tree, mostly feathers and beak, its large brown feathery plume of a tail sticking out almost three times as long as it was tall. Its eyes scanned the two as its head swung back and forth, snakelike and cunning. It clearly didn't know what to make of the mismatched pair, but it also wasn't scared enough to call the whole thing off.

It pranced, its eight terrible razor-sharp claws digging into the earth, trying to distract them. Neither of them was buying it. They knew there were several others out in the forest, waiting, ready to dive in and tear them apart. The dakotaraptor put its tail back, fluffing it up to make it look bigger.

And then it screeched a blood-curdling call, sounding the attack.

Four other dakotaraptors rushed out of the foliage at once, feathers fanned out, slack jaws of dagger teeth wide open to tear their prey apart.

Triceratops reacted, charging full speed at the nearest raptor.

Her horn tore through it like teeth through a leaf, puncturing right through its white-feathered chest, her momentum picking it up off the ground and carrying it thirty meters or so. She slowed down, whipping her head to slam the raptor into a thick tree, scraping the corpse from her horn, letting the bloody feathered lump fall limp to the ground.

Two raptors descended straight upon Ankylosaurus, the first smashed instantly to bloody, broken pulp from above by a single swing of his tail, the second getting in close enough to clamp its fangs down on one of his rock-hard armor plates.

Triceratops wheeled around to charge the one biting Ankylosaurus. She brayed, loud and angry, sounding the charge.

The raptor looked up from its failed bite just as she took her first steps.

Ankylosaurus swung around, batting him to the side. He looked up, saw Triceratops barreling toward him, and hopped quickly out of the way.

The raptor scrambled to its feet, managing to evade the

horns but not the charge—Triceratops's considerable bulk trampled him into the mud, shattering bones, crushing his spine.

The other two raptors stopped mid-charge, suddenly finding their numbers even, but the odds far from it.

Ankylosaurus lashed his tail back and forth angrily into the earth. Triceratops spun around, taking her place beside him, once more rearing back to charge.

On the ground, the trampled raptor whimpered, crying for help, its spine shattered, body bent in half. The other two raptors took careful steps backward.

And then the forest cowered beneath the tumultuous roar of Hell.

Everything stopped.

Everyone listened.

No one dared move a muscle.

The *THUMP, THUMP, THUMP, THUMP* of a tyrannosaurus rex, slowly stomping its way through the woods seemed to come from everywhere at once. But the rhythm of its steps was somehow off. This wasn't a towering predator looking for lunch; it was one of *them*. One of the dead.

Triceratops pissed uncontrollably. She recognized the footfalls. She'd seen this thing before. Even before it emerged through the trees she knew who and what it was.

One Eye was back.

The shambling mess of a beast knocked over trees and trampled bushes, the deep blood red of its scaly skin flashing through the green foliage.

The dakotaraptors backed warily toward Triceratops and Ankylosaurus, forgetting that just a moment before they were trying to make a meal out of these two. There was safety in numbers, and all things were dinner to a T. rex. So terrified was everyone that even Triceratops and Ankylosaurus had forgotten their enmity by the time the four had clustered together in a tight group.

The beast surveyed the scene with its one good eye, then slowly shambled over to the mewling injured raptor. It lowered its monstrous head and snapped up the broken thing in a single bite, swallowing it whole. The T. rex then turned its attention back to the four remaining creatures.

The raptors exchanged glances with each other before trading looks with Triceratops and Ankylosaurus. None of them was quite sure what to do.

Then the lead raptor plumed out its feathers and squawked, stamping its clawed feet in the mud. The other raptor responded by running off, coming around on the other side of the T. rex. The leader looked back at Triceratops and nodded, hoping she understood.

She did.

The other raptor charged One Eye from behind, letting out a long, aggressive squeal. One Eye turned, lumbering around, just as the raptor immediately juked, veering off into the bushes. Then the lead raptor advanced, squawking, digging chunks of earth out of the ground with its taloned feet in a bizarre, distracting dance. Again, One Eye trundled around, tipping slightly off-balance.

Triceratops saw her opening and charged with all her might.

One Eye looked down, jaw widening for a bite.

It was one moment too late.

Triceratops's horns tore through rancid flesh, the blow toppling the monster over onto its side, her momentum carrying her well past him into the forest.

Both raptors leapt immediately atop it, digging their prodigious talons into its flesh.

One Eye bucked, knocking the two dakotaraptors onto their

backs. Triceratops continued in a semicircle around a tight cluster of trees, trying to find a path back to the tyrannosaur. Ankylosaurus advanced, thwacking his tail.

One Eye staggered to his feet, unaware of the half-dozen fresh gashes in its side. Ankylosaurus smashed his tail into its side, knocking it over once more, shattering its rib cage, and spraying decaying meat everywhere.

The beast howled, but not in pain.

It was oblivious to the pain, already rising to its feet again.

The raptors danced around it in a circle, raising a ruckus, trying to keep it distracted from the two larger, more powerful dinosaurs.

One Eye lurched forward. One of the raptors charged him, then danced back. The tyrannosaur lunged, missing. The raptor rushed forward again, letting out a *ka-ka-ka-ka-ka-ka-kaw* as she did. And again One Eye snapped at her, missing. Then the raptor charged a third time, and One Eye's jaws snapped shut right on cue, cutting the raptor in two at the waist.

The T. rex threw its head back to swallow the top half of the raptor while the other half still twitched and danced nervously, blood spurting. The lead raptor, now alone and outnumbered on all fronts, sprinted off into the woods, leaving Triceratops and Ankylosaurus to fend for themselves.

Triceratops charged.

Ankylosaurus swung his club.

One Eye lurched forward, snapping at Ankylosaurus.

The club knocked One Eye's legs out from under him the moment Triceratops slammed into him.

The tyrannosaur toppled to the ground with a tremendous thud. But as it did, it craned its neck forward, biting down on Ankylosaurus, its daggerlike fangs piercing through his armored hide.

Ankylosaurus let out a terrible bray, the pain of the bite causing him to seize up and jerk away. One Eye, however, would not let go of his prize, and tore away what flesh remained holding Ankylosaurus's side together.

Triceratops lowered her head and charged, screaming.

Her horns shattered One Eye's skull and shot through to the other side, piercing his one good eye, cleaving his head from his neck.

One Eye was dead. For good this time.

Crumpled nearby in a pile of leaves, Ankylosaurus brayed in pain. He was bleeding out, in too much agony to move. His tail twitched, tears welled up in his eyes.

Triceratops slid One Eye's head from her horns, then trotted over to her friend's side.

She nuzzled his head. He nuzzled her back weakly, and made a soft, affectionate bray.

Triceratops tried to nudge him to his feet, but he was growing weaker by the moment.

She was going to be alone again.

Suddenly the forest came alive with the sound of chittering.

Triceratops looked up, recognizing it instantly. *Leptoceratops.* They'd followed them from the lake.

She turned around, placing herself between Ankylosaurus and the approaching horde of diminutive monsters. She wasn't going to leave Ankylosaurus alone; she wasn't going to allow him to die that way. No, this was where she was going to make her last stand.

Her foot patted the ground, sounding her charge.

She lowered her head, waiting for them to come into view.

The forest crunched and snapped and chittered with angry life.

Triceratops took a deep breath.

Then the earth rumbled like thunder, trembling, shaking loose like the whole world was coming apart at the seams. It was as if the earth had been struck again by the spirits in the sky.

The leptoceratops cleared the distant foliage only to be met by a charging herd of anykylosauruses. Tails thwacked and whacked and wailed into the ground, smashing some leptoceratops to bits in single swings while sending others deep into the woods. The chittering stopped, replaced by the screams of sudden death.

The undead brachychampsa emerged from a bush, its teeth snapping at a nearby ankylosaurus, three tails crashing down on it in quick succession, pulping it almost as quickly as it had appeared.

Triceratops let out her breath.

It had all happened so quickly.

She raised her head a little, suspicious of the ankylosauruses, unsure if they were alive or dead.

The lead bull wheeled around, approaching her, tail high in the air. Triceratops backed up, placing herself squarely between Ankylosaurus and the herd. The new bull stepped around her, checking on Ankylosaurus.

She knew what that meant and turned, nudging him once more.

She nudged him again.

He wouldn't wake up.

The bull approached, nudging with his own nose. Then he looked down at the wound, smelling it. His head jerked back, nostrils flared.

In a flash his tail came down, crushing Ankylosaurus's skull. He wasn't going to let him come back as one of those *things*. Then he nuzzled Ankylosaurus with the top of his head before walking past, allowing another to take his place.

One by one each ankylosaurus walked up to their fallen

cousin, nudging his belly with the top of their heads, mourning silently, then walking slowly away, a great sadness in their eyes. The procession moved quickly, and as the last one paid its respects, the herd soundlessly plodded off into the forest. Then they stopped. And one by one they turned. And each ankylosaurus gazed back upon Triceratops, waiting to see if she would follow.

She knew what that meant—Triceratops had found her new herd.

She snorted, stamping a foot in the dirt. Then she trotted up alongside them, joining the herd on their long trek across what remained of the valley in hopes of finding a safe place to sleep for the night. And despite how bizarre her world had become, for the first time in days, Triceratops felt at home.

Jake and Willy at the End of the World

What do you reckon it'll be like?" asked Willy, after taking a sloshing pull from a sweating longneck. His thumb fiddled lightly with the tattered end of the label, bottle dangling precariously over the end of the plastic armrest of his lawn chair.

"What?" asked Jake, his half-drained beer perched atop the crease between his chest and his enormous potbelly.

"You know. The end."

"I reckon it'll be like anything else. A complete surprise."

"No, I mean, do you think there'll be anything at all? Like a heaven?"

"I hope so. But then, if there is, we might have some explaining to do."

Willy nodded. "How many you calling?"

"Three."

"Only three?"

"Yep," said Jake before taking another sip.

"Why only three?"

"Because you're a shit shot, Willy."

"No, we're talking about you."

"I am talking about me."

"Well, why only three then?"

"'Cause I reckon I ain't gonna get but the three shots off before they take me out. And I reckon I'm gonna hit everything I aim at. So three. It's math."

Willy scowled. "That ain't no math."

"The hell it ain't."

"It ain't like you sat here and worked out the time in your head like you were Stephen Hawkings or something. Like some Robocop fella, all mapping out trajectories in your head."

"Who the hell is Stephen Hawkings?" asked Jake.

"Smart feller. Don't you have cable?"

"Yeah, I got cable."

"And you ain't never heard of Stephen Hawkings?" asked Willy.

"What channel was he on?"

"Most of 'em, I reckon."

"Was he on ESPN?" asked Jake.

"Naw, he wasn't on ESPN."

"Then I ain't never heard of him."

"You'da liked him. Sat around in a chair all day. Figured out a way to get the chair to do all the talking for him. Married three times."

"Good ole boy?" asked Jake.

"Close as you can get without being born here, I reckon," said Willy.

"What was his thing?"

"His thing?"

"What was he famous for?"

"Black holes and aliens."

Jake gave Willy a fierce side-eye. "You're shittin' me."

"Nope."

"Like in the movies?"

"Yep. He was like that guy that the good guy goes to who tells him everything."

"A scientist," said Jake.

"Yeah."

"But, like, for real? Like the guys who found the comet?"

Willy nodded, taking another sip. "Yep."

"Yeah, it wasn't like that at all. I just reckon I can hit three."

"You know how it works, right?" asked Willy. "If you bid too low and go over, you lose."

"I know how it works, Jake."

"Good, 'cause I just wanna make sure. I don't want to hear you screaming about how it ain't fair 'cause you didn't know the rules."

"I ain't gonna be screaming."

"You ain't?"

"Not about that," said Jake, brow furrowed.

"Well, all right then. Three."

"How many you putting down?"

"Seven," said Willy.

"You ain't hittin' seven."

"I'm calling seven."

"You *ain't* hittin' seven."

"I'm hittin' seven."

"I'll say it again."

"You don't have to say it again."

"How in the hell do you reckon you're gonna hit seven?"

Willy stroked the barrel of the Mossberg 500 Tactical edition leaning against his plastic deck chair. "Well, these here are shotguns. Loaded with buckshot. You don't have to be good to hit that many."

"You couldn't hit the wall over yonder if you pointed straight at it and sawed that barrel all the way off. You ain't hittin' seven."

"I think you undervalue my abilities, Jake."

"I think you just wrote the title to your life story, Willy."

"Nah. That ain't the title of the book. It's more like the title of the song about the book."

"You think?"

"Yeah."

"Like in a 'hell yeah, Hank Williams Jr.' sort of way?" asked Jake.

"More like a Toby Keith sorta way."

"So like it's a lot of talk about kicking ass, but then you end up all 'You guys go ahead, I'll stay here and write songs about how awesome you are.' Kick-ass. America. Yeah. That sort of way?"

"Yeah. Like that. It's a metaphor," said Willy.

Jake puckered his lips, narrowing his eyes. "A what?"

"What the hell did you have cable for if you weren't watchin' it?"

"I was watchin' it."

"But you ain't never learned what a metaphor was?"

"TV ain't for schoolin'."

"That's your problem," said Willy. "You ain't never wanted to improve yourself."

"The hell I didn't. A lot of good your mesofore—"

"Metaphor."

"Okay, *metaphor* is gonna do when that door busts down."

"I'm taking seven," said Willy.

"The hell you are," said Jake.

"I'm doin' it."

"What the hell is a metaphor, anyhow?"

"It's like a simile, but without the like."

"It's like you're speaking Spanish, but my lawn ain't mowed and my leaves ain't blown."

Willy polished off the last of his beer, chucked the bottle aside, and pulled another from the cooler between their chairs. He popped the bottle cap off with his teeth, spat it across the room with a *ting,* and took another swig. "A simile. It's where you compare two things. Like, if I was to say this cheap-ass beer you bought is like your ex-wife, Cheryl. It'll do in a pinch, but it sure don't go down easy and you spend most of your time thinkin' that maybe if you'd spent a little more time lookin', you'd have found something better."

"The beer ain't that bad."

"It's not good beer, Jake."

"And that's the title of my life story. So what the fuck is a metaphor then?"

"It's just like that, but you don't say it's like that. You just kinda *allude* to it."

"What does that mean?"

"It means some smart fella made a lot of money naming the same shit two different things."

"That's always the way, ain't it?" asked Jake.

"Yep. So, you reckon we'll know any of them?"

"Who?"

"You know. *Them.*"

"I reckon we'll know a few," said Jake. "It ain't that big a town. And the news says it's an awfully big mob of 'em."

"It just don't make no sense. Why spend your last few hours on earth breaking shit and killing people when you can be kicking back and drinking a beer?"

"It's a world gone mad, Willy. A world gone mad."

"I always figured it'd be zombies."

"You did?"

"Yeah," said Willy. "I mean, it just always felt like, if it was going to go down, that'd be the way it'd happen."

"Not just some big ice cube from outer space slamming into China?"

"Yeah."

"How's that for some bullshit?"

"That's some bullshit, all right."

"I mean, we don't even get to see it," said Jake. "It's just gonna clobber the shit out of us and we won't even get to see the light or the explosion or nothin'."

"Well, I mean, we weren't gonna *see* it anyway. Not when it hits."

"Yeah, but that ain't the point. I mean, if God really loved America so much, you'd think he'd give us the best seats."

"Maybe he just doesn't like China," said Willy.

"Nobody likes China. *China* don't like China. I mean, if they did, maybe you'd see more Americans over there doing good in their schools."

"I don't think that's how that works."

"I mean, he's still giving it to us hard. It's the end of days for us all. But they get the ringside seats. And what do we get? Earthquakes and tidal waves and acid rain. I mean, his son was American, for fuck's sake. We should get the fireworks."

"Jesus wasn't American," said Willy.

"Yeah he was," said Jake.

"No he wasn't."

"Yeah he was. You don't need cable to know that Jesus was American."

"Yeah you do, and I'm telling you he wasn't American. He was Jewish."

"That's exactly what a liberal like you would say."

"I ain't no liberal," said Willy. "How many times we gotta go through this?"

"You are the most liberal guy I know."

"One time," said Willy. "One time!"

"One time is all it takes. It's like drugs."

"It ain't like drugs."

"Oh, now you're an expert on the cocaine and the meth," said Jake. "You and your fancy cable learnin'."

"All I said was I was weighing my options. That I wanted to think about it."

"You said the black feller had some good points."

Willy nodded. "Yeah! But it's not like I voted for him."

"Doesn't matter. You turned your eyes away from God, if even for a moment. That makes you a liberal."

"You don't go to church. You can't tell me about turning my eyes away from God."

"I'm an American," said Jake before taking a powerful pull off his longneck. "That means I don't have to go to church to believe in God. I vote straight Republican. That's all God asks of any of us. The rest is just window dressing for the community. Well, I don't need no one seeing me sittin' in the first pew to know how good a Republican I am. I fear God. I love my country. Me and the big man are square. For you, there's purgatory."

"Liberals don't go to purgatory."

"Of course not. They go to Hell. *Independents* go to purgatory."

"I ain't no independent either," said Willy.

"Well, we'll find out soon enough, won't we? Anytime now that door is gonna bust down, our guns are gonna go off, and I'm gonna look behind me in line at the pearly gates, and you're either gonna be there or you ain't."

"I'm gonna be there," said Willy.

"You better be there," said Jake.

"And if I ain't?"

"I don't know if I can handle all those churchies without you. Forever is a long time without your buddies. And I only got one."

"Well, I only got one too," said Willy.

"Then you best be there. Or else I'm gonna be mighty pissed. I don't wanna have to come down there and wait around until you've seen the goddamned light."

"I don't reckon He takes kindly to that phrase, let alone when you couple it to His light."

"Well, I reckon He knew what I meant."

Outside, the din of the approaching mob grew louder, voices becoming discernible above the dull roar.

"I don't want to kill these things," said Willy.

"They aren't things," said Jake. "They're just people. People who don't think anything matters anymore."

"Well, I don't wanna kill no people either."

"Neither do I. But if we don't defend ourselves, we're committing suicide. In the eyes of the Lord, at least."

"But killing is against the Ten Commandments."

"No, murdering is against the Ten Commandments. It ain't murder if it's self-defense."

"Then I'm taking seven," said Willy.

"You ain't takin' seven," said Jake.

Something sounding like a battering ram slammed into the door, the sound like a hollow shot in a wooden box. Jake and Willy slammed the rest of their beers, chucking them aside to shatter against the walls as they finished.

"Welp, this is it," said Willy.

"Sure is."

"I just want you to know, I've always loved you."

"I know."

The door banged again.

"I mean—"

"I know what you mean, Willy. I've always known."

Willy nodded with a gentle smile, pulling the Mossberg up into his lap. Jake clutched his camouflage-patterned .357 revolver, pulling the hammer back. The door banged a third time.

"I'll see you upstairs," said Willy.

"You better," said Jake.

And the door burst open, the cacophony of mad voices screaming victory as the mob flowed in like a wave.

The Last Job Is Always the Hardest

The last one is always the hardest," said the stranger from beneath the crisp brim of his hat. He was an anachronism—a duded-up hipster with a thing for the 1930s, all pinstripes and pearly whites. Even his mustache was a thin dark stripe sitting atop his lip, unmoving above a gleaming smile. His features were sharp, his fingernails well-manicured, his wing tips polished to a high-gloss shine. There was something warm about him, inviting, like he wanted to be your best friend in the world and wouldn't stop smiling until you relented. "At least that's what they told me," he continued. "I always puzzled over what that meant, exactly. I used to think they meant that the last job, the previous one, the one before the next one, was the hardest. But it always seems to get harder for me."

He talked like someone out of an old movie, like he'd watched too many and would break out with a *you dirty rat* at any moment. But he didn't. He was more Clark Gable than

James Cagney, anyway. Not that Brian knew who either of those people were.

Brian sat sweating in his polyester suit. He wasn't used to wearing one at all, and this one was so new he could still feel the void where the hanger belonged. It was an odd thought, all things considered—the fact that this suit would know the fit of a hanger better than it ever would that of a person—what with the clatter of the train on the tracks beneath him and the stranger prattling on like he was eulogizing something Brian couldn't quite put his finger on. But there he was, dwelling upon the mortality of his own suit, thinking about how little it would get to know the shape of his body.

It was a suit with one job to do, just one day off the rack, and then that would be it forever. Early retirement, smoldering to death in a trash can.

For a moment Brian thought of all the people that had ever handled the suit, from the textile workers who wove the fabric to the tailor or seamstress who cut and sewed it together, to the shipping clerks and dockworkers and truck drivers who carried it, and the department store clerk who finally hung it on the rack. Every last person who put effort into getting it here so it could do this one thing.

What a waste of time, he thought. It wasn't even a very nice suit. But it did the job. Brian looked very professional. Just another cubicle rat on a daily commute. *Nothing to see here, folks. I'm just Brian, who works in an office and shuffles papers. No need to bother with me. No need to check my bag or ask me where I'm going. Move along, Brian. Move along.*

"You know what I mean?" asked the stranger.

Brian nodded, smiling awkwardly, fumbling for a moment through the mental tape reel in his head for an idea of what the stranger had last said. But it was blank. He'd been too lost in thought. Smoldering suits in trash cans and all.

"You're not listening," said the stranger, his tone sharper, but the smile refusing to fade.

"I'm sorry," said Brian. "I have an awful lot on my mind."

"I get it," said the stranger, still beaming. "It's a big day."

"It is?"

"It sure is. For both of us. That's a new suit, isn't it?"

Brian nodded sheepishly.

The stranger snapped his fingers and pointed in the air, waving a victorious finger. "I knew it. I always know a new suit when I see one. Suits are my thing, you know. You've got to have a hobby when you do what I do and you're on the road as much as I am. And, well, suits are mine." He nodded for a moment, sizing it up. "That's a Bell and Thompson, right?"

"A what?"

"A Bell and Thompson. Cheap Chinese racket that makes them in sweatshops on the mainland. They sell them in discount department stores over here." He reached across the small aisle between them and lifted Brian's jacket open by the lapel, fingers brushing against his chest as he did. Brian backed away, startled, but managed only to sink an inch or so farther into his seat. "Relax, I don't bite." Then the stranger smiled broadly, his eyes twinkling. "Hot dog!" He clapped his hands. "Bell and Thompson. On the money."

Brian looked down. It was, in fact, a Bell and Thompson. "Do you sell suits?" he asked, trying to puzzle out just how the stranger had done that.

"No. It's just something I picked up. In my line of work, you develop your own tricks of the trade. That's one of mine. One of my favorites, actually."

"Gets people talking, I suppose."

"Boy, does it. And how." The stranger leaned forward. He had Brian on the hook now. "Some folks, they put a lot of time into their looks. They spend a lot of money on their suits. And when you can name their tailor, wow, do they feel like a million bucks. Others, though, they don't give a thought to what they wear at all. And when they run across someone who knows what they're wearing better than they do, well, they want to know what else you might have figured out about them. Everyone has secrets. Some folks have big ones. And everyone is afraid of being found out."

Brian shifted in his seat, slowly drowning in flop sweat, his hand fidgeting against the cheap plastic handle of his banged-up secondhand brown-leather briefcase. "And what is it you know about me?"

The stranger sat back in his seat, suddenly becoming very serious. But his smile remained, somehow becoming darkly sinister, almost cold, despite not moving or changing at all. "I know everything, Brian," he said, though they'd never been introduced. "I know why you bought that suit. I know what's in your briefcase. And I know that neither of us is going to get off this train alive."

Brian tensed up, his grip on the briefcase tightening. He thought for a moment about jumping out of his seat, throwing open the door to their small sleeper compartment, and running out to throw himself off the train. But the stranger just shook his head.

"I'm not here to stop you," he said. "Quite the contrary. I hope you're successful. There're a lot of good people on this train. Nice people. Sweet people. But they have to die all the same. That's what this job teaches you. More than anything else. Death touches everyone once."

"What, exactly, do you do?"

"Same as you, more or less."

"I don't have a job. I haven't had one in a long time."

"You have a job today. A big one."

Brian looked down at his briefcase, nodding slowly. "You kill people?"

The stranger shook his head. "Not directly. But I get to choose. To decide."

Brian leaned forward. "Wait. Are you . . . with the church? Because I thought I was doing this alone."

The stranger's eyes lit up, and the sinister smile became more of an amused grin. He laughed. "No. My job's much bigger than that. Much bigger."

"Then how do you know?"

"It's my job to know. You have the stench about you, the specters of the two hundred and thirty-eight people who are about to die resting upon your shoulders. I can see them, Brian. I can hear their screams long before they've made them."

"I'm going to kill two hundred and thirty-eight people?"

"Well, two hundred forty including you and me. But we don't really count, do we?"

"I'm not going to die today," said Brian.

"Okay."

"And you aren't going to stop me."

"Whatever you say, Brian."

"What do you know that I don't?"

"Well, is that a bomb in your briefcase?"

Brian nodded. "I thought you already knew that."

"I do. Do you have a trigger for that bomb?"

Brian shook his head, smiling. "No. It's on a timer. So you can't stop me."

"I told you," said the stranger, more firmly than before. "I'm not going to stop you. I don't want to stop you, and there would be nothing I could do to stop you even if I did, would there?"

"No."

"You thought of everything."

"Yes."

"You timed this train perfectly."

"I did."

"Rode it all last week just to get the timing and route right."

"Yes."

The stranger stopped smiling. "You're lying. Why are you lying? This was all going so well."

"I'm not."

The stranger leaned forward, now very concerned as if everything had gone terribly wrong. "You are. This is your first time on this train. That's why you've got the suit. You want to blend in. No one to notice you. You even knew where to walk to avoid the video cameras. You've been very precise. It's all been planned out for you by men much smarter than yourself. You're to leave the briefcase on the train and get off at the next stop, *forgetting* it under your seat. The train stops at 4:39, leaves again at 4:44. At 4:47 the bomb goes off, right after the train picks up enough speed to ensure that even those not killed by the blast are killed by the derailment. That was the plan."

"How the hell do you know all this?"

"Because I touched every person getting on this train to mark them for the collectors. Every. Single. Person. I felt what you were going to do, saw the opportunity, and made the call. Everyone dies. Even you."

"What the hell is a collector?"

"I was getting to that."

"I'm getting off this train."

"At 4:39?"

"Yes."

"Because the bomb is going off at 4:47?"

"Yes."

The stranger smiled again. "Even though the train won't arrive until 4:50?"

"What?"

"There was an accident on another track. They've rerouted traffic to this one. As a result, our train has been traveling almost ten miles an hour slower than its normal speed. Had you actually ridden this route before, you'd have noticed. But you haven't. Because you thought you were going to be spirited away to live in the woods at camp Jesus Freak, right with God, until all this blew over. You needed to be someone no one would recognize. A first-timer. A ghost."

Brian looked at his watch. "Shit."

The stranger nodded. "Yeah."

"How do you—"

"I was coming to that, too. I was trying to tell you earlier, but you didn't care to listen."

Brian took a deep breath, steadying himself. "I'm listening now."

The stranger clapped his hands. "Hot dog! Let's do this!" He readjusted himself in his seat, now even more animated than before. "How did you choose this train?"

"I didn't. You know that."

"Right. Someone else did. You're just here to do the job, right?"

"Yes."

"So someone else did all the thinking and choosing about who dies and you just do the job."

"Yes."

"Well, that's like what a collector does, too."

"What's a collector?"

"The Grim Reaper. That thing from beyond that comes and spirits your mortal soul into the afterlife. The guy who kills you—or at the very least, sees to it that someone else does."

Brian's jaw dropped, half in disbelief, half in shock. "You're the Grim Reaper? Bullshit."

"No. The *collectors* are the Grim Reapers. Plural. There's hundreds of them. I'm a marker."

"What's a marker?"

"We're the ones who make the call. We're the angels of death."

"Oh, come the fuck on."

"Brian. How did I know your name? And what's in the briefcase? And what time this was all set up for?"

"I don't know. You know someone on the inside? You're with the FBI, maybe."

"No. Good guesses. But that doesn't explain how I'm sitting across from someone with a bomb in his hand without so much as breaking a sweat. It's a little late for me to try disarming it, don't you think?"

"Yeah."

"So why am I not afraid of your little bomb?"

"Because you're crazy?"

"Or I'm already dead."

"Bullshit."

"I don't need you to believe me now," said the stranger, smile bright, eyes twinkling. "You've got all the time in the world to think about what I'm about to tell you. Literally. All the time."

"What does that mean? Are you saying I'm going to Hell?"

"On the contrary, I might have spared you all that."

"Might?"

"I'm a marker. I choose who dies. I don't know shit about

what's . . . after. Except for this part. This is kind of the between part. I know this part really well. I've been doing it a long time."

"Since the beginning?"

"Hell no. Since the thirties."

"The 1930s?"

"Yeah."

"That's not a long time to be dead."

"You tell that to me once you've put in eighty years doing this."

"Wait. Are you telling me I'm a marker?"

The stranger nodded. "You will be. That's what I've been trying to tell you all along. You're going to die today, and when you do, you're going to take my place."

"Your place?"

"It's a limited-time gig. Each marker has to pick one million people to die. That's it. That's the job. You walk up to them, you touch them, and that's it. They're marked. Then you move on to the next one and try not to think too much about it."

"You just touch them? That's it?"

"That's it."

"And the Grim Reaper shows up and kills them?"

"The collectors, yeah. They don't . . . they don't take too well to the whole reaper thing."

Brian shook his head, folded his arms, sticking his lower lip out in disgust. "That's stupid. God wouldn't do that."

"But he'd put a guy on a train with a bomb to send a message to America that its values are out of whack? Buddy, are you in for a rude awakening when you get to the other side."

"I'm not dying. Not today."

"It's already done."

"I could jump."

"The fall would most likely break your neck. Or you'd bang

your head on a rock. Or whatever. Collectors are devious little fucks. Once somebody is marked, they're like the Mounties. They always get their man."

"I'm not marked yet."

"I told you. I've touched everybody on this train. Everybody." He pointed for a moment at Brian, as if surprised by something. "That's a nice suit. Is it a Bell and Thompson?"

"You already—" Brian's jaw went slack once more. "You're full of it."

"So here's the rules. One million. Any one million will do."

"I'm not listening to this."

"You'd better. Otherwise you're gonna be lost when your ticket gets punched. One million souls. That's the debt you owe the world. The millionth soul, that's the one who replaces you. You'll feel it when it's coming. The minute his or her time is up, you're off the hook and on your way to whatever reward you've earned. Everything else you'll be able to figure out on your own."

"How many have you touched?"

"Including you?"

"Yes."

"One million. Haven't you been listening?"

"Wait! You chose me?"

"Of course I did."

"Why?"

"Because I don't like you."

"You don't like me?"

"No," said the stranger, disgusted. "Why would I like you? You're a Jesus freak without the Jesus part. You hate more than you love. You believe that a bomb will teach people a lesson. And you're stupid enough to listen to a group of church elders who told you that this was all going to work out okay, but didn't bother to check on any of the details yourself. You are a bad person. And that's before we even get to the way you treat waitresses—women in general, really—and the terrible stuff you look at while touching yourself. You're lazy and boring, you insult strangers, and you believe anyone who doesn't buy into your own brand of fundamentalism is destined to burn. But worst of all, you were willing to walk onto a train with a bomb without having the common decency to die along with everyone else. Simply put," said the stranger with a shrug and a limp finger, "you're an asshole."

"You're gonna kill me for all that?"

"No. The bomb will kill you. The collector will see to that. I just marked you. And once you're gone, my million chores are up."

"But you chose me. That's as good as killing me. How can you live with yourself?"

"Ah! Now there's an excellent question. You're going to be asking yourself that a *lot* over the next few years. Decades, really. You'll figure it out. We all do." He paused for a second, trying to find the words. "Look, it's a shit job. I've had to mark an awful lot of good people. Nice people. People who deserved better than they got. But people have to die. I was choosy at first. Got to know people. Only marked the ones who really had it coming. But that could take you forever. You could go days without really finding someone deserving. I've done this for eighty years. *Eighty years,* Brian. You know how many people a day that is?"

"No."

"Thirty-four. On average. I took some days off here and there. Other days you'll make up for it. You'll find it hard to mark people on Christmas or on particularly sunny days in spring. So you'll give some folks a pass you probably should have marked. And man, do the collectors get pissed."

"Why would they be pissed?"

"They've got a million souls to deliver too. Only they've got to wait on you. The collectors start nagging, time starts dragging, and the next thing you know, *BAM!* You're marking a guy for leaving a shitty tip and snubbing a homeless guy on his way out the door. You'll start to invent reasons. Then eventually you realize that the world isn't supposed to be fair. If it was, you wouldn't be spending your afterlife deciding who lives and who dies.

"Once I spared someone only to watch another marker come by and tag her ten minutes later. The first time something like that happens, you realize the futility of what you do. It's all so random. This whole world, this whole system, every last bit of it. I was making decisions based on my own judgments while another guy was running around touching his daily quota of a couple hundred people just to get it all over with. There's no rhyme or reason to it all. Then one day, without even realizing it, you're marking your first kid.

"Brian, the first time you watch a kid you marked die changes you forever. Don't stick around if you can help it. Never stick around. You'll see some eventually. Collectors will take to following you when they're caught up on things. They'll kill someone seconds after you tag them if they can—run them down in the street with a bus or pop an artery in their head if they have to. Watching it is the worst thing. It makes you feel connected. Responsible. You'll try to give people a death with meaning, but it will rarely pan out. You'll just feel bad."

Brian glared at the stranger, starting, for a moment, to believe him. "Were you an asshole?"

"What?"

"Is that why the guy before you chose you? Did he hate you too?"

"Me? No. He liked me. Felt sorry for me. I'd just walked in to find my girlfriend in flagrante delicto with her neighbor. She told me it had been going on for a while and she was glad I knew. I was going to toss myself off a bridge. Damn myself right to Hell. He talked me out of it. Patted me on the back. Told me about my million souls. Told me he had been watching me, thought I'd make a good judge of character. He posited that someone with a kind soul might choose the right people and leave a world filled with the just and righteous. Slipped on the ice on my way home, cracked my skull right open. And that was it."

"So why don't you choose someone kind?" asked Brian, sweat soaking all the way through his shirt and now seeping into his jacket.

"Because this is a special kind of hell all its own. There's no goodness to this job. You don't leave behind a kind and righteous world. You spend all of your time in war and hate and poverty. You mark children as they come into the world. You mark their mothers so they die on what should be the happiest day of their life. You mark fathers on their way home from work and lovers on flights home to be reunited with their one and only. You mark hopeful people looking forward to tomorrows you don't allow them to see. And you'll do all of this at a brisk enough pace to make sure you don't spend more than a century doing it.

"Thank the maker—or whatever machine-tending thing is waiting for us on the other side—that it had the foresight to split it between two jobs. Could you imagine, even for a minute, having to choose who lives and who dies only to have to kill them too?" The stranger looked down at the briefcase still gripped tightly in Brian's hand. "That's how you were going to sleep at night, right? You were just the guy who brought the briefcase. You didn't choose these people. You didn't choose this train. You didn't make them get on it. You didn't even make the bomb. You just delivered it, like God *told you to*."

Brian nodded.

"We tell ourselves a lot of things to make what we have to do palatable. We find a way to justify it. To make it through the day. And that's why I chose you. You're an asshole. A real cocksucker. You don't deserve to live. And you don't deserve a quick death either. But you're willing to do what God wants you to do. You're willing to kill for Him without question. And that, my friend, makes you perfect for this job."

"But I don't want it."

"No one wants it. That's the point. At least I hope it is. I hope I didn't do this all for nothing. I hope the people who have gone on before me, the people I shipped off, I hope they can forgive me. That they understand."

"What about me? I won't forgive you."

"Shit, Brian. After today, after that bomb goes off killing two hundred and thirty-eight other people, after you wake up to find that no one recognizes you and that you can walk unseen through the world if you want to, after you see the devastation you caused and the pain and suffering you inflicted, you won't even be able to forgive yourself. And all that is *before* you realize that the fact that you chose to do this is why I picked you in the first place. And once you come to terms with that? You'll realize you have to do it all over again a million more times before you can see what's on the other side—to see if you even get into Heaven or Hell. So ask me again: do I give a shit if you forgive me? No. No I don't. And that's why I picked you. My last selfish act in this world. Hopefully you'll find it easier to mark your million than I did mine." The stranger took a deep breath and looked at his watch. "Four more minutes. Four more minutes and you get to find out whether or not I'm full of shit." Then he closed his eyes, relaxing, and settled in as if ready for a mid-afternoon nap.

Brian looked at his own watch, panicked. The man was right. It was 4:43. The train was five minutes late to the station, and though it was beginning to slow, it still wasn't quite slow enough for him to jump off. He looked up at the stranger, holding the briefcase a few inches off the floor. "How do I turn it off?"

"You don't."

"But I want to. I want to stop this."

"You can't," said the stranger, eyes still closed. "It's already done. Everyone's already been marked. All that's left is to wait for the collectors to come."

Brian set the case gently back on the floor and sighed. "What was your name?"

"I don't remember."

"Why the hell not? It's your name, not a locker combination."

"This job is easier when you forget yourself. You'll remember the big stuff, but it's hard to remember a name when nobody else ever bothers to call you by it."

"Are you a religious man?"

"Was I or am I?"

"Are you?"

"There's no use for religion in the afterlife. There's only truth in death. You either go on to your great reward or you stay here for a spell as one of God's pencil pushers. Belief is the wrong word. It's a knowing without *really* knowing. You know what I mean?"

"No. I've always believed."

The stranger smiled, opening his eyes, laughing a little. "A few nights doing this and you'll begin to question everything. Even that."

"Never."

"Trust me. Bomb-briefcase Jesus won't be there on the dark nights when you stagger into a children's cancer ward. He won't be there when you find out about the awful oil heater fire a collector used to take out a whole family you touched the week before. And he sure as shit ain't gonna be there when you realize you've got decades left to serve before you meet your quota. When this job is done with you, there won't be a thing left you believe in. You'll be lucky if you even find any hope left to cling to."

"Did you?" asked Brian.

"Did I what?"

"Find hope?"

"Only that this would all make sense one day."

"Does it?"

"I'm about to find out. Like I said, it's a big day for both of us. I hope you like that suit."

Brian looked down sadly at his jacket, pulling the lapels away with his sweaty hands. "I hate this suit."

"It is a terrible, terrible suit. Eighty years of that will be a punishment all its own."

The door to the small sleeper compartment opened, and a balding, bespectacled man in a tie-dyed T-shirt and blue jeans loomed over them with a wry smile. "Is this the new guy?" he asked, looking at Brian.

"Yep," said the stranger.

"Two hundred and thirty-nine," said the strange little man, smiling queerly. "I could take the rest of the week off if I wanted."

"But you won't."

"Of course I won't. But it's nice to think about."

"It really is. You're a bit early, don't you think?"

"Nah. The timer in his case is off by two minutes."

"Oh!" said the stranger, caught entirely off guard. "I thought we had a little mo—"

Hell They Call Him, the Screamers

He cuts. It's what he does, what he always has done. First the long blade across the neck to spill the blood. Then with the paring knife, down the spine, across the upper buttocks, through the love handles and back up the sides; down the leg and through the ankles, back up and around again. Then with the hooks, in just beneath the skin, peeling it back away from the muscle with a firm tug. He's timed it just right, learned when their reflexes will jerk them away, giving the extra force needed to peel it off in clean, perfect sheets.

They scream. It's what they do. It's what they always have done. First with the protests. The *No!* The *Don't!* Then with the swearing. Always the swearing. Even the churchiest of them— the blue-haired old biddies with crosses around their necks and knuckles bleached white from gripping their Bibles too tight, blurting out the foulest "cuntfuckingmotherfucker" when the knife goes in. Then comes the begging. The pleading. The bargaining. They offer houses and cars and riches beyond imagining. The young ones offer blow jobs, then fucks, and when that doesn't work, all manner of depravity. "Please. You can fuck my ass. No one's ever fucked my ass. It's yours. Just don't cut me. Don't hurt me, please. I'll like it, I promise. It'll be so tight for you. You can shit on my tits if you like. Shit on them and then cum. You look like you'd like that." But he doesn't. Next they beg for their children. "Please, I have children," they say. Some of them actually do.

Then there's the *Why?* They always ask why. "Deargodplease, why are you doing this?" The butcher doesn't say a word. He just cuts. Just as he's always done. He tried at first to explain it. But it never took. It doesn't make sense until the end. He would talk over their screaming. Their pleading. Their offers of ankle-grabbing ass-fucking. First eloquently, then bluntly, but it never took. The fear. It stoppers the ears and twists the stomach, making the brain useless. He'd try to tell them that. But they scream more than they listen.

He is nine feet tall, with slabs of pallid flesh dripping down with hairy-nippled mantits over half a ton of solid muscle, a thick layer of musky sweat, and a useless skin-leather apron dangling from his thirty-two-inch neck. His eyes vacant, black without a speck of white. His mouth ever yawning a voiceless scream. His teeth narrow, filed to points, and a square jaw powerful enough to snap bone. Hell, they call him, the screamers. He is The Butcher of Fleshtown. One of a thousand. The one with the steadiest hand. The cleanest cuts. Able to hold down the strongest man with a single meaty mitt, carving him apart while he struggles and screams. There are many butchers, but he is the only one they call *The.*

Fleshtown. A grim, cavernous concrete box, fifty carving tables wide, twenty deep. The floors stained a permanent red;

the walls a flat, blood-peppered gray. Drains set in the floor every ten feet. The granite carving tables scarred by knives, their centers polished to a slick sheen from all the writhing bodies. A thousand butchers hacking away at once, their screamers howling, their attendants handing them freshly honed blades or trundling bins off to the furnace. And in the back, nearest the exit, stands *The*.

At his feet blood congeals, hundreds of gallons of it an hour. It sprays out the neck onto the growing pile of crimson pudding, thick, dark, the bottom turning black before day's end, when the sweepers come by with hoses to spray it down the drains. In the morning it rises to his ankles, by noon to his waist.

After the flensing comes the carving, the slices deep, down to the bone, down the left side of the leg, then up the right, again on the other leg, the arms, deep along the muscle of the torso. The cuts nicking bone, slicing sinew, loosening its grip on the flesh. Then he digs in, his fat fingers tearing, fingernails worn down to the nubs, pulling the meat off in chunks. He peels the flesh away, the light sprinkle of remaining blood spattering against his apron, his arms, his cheeks. And still they scream, their voices shrill and heavy—loud despite the meat absent from most of their bones.

He casts stray pieces behind him, the bones, the muscle; whatever comes off goes into the large gray plastic bin, streaked crimson with blood. And when the bin is full—after two dozen or so screamers—it is wheeled away to the furnace, dumped, the pieces scattering at once to ash in fires as hot as the sun.

Then when all the meat is gone, and only the chest and head remain, out comes the cleaver. He swivels the torso around, holds the blade high above his head, brings it down in a single mighty swing. The head splits in two, cracked open like a coconut against the stone table. Raising the cleaver again, he brings it back down into the sternum. Then he slips fingers the size of pop bottles into the chest, prying the rib cage open with a single crack, his hands quickly scooping out guts and brains, tossing organs sloshing with shit and piss back into the bin.

And once all the meat is gone, and every last limb is severed and all that remains is the split-open shell of the screamer, he reaches in and peels away a thin layer of soul. It glimmers, glows, and sparkles, shimmering for its first few moments in the light. Then, and only then, do the screamers finally stop screaming. Their souls swell, no longer trapped inside a mortal shell, filling out, drawing their first real breath of freedom.

Then The Butcher throws a meaty fat thumb over his shoulder, pointing toward a simple cinder-block passage in the back of the slaughterhouse. "What's down there?" they ask.

"Peace," he says quietly, his voice deep, resonant, like a father speaking to his child.

"What's it like?" they always want to know.

"I don't know," he says. "I've never been there. I'm just the butcher." Then he bellows to the foreman, "Next!" as the liberated soul wanders confused off toward the passage.

The flesh, it hungers. It thirsts. It fucks. The flesh is where the fear is. There is no soul that grows hungry or tired or scared. Only flesh does that. And the flesh is not the soul. But it's easy to forget that, to think the soul wants to feed and fuck and fall asleep. What the soul wants is bigger than that, simpler than that. The soul only wants peace. And there is no peace for the flesh. No respite. It eats, it sleeps, it cums, and then it starts the cycle all over again. It's why the screamers offer so much. They think The Butcher meat and bone, just like them.

They don't understand The Butcher. Not until the end.

I Am the Night You Never Speak Of

Author's note: The following story was originally published in Midian Unmade, *a Clive Barker–approved short story collection set in his Nightbreed universe (based upon his novella* Cabal*) after the fall of Midian. This story takes place there.*

It's banging in my skull again. The hunger. It starts as an itch on the other side of the bone, behind the earlobe, just where I can hear it. Scritch, scritch, scritch it goes in the night. I don't notice it when it's just a tickle. I've trained myself not to. But when it's a scratch, I know I'm in for it. I know that it will get so bad it'll curl my fingers, curl my toes, paint my knuckles white, and choke my fingertips red. It'll arch my back and make me want to bite my own tongue clean off. I'll start beating a balled fist against my skull, want to drive a knife or a screwdriver or a power drill—whatever I have on hand—right into the spot to scratch it.

But that's just how it starts. And it only gets worse from there. Next comes the pounding, a screaming headache like a hangover from three solid days of tequila and nothing else. My brain throbs against a skull full of exposed nerves and I want to tear my skin off my arms just to feel something else for a change. I want to pull out my hair in clumps, bits of flesh dangling from the ends, rip my ears off both at the same time. But that won't help. That won't be but a distraction, a momentary dalliance from the scratching and the pounding and the bleating of my hunger.

I have to feed. To eat. To devour whole the dark of night. Its sins. Its memories. I have to feast upon the guilt and glee of a hundred carnal pleasures, to drink and fuck and finger and sink low into a junkie sleep rich in the glow of a peaceful head and the taste of cock and quim and filth on my mouth.

Not that I love that shit. I hate it. It's fucking cotton candy for the soul. A second on the lips, a flash on the tongue, and then vapor—an unsatisfied memory of a moment you can't ever get back. You need more. You gotta have more. That's where it started, for me at least. And it never ends. It never ever ends.

I don't eat people, not like the others. Some of the others, at least. I eat the sin. The act. I dine off the moment that the soul crosses the line from one side of morality to the other. But it ain't like you think. A sin ain't found in the lines of a book. It's found in the heart, the soul. A sin is found in shame. Or in that dark enjoyment of something made better because you think it's wrong. That's where I eat; that's where I live. That's where I come for you.

Getting people to sin is easy. Everyone wants to be around me. I'm fucking beautiful. Not hot. Not sexy. Beautiful. They can't take their eyes off me. You. You would fuck me. That's how beautiful I am. I haven't even told you if I'm a man or a woman yet, and I don't know if you're gay, straight, or married. But you'd fuck me. You know you would. You're starting to picture me now, see my features through the fog, feel the tickle in your groin as you rub your thighs together hoping no one else in the room notices how hot you're getting. That's how fucking beautiful I am. And that face you're seeing. That's what I look like. That's what I always look like.

And everyone sees me different. Everyone but the monsters. To them I always look the same.

In Midian they called me Bacchus, the god of lust and ritual madness, of ecstasy and wine and all the filthy fine fucking things folks love. Most thought I might actually be him, or at least the inspiration for the story. But I ain't him and he ain't me. I ain't half that old. It's just a name, good as any other. But now, now that they know me, now that the walls have come down and so many truths have been revealed, they don't speak that name in jest. They don't think about me that way anymore. Now I'm something else. Now that word has a whole new meaning.

Now they know that I eat sin and a monster ain't nothing but.

People think of psychopaths and equate them to monsters. They think of the cruel, emotionless detachment and see the awful things they've done and scream *A MONSTER! A MONSTER!* But that's no monster. A psychopath is just a thing that's broken. They're not men; they're animals—devolved brains that have ceased feeling and turned to instinct. Animals, those are the only things that will do something cruel without remorse. They'll bite their best friend for a morsel and never give it a second thought. You can smack 'em upside the head and they'll come back to you—if you've broken them right. That's no monster. Monsters know. Monsters feel. They know exactly what the fuck they're doing; they know the things they do are wrong but savor it anyway. Every. Delicious. Moment.

Until you've watched a monster eat a man, head and all, tear out its entrails, and dance beneath the moon with a delighted blood-smeared smile, you don't know. You can't know. They love it. They love the shit out of it. That's a monster. And that shit gets me harder than anything. A monster, a good and proper monster, will sate my hunger for a decade or two. I'll gut 'em like they would a human and gobble up every sinful morsel; I'll crack their bones and drink the marrow. Once I ate one so foul that I didn't get hungry for another thirty-four years. But that time I got lucky. A beast like that is craftier and more cunning than anything you've ever known. To get one like that you've got to catch 'em at their weakest. At their hungriest. When their insides pound as hard as mine do now.

But I ain't seen a monster like that for a very long time. Not since Midian. Not since the walls came down and we scattered to the winds. Midian was good to me. I could watch and wait and learn the routines of the worst of us. Then when the hunger or boredom got to be too much for them, I'd follow them out, wait for them to break the law. And then I would break it myself. Had to do that only a few times. The rest of the time I could live in peace. Quiet. The demons screaming in my head sated for years. I could read, have real conversations in which I didn't have to pretend so much, maybe even watch a little TV. I never had to drink, to feast, to find myself throwing up in some back alley, needle in my arm, unshaven junkie on my cock working for his fix. Not unless I wanted to. Those were good days. But they're gone now.

So I have to fill the new ones. I have to feed. I have to gorge on whatever weak-ass human sin I can find, which means most of the time I have to make my own. It's awful. A single night of human debauchery is like a thimbleful of water after three days in the desert. It'll stop the pounding, all right; it'll stop the itch.

But it'll only buy me a few hours of peace, a few hours of quiet, a few hours without the walls of my sanity tumbling down. Just enough to sleep. But most days it's the itch that wakes me up.

So my life is a constant party. A night train of debauchery with no stops until dawn. Booze. Sex. Drugs. Gambling. Theft. Violence. Whatever your kick—your real kick—I aim to supply it. To be that silent dream drifting into the bar to grab you by the short and curlies and tug you into a smoky backroom corner to finish you off in the dirtiest, filthiest, most perverse way you can imagine. But don't get too excited. I ain't your fucking fantasy. No. That would be too easy. I don't get off being everything you wish I was.

Who the fuck am I?

I am the night you never speak of. The porn you jerk off to but could never tell anyone about. The tryst when your wife is out of town. The drunken night after five years sober that leaves you lying in a pile of your AA anniversary chips. I am the memory that makes you cringe in the shower, the lie that ruins your marriage, the truth that makes you put a gun in your mouth after midnight when no one is awake to take your calls. I am the dark deed that hollows you out and leaves you like a husk to be filled with booze or sex or love or excess or consumerism or religion or fitness or parenthood—whatever your vice may be. That's who the fuck I am.

And tonight my head is pounding again. The sun is setting and I'm running out of smokes. It's time to hit the town. It's time to eat. It's time to ruin someone's life.

I'm staying in a shithole motel in a know-nothing town that is the pimple on the ass end of Texas. I've just finished a long run in Vegas—which I can only handle for so long. There's no night in Vegas, not inside the city limits. Not where the hunting and feeding happens. It's all lights and noise and six-dollar steaks, all day, every day, in a way that it eventually makes the sunlight feel wrong. It flips the whole world on its head. I lived underground beneath the dirt and graves for ages, and even I can't handle Vegas for longer than a month or so.

I hitched my way as a lot lizard, blowing truckers in their cabs, feeding off the really dark shit they daydream about on the long hauls. It's not that I'm poor. Cars can be tracked. There are always people looking. Monsters looking. And I don't like anyone to see me coming. Or going. It's why I'm still here after all this time. Remember what I said about clever monsters? I was being humble.

So here I am in some shit-smear Panhandle town with my head on its way to making me cry out loud and I'm dying for a smoke.

I'm thinking there might be a bar nearby. I've been to this town before. That's why I hate it so much. I always forget its name. It's something stupid like Oatmeal or Friday or Happy or Paris—you know, one of those cute co-opted bullshit names Texas loves. But I think there's a bar, and I think it should be open, so I hoof it across the dusty, yellow-grassed plains to cut an hour or so off my walk.

And I'm right. There's a bar. And it's open. More or less.

It's one of those concrete box buildings that just looks wrong all by its lonesome. Sharp angles, whitewashed cinderblock walls, a sign hand-painted by someone with aspirations of leaving this town but lacking the talent to actually do so, a big black metal door and no windows to spoil the neon-drenched insides. It's got one of those stupid lighted arrow signs out front with slotted letters falling off that no one gives enough of a shit about to straighten after a storm. Why bother? I wonder. It's not like you could miss this pathetic structure along the road with nothing but telephone poles and a gravel parking lot to keep it company. But there it is, inviting you in for CHEAP BEER and FRIDAY NIGHT POOL TOURNAMENTS.

It's Tuesday. But thankfully there are half a dozen cars and trucks in the lot. Probably the only alcohol for fifty miles.

The inside smells like stale smoke and dirty mop water. It's exactly as I remember it. Cement floor covered by a stained, tattered rug—the thin, rough kind you find in cheap strip center offices. It's lit almost entirely by neon advertising, some corners brightened by beers that haven't been available for decades. It's not so much a bar as a coffin where a lonely few escape their somehow even worse lives.

I smell the guy right away. I can taste his longing on the tip of my tongue, the want lingering at the bottom of his heart, buried under ten years of single-position Saturday-night sex. He wants a turn. He's waiting for it. The rest of the bar is slim pickings. You'd think that everyone could be broken by something, could be lured away with just the right offer, but I'm telling you now, that ain't the case. Some people want for things they'll never allow themselves to have.

But this guy, this guy has it bad. He's a stained T-shirt barely squeezed over a spare tire, with salt and pepper stubble sprawling across two different chins. He's daydreaming over his beer, thoughts lingering over freshly dusted memories some fifteen years old. This guy's special. Sure he'd love a roll in the hay—a good, righteous fuck or even a quick handy out back. But that wouldn't even register. That'd be the pitiful highlight of his fucking year, and he might go so far as to tell his wife about it just to piss her right the hell off.

No, this guy is looking for something else, a different brand of vodka altogether.

I sit two stools down and don't make eye contact. That's the key. People get suspicious when they get everything they want without having to work for it. So I make him work for it. He nurses his bottle of beer for a while, checking me out in the mirror hanging on the wall behind the bar, mindlessly picking at the label.

I wonder for a second what I look like to him. I never get to know. I get an inkling, a few of the details—young, old, black, white, male, female—that kind of stuff. And I know that only because I know what they want. But I never see myself, not as they see me. I know he thinks I'm a man, I know I'm in my twenties. But I know shit else. Hair color, eye color, beard or clean-shaven. None of it. I look across the counter at the mirror and see nothing but the monster, a withered old husk, partied out like a drooping, wrinkled party balloon. It's a good thing no one ever sees my eyes, my real eyes, bloodshot and yellow with a thousand-yard stare that'd just downright chill you to the bone.

"Can I get a pack of smokes?" I ask the frumpy, dumpy white-trash owner of this fine establishment. She nods and tosses me a pack from behind the counter. "My brand," I say with a smile. At this point, they're all my brand. I light up, the smoke only the faintest relief against the din in my skull. But I draw in a drag like it's fine wine, smiling and letting it roll over me. Headache or no, the show must go on, or else the headache will just get worse. And it will get worse. So I'm all about the show now.

In the mirror I see a flash of razor teeth.

I hate seeing myself in the mirror.

"You still play?" he asks, drifting back in from out of his daydream.

"What?" I ask.

"You still play?"

"Ball?"

"Yeah, ball."

"How'd you know?" I ask, already knowing the answer.

"The way you carry yourself. A guy who plays ball, if he's the real deal, if he gives himself to it, it gives him a walk."

"My posture gave me away?"

"Yeah. I'm guessing . . . running back?"

"Tight end. You?"

"Quarterback. Up through college." He lifts the sleeve from his bicep, revealing the number 27 in big block letters and local high school colors. "Till I blew out my knee."

"Who'd you play for?" I ask, the lilt of my voice showing genuine interest.

Bam. He's on the hook and moving two stools down to sit beside me. He wants it bad. I can taste his thoughts, the stench of his desire reeking like a bloated corpse. Middle age is making him weary, sad, putting the creak in his bones and a layer of fat on his belly. He wants to be young again, but even I can't do that. So he talks about it. And he talks about it. And beer after beer he keeps talking about it, reliving every glorious moment.

His name is Bill.

It's an hour in and he's recapping the final quarter of the big state championship. I know when he's lying, but I don't mention it. The embellishments are the only thing making the story listenable. Otherwise it's the standard claptrap that I try to choke down with as much alcohol as I can stomach, half a pack of smokes, and the hope that this headache will soon be gone. Every once in a while I break in to tell my own lies, stories I've lifted from a hundred other guys just like him, details that sound right because they actually happened to someone else.

But none of this is going to chase away the hunger. It's all just foreplay. I gotta get this guy out of the bar so we can get down to business.

"Man," I say before killing the last few swigs of a beer, "I wish I weren't so far from home. I could really go for a round of shooting right now."

"Shooting?" he asks.

"Yeah. Me and the boys like to go out after a game, get completely wrecked, then line up our bottles and shoot shit until we pass out. All this talk about playing has me wanting to shoot."

"I got a couple shotguns in the truck. Maybe fifty, sixty rounds."

"Bullshit," I say, pretending that I haven't been smelling the gunpowder on him for the last hour.

"Ain't no lie. You wanna shoot?"

"Yeah, I wanna shoot." I look up at the bartender. "How much for the rest of that bottle of whiskey?"

Bartender shakes her head. "I can't let you walk out with anything open. Not so much as a beer."

"Then how much for an unopened bottle?"

"Ain't got a license to sell you that, neither."

Bill waves a fat finger at me. "Let's do a few shots now and it'll hit us just in time to shoot. Trust me. I do this all the time."

He was right. He does. The whiskey hits us just as we've lined up trash on a fence out in some disused field miles away. He's a good shot. I pretend not to be half bad. Truth is that I've spent an untold number of drunken nights getting hillbillies and rednecks to shoot at things that shouldn't be shot at. It's not all about college girls, struggling ex-addicts, and cheating husbands. I gotta dig deep to keep on keepin' on. Some nights it's getting spanked by a priest, others it's getting someone to cheat at cards, and yeah, still others are spent shooting cans out in the sticks, talking a drunk idiot into going down on his drunker sister or . . . putting some buckshot in his asshole neighbor.

So, yeah, I've done this once or twice.

We shoot until we've almost run through his ammo. I get pretty close most of the time, but as the shells start running thin, I start nailing my shots one after another after another.

"Damn, son," he says. "You're getting the hang of it."

"I'm getting sober is what I'm getting."

"Young man like you can hold his liquor. I'm drunk as hell."

"Well, I ain't anymore. Let's go get some more to drink."

He looks at his watch. "Bar's closed. Missed it by ten minutes."

I make a pained face and look up at the wide dark sea of stars above. We really are out in the middle of nowhere. "There's a house along the road about a mile back. What do you say we raid their liquor cabinet?" I shoot him a playful smile, but cock my brows just so to tell him I'm serious.

"That's breaking and entering."

"Yeah."

"No way," he says.

"What? Do you know 'em?"

"No."

"Well, ain't you never raised hell before? I thought you were cool."

That hits him like a fist to the gut. He tries to hide it, but his eyes give him away. He thought he was cool too. For a while there he was feeling like a kid again, just one of the guys.

"We ain't gonna hurt nothin'," I say. "Just peek in their liquor cabinet and take some for the road. You never done that?"

He has. But not in a long time.

I can feel it in my bones, smell it on his breath. He hesitates, temptation gnawing a hole so big in his gut you could drive a truck through it.

He smiles. "Fuck it. Let's do it."

Release. It's like that moment you stand up after drinking when it hits you all at once, coupled with the tingling opening salvo of a full-force orgasm. The headache vanishes in an orgiastic rush, with even the itch banished to the back of my skull for another hour or so. If he goes through with this, I'll be good till sundown tomorrow. If not, I've got a few hours' reprieve to figure out my next move and find my next victim.

But this guy's gonna go through with it. I can tell. I can always tell.

But that ain't the worst of it, not for him.

This poor son of a bitch has no idea what he's walking into. You see, there are a couple of things I haven't told you yet. Firstly, I know exactly where we're going and I know who lives in that house. I smell 'em every time I end up here. Secondly, I didn't end up in this town by accident. Not this time. And lastly, we're not going there for booze. We're going there for peace.

Who lives in that house?

UHF and the FM Girl.

That's what we called them anyway, in Midian, behind their back. Their names are Humphrey B and Sylvia, but the first time you see them you can't think of them as anything but UHF and the FM Girl. UHF is a tall guy, six feet at the shoulder, with an old nineteen-inch black-and-white CRT television for a head. There's all this sinewy muscle wrapped around cables running up from his chest and neck into the TV, but the back of the set is blown out, like it was hollowed from the inside by a shotgun blast—jagged plastic surrounding a seven-inch hole. Inside there's nothing, nothing at all. But the TV screen is always lit, a disembodied head in fuzzy black and white, ever floating, reacting, just as you'd expect his head to react.

The FM Girl is different. She's lithe, willowy, easily five-foot-nothing, her skin wrinkled and desiccated, as if she were mummified, her eyes and mouth sewn shut with ratty black thread. While she can't speak, she's always broadcasting her thoughts, and if you've got a radio nearby tuned to the right station—89.7! The screaming sounds of Hell!—you can hear her just fine. So she carries around an old beat-up hand-cranked emergency radio that she'll wind to life if she ever has anything to say.

They're a fine couple, as married as us monsters can be. FM Girl needs flesh to feed; UHF just needs to watch. He can go a little longer than she can, but neither can go more than a year or two without a good honest-to-God murder. I've been keeping track of them for a spell. They've been picking off truckers over the years, catching them overnight, murdering them in their cabs before driving their trucks off into oblivion. But it's been a while. And they must be getting hungry.

So I'm bringing take-out.

The windows of the house are blacked out for obvious reasons, but Bill doesn't notice. It's a run-down, single-story ranch-style affair with peeling blue paint and the rusted-out frame of a mid-seventies Oldsmobile oxidizing into nothingness out front. It is, as far as Panhandle homes go, entirely ordinary.

We slip in through the back door into a hallway that splits off to the living room and the kitchen. I point to Bill and then the kitchen, then at myself and the living room. He enters the kitchen completely unaware that there's an open door to the cellar in there, and that under this house there be monsters.

They hear him come in. He's about as silent as a raccoon in a trash can.

A pale blue light creeps up the stairs, but Bill's too busy picking through the cabinets to see it.

Behind him, not six feet away, is the FM Girl, her husband

standing silently, ominously, behind her. Watching. The kitchen fills with the blue light of his flickering set, and Bill turns slowly around.

His eyes go wide with fear. He's paralyzed, unable to process what he's seeing.

The FM Girl reaches up to her sewn-shut mouth and yanks at the thread, pulling it out in one slow, deliberate motion. Then her cheek splits, splaying her ear to ear, rows of needle-teeth glistening in slobber as her massive jaw unhinges. Her mouth is so wide it looks as if it could swallow Bill's head whole.

Behind her, UHF's head vanishes from inside the set, his display showing his view of his wife and her soon-to-be meal.

The FM Girl reaches down and cranks her radio, winding it up furiously. It crackles to life, thick static shrieking murderous thoughts along with the phrase *Wrong house, motherfucker.*

My machete cuts her in half from behind before UHF can speak up to warn her, his flickering screen showing every horrible second of his wife's demise. Her body topples to the floor with two wet slaps.

I dive in like a rabid beast, razor claws rending her flesh into fistfuls of meat that I greedily shove into my mouth. Blood coats me in seconds, the floor growing slick with it.

I look up at UHF and smile. He's feeding. He's feeding watching his own wife devoured handful by delicious handful. He feels awful about it, can't decide whether to run for safety or stay a few seconds longer to taste the end of the love of his life. The thrill of his sin is the cream gravy on the chicken-fried steak of my meal.

"You should go, Humphrey," I say through a mouthful of his wife.

His head reappears on the screen and his voice crackles through his tinny mono speaker. "Are you going to kill me next?"

"Do I have to?"

He shakes his head back and forth, the television remaining perfectly still. "No."

"Then go. Run. Before I change my mind."

He thinks for a second, knowing he should probably fight, should stay and defend the last remains of his beloved Sylvia. But he doesn't. He runs.

And I turn back to my meal, savoring every last bit of murderous sin that remains of the FM Girl.

Bill is slumped on the floor, staring at me slack-jawed, eyes wide, unblinking.

So I turn to him. "You're not going to say a word about this, are you, Bill?"

He shakes his head, terrified, a few seconds shy of pissing himself right there on the floor.

"Good. Now get the fuck out of here."

He stands up and scampers out the door without looking back. Frankly, I don't give a shit if he tells anyone. Who's going to believe him? He walked out of a bar drunk with a stranger, and the next time anyone sees it, this house is going to be on fire. Telling stories about monsters in the basement will get him branded either a crackpot or an arsonist.

He'll choose neither. He's going to spend the rest of his life trying to forget what he saw tonight, and maybe, just maybe, he'll stop trying to live in the past.

I don't have anything against humans, really. I don't ever make anyone do anything they don't want to do in the first place. Not really. I just give them a nudge. The interesting thing about doing this is seeing what comes after. My gift to them is they get to find out who they really are, deep down. And what they do with that knowledge defines them from that point on. Some folks can't handle the memories of their night with me, but others come out all right on the other side. They make peace with themselves. They become better people. But it's their choice. Everything is their choice.

So in case you were wondering, that's how I sleep at night.

And I'm going to be sleeping a lot better now knowing I won't have to be that guy for quite some time, that I won't wake up with an itch in my head that turns into a rumble that turns into a scream. All my drinking I can do for myself now; all my sins will be my own. At least for a while.

But now that my head's clear and I've got the taste of monster on my tongue, I'm wondering. Just how much more time can I buy myself if I run ole Humphrey down as well? I think I might do just that. He smells delicious.

A Clean White Room

Scott Derrickson and C. Robert Cargill

THE LOBBY

The *clack-clack-clack* of his wing-tip shoes rings out stark and steady against the polished marble floors, echoing with a tinny din through the cavernous old lobby. At one time this place was the height of luxury, but now the wallpaper is decades old, yellowed with water stains, peeling in places, the mahogany front desk chipped, abused, languishing just this side of total ruin. Yet somehow the browns, yellows, and whites blend together into something homey, comforting. In the right light it might even seem quaint.

But it never quite holds the right light. In fact, it is rare that this building has exactly the right light at all. Quirky. That's how the Landlord had put it. The wiring is quirky. Damned inconvenient is what it really is.

He's pacing again, counting his steps again, each stride just shy of covering the breadth of the black-and-white checkerboard pattern splayed from one dingy wall to the other. Eighty-seven and a half steps wide, 112 from door to desk. But it feels bigger. Sounds bigger. It seems to change shape in the night, the walls growing farther apart or contracting inches at a time. But it is always $87^{1}/_{2}$ steps wide and 112 steps from door to desk. No matter how many times he counts, it is always the same.

He stops. He turns. And there are his groceries. Two large paper bags filled with the same items they held last week. And the week before that. And as many weeks back as he can remember.

He didn't hear a knock or a key in the tumbler, and the delivery boy made no announcement. He'd always assumed the delivery boy was scared of the place, creeped out by the images on the carved ebony front doors, chased off by the eerie silence that always pervades this place. But he never saw him, never spoke to him, couldn't say with any certainty that such a delivery boy even existed. Groceries simply appeared, always when he wasn't looking. So he walks back 112 steps, picks up his groceries, and walks 43 steps back toward a large oak door with a small, slightly corroded brass plate that reads SUPERINTENDENT.

The Superintendent fumbles in his jacket pocket and keys clatter into his hand, several dozen different cuts and shapes and metals all bound together on a single large brass ring. He thumbs through them, finding the right one by touch. The key goes in smooth and silent, the lock clicking only faintly, the knob whispering gently as it turns. It is the quietest door in the building. It has to be, for it hides its greatest secrets.

He opens the door, slides quickly in, and sniffs deeply at the air of the place.

The apartment beyond is opulent, almost ridiculous, both in size and architecture. While all of the rooms in the building are unusually large, the Superintendent's dwelling is second only to the penthouse in size. In any other building it would sell for millions, but in this one, nothing—a prize instead only for someone willing to hold the building together with spit, baling wire, and moxie alone. The ceilings are vaulted, ebony beams running across them, chandeliered lights dripping from the center of nearly every room. The floors are hardwood, dark, scuffed, the wood soft in places from the tread of a century's worth of traffic. The walls had once been white but are now a sort of eggshell from the smoke of five previous superintendents. The fireplace is massive, brought stone by stone across the sea from some ancient residence. And the kitchen is large, designed with servants in mind, updated just enough to be modern, but not so recently that everything worked properly.

Despite the opulence, the apartment on the whole is spartan. No art, no photos, no statues or sculptures, just a simple table with a single chair, one red suede couch—well worn—a rocking chair by the fireplace, and a bed, a wardrobe, and a nightstand in the adjoining master bedroom. It is otherwise stone, wood, and wallpaper. Nothing more.

The Superintendent methodically puts his groceries away in the kitchen, each sundry finding its way to a very specific, well-rehearsed location. There is an order to it, almost a ceremony. The flour goes in a perfectly sized clean spot amid a dusting of scattered meal where all of the other bags of flour had rested before; the oil in a spot flush against the cabinet's back corner; the carton of milk immediately below the refrigerator's bulb. Each item in its exact place despite there being no lack of room for them to find another home. It is as he wanted and no other way.

THUMP.

He looks up, eyes narrowed, at the room above him. Apartment 202. The one with the ironwood door. Another thump.

Then a series of rumbles and rattles like an awkward tap dance by large, clumsy, untrained feet. The Superintendent sighs deeply.

It shouldn't be time yet, he mutters to himself.

He quickly puts the last remaining groceries away before adjourning to his bedroom to get changed. Strips out of his sweat pants, jacket, and T-shirt, opens the doors on the antique mahogany wardrobe. Inside, a single gray wool suit. Three-piece. Single-breasted. A narrow gray wool tie. And a cotton shirt with bone buttons. The Superintendent dresses quickly, leaving neither a hair nor a fiber out of place.

He opens the bottom drawer, digging through a pile of T-shirts and pants, drawing from beneath them a small fifteen-inch ebony lockbox, carved seemingly from the same wood as the front doors and almost identically decorated. Angels upon demons upon knights and knaves. The Superintendent takes a deep breath, cracks his neck side to side, and leaves his apartment, grabbing his key ring on the way out, locking the door silently behind him, and making his way across the lobby to the elevator.

THE DESERT

He was swallowed by the moonless black so deep and far-reaching, the only way to tell the difference between the earth and the sky was by where the stars began. The sky was riddled with them. More than he'd ever seen at once. It was the type of sky one expected to see only in the still quiet of an uneventful night. But this was far from that.

There was shouting, screaming. And when a mortar exploded half a football field away, the *BOOM* rattled his bones and the landscape lit up with a flash of daylight. But just for a moment, a scant terrifying moment. He scanned the ground for shadows, for bodies, for the things that might be hiding, waiting for him in the black. His breaths were measured, controlled, desperate for calm, and he counted his paces—253 of them in total between the latrine he'd just left and his bunker.

He had to find his way back, had to get back to the concrete bed beneath which he could cower and cry to himself, more afraid of the things that might be lurking just outside the light than the explosives and shrapnel that might shred him into a puff of pink mist. Only fifty more steps to go. Only forty-seven more steps to go. Only forty-three more steps to go. Only forty more steps . . .

202. THE IRONWOOD DOOR

The lift key turns and the tiny antiquated brass and iron elevator rattles to life. It jerks and sputters in fits on the way up, but it's better than taking the stairs. You never know how long the stairs will take. The insides are polished to a high shine, and the Superintendent eyes his reflection, nervously adjusting his tie before brushing a bit of stray dandruff from his shoulder. It takes nearly a minute to get to the second floor, and when the doors open, he quickly steps out, staring headlong into a mirror. He looks both ways down the hall, unsure where 202 is today. These halls are tricky. They coil around like snakes twisted up in themselves, the lengths seeming sometimes impossible, other times merely improbable.

To the right the overhead lights shine bright and steady, but to the left they dim ever so slightly every few seconds before brightening back up, an ever-present buzz oscillating along with them. The lights are always stranger near 201, so he turns to the right and begins a winding tour of the second floor. One hundred twenty-four steps. It is always 124 steps. Three turns and a long corridor later he finds it. Just as he remembers, 124 steps in. The ironwood door. Three small brass numbers. Two zero two. And a brass knocker, a small piece of note card slotted into it with the tenant's name: Mr. Fitzpatrick.

The Superintendent jangles his keys, searching for 202. He hasn't used it often yet, still hasn't memorized its shape, and tries three different keys, all black stainless steel. The first two get stuck halfway in; the third slides in like cutting through butter. The knob creaks a little as it turns but not too loud, and the hinges whine softly as the door swings open.

The inside of the apartment is even more spartan than his own. White walls. No table. No fireplace. Just three mirrors, each on a wall of its own. And a single wooden chair.

Tied to that chair with brown leather straps is Mr. Fitzpatrick.

Fitzpatrick is a nebbishy man. A small man. Wiry. Like a bundle of sticks pieced together beneath khaki pants and a polo shirt, each stick ready to snap under the slightest pressure. His hair buzzed close, balding around an ailing widow's peak. Skin pale, chin weak, eyes a little too close together. Trembling, he looks up at the Superintendent, lip quivering, a scream caught in his throat.

"Please don't kill me."

"What did I tell you?" asks the Superintendent, his voice croaking, deep with bass.

"Please, God, don't kill me. Just let me go."

"What. Did. I. Tell. You."

Fitzpatrick looks shamefully down at his ragged tennis shoes. "Not to make a sound."

"So why am I up here?"

"I made a sound."

"You made several."

"You're just going to kill me anyway."

"I don't want to," says the Superintendent.

"But you will."

"I don't have a choice. Not now."

"You don't have to kill me."

"This is all on you, and you know it."

"Please," begged Fitzpatrick, "I have a family."

"No you don't," he says coldly. "Not anymore."

Fitzpatrick's eyes go wide, his mouth yawning in terror.

"What did you do?" he whispers.

The Superintendent slowly opens the ebony box, eyeing Fitzpatrick all the while. Inside is a twelve-inch wooden dagger, blackened by fire, sharpened from hilt to tip, decorated with symbols and scrawl, letters from a long-dead language. He grasps the hilt, squatting to set the box gently on the hardwood floor. Then he springs across the room, holding the blade against Fitzpatrick's neck, rage spilling out from calm waters. "Who are you?" he bellows.

"Jerry Fitzpatrick!"

"No! I didn't ask who you were. Who are you now?"

"Jerry!" Fitzpatrick bounces around in his chair, screaming. "I don't know what you want me to say! Tell me and I'll say it! I'll say anything! Please!"

"I want the truth."

"I told you the truth. You want me to lie."

"You're full of lies. Nothing but. Tell me who you are and this can all be over."

Fitzpatrick looks down at the knife. Wooden, but carbonized and razor sharp. He wets himself.

"Jerry Fitzpatrick," he says meekly, knowing full well what was coming.

The Superintendent clenches a tight fist, punches him square in the jaw, knocks the chair over onto its back. Fitzpatrick's head bangs against the floor, the sound like a hollow being hit by a hammer. Tears stream down the side of his face into his hair, piss turning half of his khakis a deep soaking brown.

The Superintendent looms over him, pointing the blade like a wand directly at his heart. "Who are you?"

THUMP. THUMP. THUMP.

They both look up, Fitzpatrick's eyes wide with surprise, the Superintendent furrowing his brow, scowling at the ceiling. Three oh one. Goddamnit. The Superintendent leans over, grabs the back of the chair with his free hand, flinging it upright in a single motion.

"Stay here," he says. "Stay quiet. Or this will all get worse. Much, much worse."

Slamming the door behind him, he stares down the hallway at his reflection in the mirror. He seethes, breathing heavy, teeth clenched, dagger clutched tight in a white-knuckled fist. Then he storms down the hallway, his shoes sounding a far brisker *clack-clack-clack* than before, his mind desperately retracing the steps back to the elevator in order to then find his way to 301—the one with the Spanish cedar door.

THE DESERT

The daylight was harsh, the heat unbearable, barren earth stretching as far as the eye could see, broken only by shacks and stone buildings. His team leaned back against the mud-brick wall, crowded around the door, M4 carbines held close against their chests. Their packs were heavy on their backs, sweat pouring down their brows, dripping onto their hard plate vests.

Miller nodded, his pale blue eyes revealing only confidence. Jackson nodded back, kicking in the door before he could even finish the nod. The wood was old, barely serviceable, and it shattered around the knob as the boot came crashing through. Splinters rained down as the team barreled in, shouting, rifles trained. Arms went into the air, white and black and cream-colored robes hitting the floor, begging in Arabic for mercy. Claims of innocence; accusations of a mistake.

It was shadowy inside. Some of the rooms didn't have lights. The Superintendent wasn't sure what he was more afraid of—someone dangerous lurking back there . . . or something. He remembered his training, fell back on instinct, tried to bury the images of claws and lithe oblong shapes back into their deepest recesses so he could focus on his job. His job was what mattered, it was all that mattered. Everything else was just fear. And fear is only in the mind. Do the job, do the job, do the job.

He crept slowly on unsure feet into waiting dark.

301. THE SPANISH CEDAR DOOR

The key crowds into the lock like a drunk in a packed subway car, bumping and scraping against every tumbler along the way, trying to settle in, find its place. The door is plain, a polished sandy blond with only a handful of nicks. Everything about it seems as if it has seen very little use at all, as if it were either long neglected or a recent cheap replacement. It swings open slowly, a bit crooked on its hinges, squeaking rather than creaking.

The inside is as plain as the door, and every bit as plain as 202. Three full-length mirrors, one mounted on each of three walls, and a chair, facing the doorway. Strapped to that chair, much like the one before it, was a woman: thin, pretty, with high cheekbones and hair almost as sandy blond as the door. Her eyes closed, lips drawn tight.

"You moved your chair," says the Superintendent, waving

the dagger in one hand as he talks, closing the door behind him with the other.

She says nothing.

"We talked about this." He walks over, spins her chair 180 degrees so it faces the mirror on the opposite wall. "You're not to move. Not a muscle. Not an inch."

"I don't like looking at myself."

"You're not supposed to. That's the point."

"Just get it over with."

"Not yet. Not until you tell me. Not until you show me. Tell me the truth and it'll all be over."

"You think you know, but you don't. You don't know anything."

"Who are you?" he asks.

"Emma."

"Emma what?"

"Emma Goerte."

"When were you born, Emma?"

"What? What does that matter?"

"When were you born?"

"In eighty-seven."

The Superintendent sighs. "Which eighty-seven?"

"What?"

"You heard me. Which eighty—"

Bzzzzzzzzzzzzzzzzzt! sounds the old intercom, cutting him off midsentence.

"You should get that," she says.

The Superintendent clenches his fist, punches her square in the back of the head. The force lifts the back legs of the chair off the ground, her head flopping around limply as if her neck was broken. She doesn't move.

Bzzzzzzzzzzzzzzzzzt!

He walks over to the old brass intercom, presses a well-worn button, leans in to the corroded old speaker. "Yes?" A soft, lingering silence hangs in the air, small pops crackling over a light static. In the background, just beneath it: wails, moans, tiny distant screams. "YES?"

Nothing. That could only mean one thing. The Landlord.

THE DESERT

"She was great, you know," said Burke. He smiled so wide that all thirty-two perfect teeth showed. His hair was black, cropped short but styled, his eyes always glassed over as if they didn't give a shit about anything they had seen. "Really fuckin' great."

"I don't want to hear about it," said Miller, his hand gripped tight on the wheel, the Humvee rattling with every bump on the bomb-blasted, rubble-strewn road.

"Well, what the fuck else do we got to talk about?"

"I want to hear it," said Jackson, who sat in back with Burke.

Miller swore beneath his breath, shook his head a little.

"We're talkin' tits out to here, beautiful big brown nipples— you know, like perfect slices of thick meaty cooked sausage— narrow waist, a stomach like she was doing Pilates, and one of those yoga asses. You know what I'm talking about? The yoga asses? With the pants?"

Jackson giggled like a thirteen-year-old boy. "Yeah, man. I love those." He did. He'd seen them online but never in person. Not out of the pants at least.

"And she was tight. Hairy as fuck, but tight. I mean virgin tight. That pussy just gave and gave and gave like it had never felt a dick before. Gripped me like a fucking pro. It was like being in high school again. That's the thing about these fucking haji girls, man. No one knows what they've got hiding under those burkas. I was probably the first one there. Her face wasn't nothing to look at, but those tits, man. Just thinking of those perfect fucking nipples is getting me hard all over again. And the jiggle and bounce of those tits. It was like porn-star shit. And man, do they train those girls right. They just lie there and let it happen. Wait for it to be over. Whisper haji talk in your ear. It sounds like they're begging for it."

"Burke! Goddamnit!"

"I bet she was," said Jackson.

Burke's head bounced up and down like a dashboard bobble toy. "That's the thing, man. American girls. You've got to fucking woo them. Empty your wallet just to get them to lie there like a limp fish. But these girls, all you need is a firm hand and a gun. And they'll fucking writhe in all the right ways."

"You listening to this shit?" muttered Miller, glancing at the Superintendent. He wasn't, not really. He only pretended to. His eyes were out on the road, watching the setting sun, hoping they got back to base before the dark set in.

"Did you get her number?" asked Jackson.

Burke laughed. "Nah, I did the only thing you can do. Did her in with a rock and set her on fire. You know she has four or five angry brothers. When they find out sis isn't a virgin, they always go out and waste some poor sap in a uniform. Can't have that on my conscience. Waste of a perfect set of tits."

THE LANDLORD

He wears a white cotton suit, a pair of horn-rimmed glasses, speaks with just the hint of a southern accent, all lilt and no twang; sits in the rocking chair, next to the fireplace, where a blaze now roars; pulls his glasses down from his face, steams them up with a breath, cleaning them with a handkerchief. "How's occupancy?" he asks.

"Fine," says the Superintendent. "A little busier than usual, but nothing I can't handle."

"Anyone new?"

"Two oh two. Fitzpatrick. I don't know much about him yet."

"Right upstairs. That's cutting it a little close, don't you think? I don't want this building full."

"I'm taking care of it."

"Taking care of it?" he asks sharply.

The Superintendent nods nervously. "Yes."

"Do you want me to take you back? To where we found you?"

"No," says the Superintendent. "I don't."

"Why haven't you done it yet?"

"It's easier if I wait."

The Landlord finishes polishing his lenses, then slowly slides his glasses back onto his nose. "No. It's harder if you wait."

"It's trickier if I wait. But it's easier once I see who they really are. The longer they're here, the more real they become, the more their true nature shows through. It's easier to kill someone when you know he's not innocent."

"No one is innocent, especially not them."

"But it's easier when I can see it for myself, see what they're willing to do, how far they are willing to go to get out."

"The more of them you have and the longer you wait, the more dangerous this all becomes."

"I know why I'm here. I know what I was hired to do."

"Because we can put you right back where we found you. In a bus station, shivering, covered in your own piss, your last few worldly possessions clattering around in a tattered old pillowcase. I will drive you there now and this can all be over. You can beg in the streets and chase the light after sunset to hide from the things that call to you from the shadows, that tell you all of those horrible things, that show you all of those horrible things."

The Superintendent shudders. "No."

"What is it you want?" asks the Landlord.

"I want to go home," says the Superintendent, his voice cracking with a childlike tenor.

"You don't want to go back there. Not after how they treated you, the way they cast you out, tossed you into the streets like garbage. Tell me what you really want."

"I want a clean white room. With a bed and a desk. A window would be nice, but I don't need one. A rec room with a good TV. My medicine. The kind that makes everything quiet, not the one that makes me tired all the time. I want the voices gone. I want the noises gone. I want the things gone. I just want to be left alone in my room, my clean white room. And maybe watch a little TV." The Superintendent scratches his head, eyes cast down in shame.

"And we'll give you that room. That was the deal. We'll pay for that room for the rest of your life. But you have to do this for us first. You have to go upstairs. You have to kill them. You have to kill every last one of them."

"It's hard."

"If it were easy, then everyone could have his own room, his own quiet. It takes a certain kind of person to do this job, a certain kind of person who doesn't come along every day. You're that certain kind of person. That's why we chose you."

The Superintendent purses his lips, nodding slowly.

"I'm your man."

"All right. Take that knife. Go upstairs. And do what you have to do. Do your job." The Landlord looks around the room, listening closely to the creak of the building, the pop of the embers in the fireplace. "Sometimes I think there's very little life left in this old building. I'd hate to have to start all over again. From scratch."

THE DESERT

The Humvee smoked, broken, tires flayed by shrapnel, fires crackling, moments away from exploding. Jackson hung half out of the window, body crushed, guts showing in places, eyes wide like he was still surprised—like he could still feel surprise. Miller hung upside down, still strapped in, chest blown open.

It was dark now and the smoke billowed, disappearing above them into the night.

The M4 jumped in the Superintendent's hand, gunfire popping. He wasn't aiming at anything in particular; he just wanted everyone away from him. He prayed silently for the choppers to arrive, to spirit them away, to take them back into the light.

Burke screamed, firing, laughing, the bullets tearing through two men as they ran. "Get them! Don't let them get away!" His rifle roared, his teeth clenched tight.

"We don't know they did this!" the Superintendent called back.

"Yes they did! Yes they fucking did! They all did! Ain't none of them innocent! Not a goddamned one of them! Get 'em! Fucking get 'em!"

And that was the last thing he said.

The sniper's bullet tore through his neck, almost taking his head clean off. He fell to the ground, knees buckling like jelly, legs bent backward beneath him, boots to ass, his arms wide like he was crucified into the dirt. His mouth hung open, gurgling, throat shredded.

The Superintendent dove for cover, not even bothering to scan for the sniper.

The night went quiet, only the Humvee making any sound. It would blow at any moment, he knew it. It was all over.

Then it came. Shrieks. Howls. The bloodthirsty slavering of a gibbering beast. He'd heard it before. Cowered from it beneath his covers since he was a kid. It was a thing from the shadows. He knew what it looked like even before it crept out into the flickering firelight.

It was tall, terrible, impossibly thin. Mangled hands with razor claws as long as its fingers. Bulbous eyes like black glass set in umbral, pallid flesh. Wings three times the size of its body. Once out of the shadow, its gray skin seemed to glow even in the slightest illumination. The thing pounced upon Burke, tore his chest open through his vest, pulled his screaming soul out through a shattered rib cage. Its head splayed, a mouth that wrapped around from cheek to cheek growing wide, rows of razor-sharp needle teeth glinting.

And it shrieked again, long and loud.

Then it leapt into the air—straight up twenty feet—diving right back down into the shadows behind the Humvee, Burke's soul grasped tight in its arms.

The Superintendent wrapped himself into a ball, tears streaming, begging quietly for help into his radio as he waited, desperate for the choppers to arrive. He whimpered, he cried. But he couldn't hear the choppers. Not yet.

202. THE IRONWOOD DOOR

The door flies open and the Superintendent bursts through, his right hand tight on the dagger. "When were you born?"

Fitzpatrick startles in his chair, wriggling against his leather restraints. His skin cold and clammy, the smell of his piss hanging stale in the air. Narrow-set eyes look up at the Superintendent, pleading.

The Superintendent puts a firm hand on Fitzpatrick's shoulder, holds the blade inches from his chest. "When were you born?"

"I don't know!"

"What do you remember?"

"About what?"

"Don't be an asshole. Before you got here. What do you remember from before you got here?"

"Pain," he whimpers.

"What kind of pain?"

"The worst kind."

"Fire?" asks the Superintendent. "Burning?"

Fitzpatrick nods. "And cold. Terrible cold."

"Why were you there?"

"I don't remember. Please. Please don't—"

"Stop begging. You're only making me angrier. Why were you there? There must have been a good reason."

"No. I didn't do anything. I swear. I . . ."

The Superintendent's eyes squint, his countenance darkening. "Now I know you're lying."

"No! Please—"

The knife goes straight through his sternum, deep into his heart. Black, frothing blood spurts out, foaming around the edges of the wound, spraying the Superintendent from face to stomach, soaking his gray wool suit. Fitzpatrick bounces in his chair, the last few seconds of life spent wrestling against the restraints, black blood gurgling in his throat. The Superintendent knows that sound, remembers that sound. He shivers, memories washing over him, the grip of the knife loosening in his hand.

Then he falls to the ground, listening silently to Fitzpatrick's last gasping breaths, knife still deep in the man's chest.

For a moment he listens past the gurgles and the breath, past the convulsions and the death rattle, listening close. Expecting, if only for a moment, the sound of choppers.

301. THE SPANISH CEDAR DOOR

He stands in the doorway, gray suit stained black, blade dripping. She was facing his way again, sandy-blond hair limp and greasy on her shoulders, eyes trained on him, seething. For a moment they just look at each other, each waiting for the other to say something.

"Eighteen eighty-seven," she finally says.

"What?"

"I was born in 1887. But that doesn't matter now, does it?"

"No. Not anymore."

"I heard what you did. I heard the screams. Then the quiet. It's my turn now, isn't it?"

"Yes."

"You didn't eat him, did you?"

"What does that matter?"

She laughs. "That's all that matters. He'll be back, you know. He'll be stronger."

"What do you know of it?"

Her eyes go black, glassy black like the things that creep in the dark and the shadows. Then her hair blows back, as if caught in a gale-force wind, and she croaks, long and loud, like steel being dragged across concrete. Her chair begins to rattle, each leg jumping an inch off the ground, and the mirrors shake on the walls and the room itself quivers from some unseen force.

"Meshalok beluh kommorah! Betak mek anshorti!" she cries out.

The room echoes with the voice of Hell, growing at once cold, and the lights flicker as the whole building stirs, seeming to settle in on its own bones, threatening to topple over, crumble to dust.

The cabin melts in around him, the air crisp, almost frozen, a weak fire struggling against it, failing. Shadows flicker in the light. Everything wood, iron, rustic. A baby cries atop a table, its mother in tears above it.

She's angry. Angry at the man who left them. Angry that the last scraps of food were gone days ago. Angry that her baby WILL NOT SHUT UP!

She grabs it, throttles its throat, choking it hard, fingers so tight they crush the windpipe; shaking it so hard that she snaps its little neck. *BANG! BANG! BANG!* goes its skull against the tabletop. *BANG! BANG! BANG!* until the crying stops.

And it does stop.

And the silence wails instead.

It's cold. Frozen. A wooden shack in an icy wasteland, miles from town. Miles from anything. From anyone.

And the woman with sandy-blond hair strips off her clothes, her milky-white skin pulled tight over visible bones, her breasts raw from feeding. She opens the door, wind howling in, three feet of snow piled up outside.

Then she steps out, staggering into the night, half dead before the door swings shut in the wind behind her.

And the apartment melts back into place, the cabin gone, the dead struggling in her seat.

She pushes against her restraints, the leather giving way, stretching, about to burst.

The Superintendent braces himself against the doorframe, grabs the door, slamming it shut.

"Hell is waiting for you, sin eater!" she shouts in a second voice, the first one still shaking the world apart. "There isn't a sin eater born who finds his way to any other place!" Her restraints snap. She bolts upright.

But the Superintendent is quicker, if only by a fraction of a second. The blade sinks deep into her belly and the voice stops, her eyes melting back into a pale brown rimmed by a blood-shot white. "Not today," he says. "Not ever." He jerks up on the knife, slicing her open from stomach to sternum. The black blood gushes like a geyser, hosing him down in a sticky ichor, its smell like stinking carcasses, her sins too numerous to pick out from the scent alone. Entrails slop on the floor, rancid and foul, maggots writhing in black like twinkling stars.

"See you soon," she gasps. And the world falls quiet again, the building once more at rest, once more at peace. It's a cold, eerie silence, like standing in the middle of an empty freeway at midnight.

The Superintendent pushes her off the blade and her body collapses to the floor, her eyes staring lifelessly into the darkest corner of the room.

THE CHOPPER

The blades whirled overhead with a *WHUPWHUPWHUP* that shut out the rest of the world. Beside him in the belly of the air-craft lay the rest of his unit, each torn apart or crushed, covered in silver blankets so he couldn't look at their faces and see soul-less eyes staring up at the roof. He was the last one left. His skin was pale, his stomach roiled, and he would have thrown up had he not already vomited everything left in his system.

He looked down out the window at the darkness below,

knowing that they were there, creeping, jumping on anything they could find—he could almost feel them, skulking, braying, waiting for him. Screeching at the stars, wondering where he was. They were down there claiming the dead, dragging their souls headlong into Hell. And he was next. He knew it. They wouldn't wait forever.

There had to be some reason he could see them, hear them, smell them. He just didn't know why. And he didn't want to.

The Superintendent took a deep breath, counting silently to himself, wondering how much longer it would be until they made it back to base, made it back to the light. There was a comfort in the light, even the cheap fluorescents that lit up the plywood and sheet metal structures. Even those lights were strong enough to chase the things away. Even those lights could be trusted to let him sleep. That's all he wanted to do now. Sleep.

THE STOOP

The Superintendent sits out on the front stoop, drinking in the afternoon light, smoking a cigarette. He normally hates it outside. There is too much commotion, too many people. It is too easy to get confused, find himself screaming again at some poor fool who has gotten too close, find himself swinging angry fists at a mother just trying to soothe a crying child. Loud noises mess with him, bring too much back. He likes it quiet, likes being alone, likes the night when it isn't so dark.

The air has a comfortable chill to it, the trees holding tight their last bursts of autumnal color. He sits in his suit, still soaking in sticky black. No one would bother asking about it, no one is likely even to care. After all, he has the kind of face that makes people uncomfortable. Something about the way he never smiles, or his eyes wandering nervously looking for roadside bombs or beasts with snarling maws. It probably just looks like a sewer backup anyway, like he was some unlucky sap who had been standing in the wrong place at the wrong time.

That's how he always feels anyway. He might as well play the part.

He takes a moment and drinks in the building, its stone a roughhewn onyx, its glass gleaming, polished, and almost as black: an ancient, crumbling, broken monolith with rusty wrought-iron fire escapes and two massive doors made of solid ebony. It is an eyesore, to be sure, the sort of building no one pays any mind to when they pass, as if something primal inside of them whispers in the back of their brains to just keep walking. Maybe they can't see it for what it is, or maybe they can and just can't admit it to themselves.

He stares at the doors, each intricately carved with figures and scenes like a Rodin sculpture he'd once seen. They appear at first glance to be art deco re-creations, but the wood somehow hints at them being far older than that. One door has finely polished angels, cherubs, and seraphim; the other crudely carved demons, devils, and despots. Between them, along the inside edges, stand knights and knaves fighting for both sides. It is a war between Heaven and Hell, but if you look closely, examine the expressions worn into the wood, count the bodies piled on the ground, you could see that Hell is clearly winning.

The Superintendent smokes the last few puffs of his cigarette, enjoys his last few moments of daylight. He still has two bodies to drag down to the incinerator in the basement. They can't be up there when the Landlord returns. He can't do what the Landlord wants. He just can't. Not anymore.

201. THE KNOTTY ALDER DOOR

He hears the bump, smells cheap cologne, musk, and beer in the air. The smells of the previous tenants linger in the hallways, but he can always smell when something new is coming through. What he doesn't understand is what it is doing so far down the building. These things keep creeping closer to the ground. They are supposed to stay up high, as far away from the crack as they can, but now the lower rooms are filling up instead. This isn't a good sign. Apartment 201 was the last one left that wasn't his own. And they can't manifest in his own room, can they?

The door is made of knotty alder, a rich, vibrant, expensive-looking wood. He fumbles through the keys, trying to find its match. He still doesn't know what half the keys do, if they even do anything at all. Maybe they are for old doors; maybe they are for doors yet to be put in. He tries half a dozen keys until the seventh, a small copper one with only two teeth, fits like a glove.

He turns the key and the lock sounds out like a small-caliber gunshot. Shit!

He doesn't have much time. If that thing is standing already, it might make a run for the door. He hasn't brought the knife, hadn't even thought to. Those things never know that he is coming.

The Superintendent swings wide the door, jumps through, slamming it loud and angry behind him.

The thing lies on the floor, trying weakly to stand, still coming to its senses.

The Superintendent grabs the chair from the corner of the room and some leather straps tucked into his waist. He places the chair in the center, facing a mirror, and hoists the thing on the ground up into it. It wears fatigues and a hard plate vest. It has a holster but no pistol for it. Its hair is black, cropped short, but styled. It looks familiar. Very familiar. And then the Superintendent freezes, jaw dropping, eyes wide with shock. He can't even bring himself to finish tying the straps.

"I know you," Burke says, still groggy, eyes struggling to give his face a name.

The Superintendent quickly regains his senses, tying the straps so tight that it might cut the circulation of a living man off entirely. "We served together."

"We don't anymore?"

The Superintendent steps back, giving himself a wide berth. "Not for a while now, no. I got out. So did you."

"I don't remember that."

"You will. It'll come. With time."

"With time? What the fuck does that mean?"

"It always comes. It just takes a while."

Burke looks around the room. "What's with the mirrors?" he asks, eyes avoiding them.

"The dead hate mirrors. It confuses them, angers them, reminds them of what they really are."

"I ain't dead."

"Yeah. You are. You have been for a long time."

Burke eyes him suspiciously. "What the fuck is going on here? Where are we?"

"Just a building. A very old one."

"What kind of building?"

"The kind you build on top of a crack in the world. The kind meant to keep things in."

"I don't . . . I don't understand."

"You will. You'll remember. You'll remember everything.

Iraq. The girl. The thing that came out of the darkness. Everything. And then you'll remember what came after."

"What came after?"

"Hell."

"No." Burke squirms against his restraints. "What the fuck
is going on here? WHAT THE FUCK IS GOING ON HERE?"

"You came back. You found the crack. And I have to send
you back to where you came from."

"No. No. No! Fuck no! That ain't right. That ain't fucking
right!"

"Nothing about this is."

The Superintendent withdraws, opening the door, slipping
quickly, quietly into the hallway.

The door closes behind him, his heart pounding, head swimming. He can hear the chopper—the blades right above him. He
can see the bodies, smell the bodies. Remembers them looking
right at him. Remembers the bullet that tore out his throat, the
thing that tore out his soul, the smell of his corpse on the chopper. The war comes rushing back. He punches the wall, his
vision red . . . screaming, wailing.

Then black.

THE DESERT

"Get a load of this little shit," said the brutish ox. He was big—
easily six-four—and ugly, his body a layer of thick fat laid over
well-hidden muscle. His speech was slow and slightly affected,
making him sound as beef-witted as he looked. Everything about
him pointed to him having no other choice but to go to war—it
was that or move heavy things around all day under strict super-
vision lest he hurt himself. Nodding, he laughed as he pointed at
the Superintendent. "What's wrong with your eyes, little shit?"

His voice bellowed through the canteen, its deep bass resonating through the prefabricated fixtures meant to give the boys a little taste of home.

The ox's friends laughed with him. Another piped in, "Yeah, he's like one of those shaking little rat dogs."

"Chihuahuas," said another.

"Yo quiero Taco Bell?"

The Superintendent ignored them. It wasn't the first time he'd been treated like that; it wouldn't be the last.

"Hey! Chihuahua!" said the ox. "You hear me? You fucking listening, boy?"

"He hears you," said Burke, standing up from his chair. "I hear you too. And if I keep hearing you, I'm going to put so many of those nasty, twisted backwoods teeth down your throat you'll be shitting dentures." He cracked his neck to both sides. "Now, do you hear me, you sorry shit-for-brains piece of shit?"

The ox stood up. "You said shit twice."

"Only because I didn't think you could count that high."

The ox swung hard, but Burke was faster. Burke ducked low, threw a wicked uppercut to the ox's balls, then followed it with a haymaker to his jaw just as he doubled over in pain. The ox spun around, hit the ground with a loud crash, dazed.

An officer poked his head through the canteen door. "What the happy fuck is going on in here?"

"He fell," said the ox's friends.

"Yeah," said Burke. "I was just getting up to help him to his feet."

The officer nodded, knowing better but not really giving a shit. "All right. Carry on."

Burke helped the dazed ox to his feet. The ox flinched but accepted the help.

"Don't fuck with my squad," said Burke, "and you and I will get along just fine."

The ox nodded, returning to his chair slow and easy, his bell thoroughly rung. Burke sat back down next to the Superintendent.

"Thank you," said the Superintendent.

"No worries, brother. With all the hajis out here trying to kill us, no reason for us to be shitting on each other like that."

THE LANDLORD

The Superintendent lies faceup on the red crushed-velvet sofa next to a roaring fire in the peaceful quiet of his apartment. The last thing he remembers is standing in the hall, assuming he might wake up to find himself lost in the maze of the second floor. But he isn't. He is here. Across from him, once more in the rocking chair, sits the Landlord. And he doesn't look happy.

"Did you really think I wouldn't know?"

The Superintendent sits up, gathering his wits about him. "No, I . . . I mean—"

"The job was simple. Kill the things that come through and consume them so they can't come back."

"They haven't come back."

"When was the last time you went up to the fourth floor? Or the penthouse?"

He couldn't remember. It had been weeks. Months, maybe.

"The building can only keep them for so long. They'll work out the mazes, find their way down the stairs. They'll find the door. They'll find a way to open it. And then they're out in the world. We work very hard to make sure that doesn't happen. We keep Hell where it belongs. That's the job."

The Superintendent nods. "I know, I just . . . I didn't know how hard it would be."

"That's what you get for associating with the hellbound. Why would you even know someone like that?"

"I went to war."

"Fair enough." The Landlord leans over, picks up a wooden box, slightly larger than the one that holds the knife, sets it in his lap.

"If you thought this was hard before, it's about to get much, much harder."

He opens the box. Inside is a revolver—an old-style single-action Peacemaker with fancy inlay and a metal grip—a leather holster, and several rows of wood-tipped bullets.

"I thought bullets couldn't kill them. That's the point of the knife, right?"

"The dead can only be affected by the dead. It's the reason for the doors, the wood floors, the chairs, the leather, all of it."

"If you had this all along, why have I . . . why did you make me do it with a knife?"

"You said it yourself. This is a hard job. Some superintendents can't handle it. It just becomes too much for them. We found that leaving a gun lying around, well . . . it's easier to pull a trigger."

The Superintendent nods. "I understand."

"You know what you have to do?"

"Yes."

"You know how hard this is going to be?"

"Harder than anything else."

"Right." The Landlord stands up, hands the box to the Superintendent. "It's going to get harder the higher you go. Those things have been here far too long. I'd start with your friend."

"I didn't say—"

"You didn't have to." He pauses, standing, straightening his jacket. "Go put on your suit."

201. THE KNOTTY ALDER DOOR

The Superintendent drags his dining room chair into the room behind him with one hand, the other resting on the grip of the pistol on his hip. Burke still faces the other way, eyes closed, head turned to the side. The Superintendent was right: Burke can't stand to see himself in the mirrors.

"So this is it, then?" asks Burke.

The Superintendent spins Burke's chair around toward his own and takes a seat, the two sitting face-to-face, though several feet apart. "It is."

"Why are you doing this?"

"I didn't have anywhere else to go."

"You could have found something better than this."

"I was born to do this."

"Who told you that?"

"Not everyone can see you, you know. Almost no one can. You're the thing that goes bump in the night. You're the thing that slams doors and crawls inside little girls and makes them swear and spit and do awful things."

"That's bullshit," says Burke. "I'm not any of those things."

"Not yet. You aren't strong enough. You're still coming through. Once you're all the way in, you'll be nothing but hate and anger and pain."

"So why don't you just get it over with? Shoot me and be done with it. That's all you have to do, right?"

The Superintendent doesn't answer.

"What the hell else is there?"

"The things that come through—"

"Stop calling us things."

"The things that come through. I have to eat them."

"What the actual fuck?"

"I have to eat them. Swallow their sin. Purify them."

"You fucking do that?"

"I used to. But I haven't in a while."

"Why not?"

"It's hard. Hardest thing I've ever had to do."

"Why the fuck do you have to eat them?"

"Limited transubstantiation. Or at least that's the word they used. It's supposed to cleanse them. Send them back clean so they don't have enough power to come back through. I don't really understand it. I still get confused sometimes and the words get jumbled. I just do what I'm told. What I can, at least."

"Like Iraq," says Burke.

"Like Iraq."

Burke leans forward, genuinely curious, speaking softer than before. "What's it like? The taste, I mean."

"Sweet at first. Savory. Like good pork." The Superintendent pauses, mind swelling with unpleasant memories. "But then you can taste them. The things they did. The things that rotted them from the inside out. All the evil little things pile up, and it's like eating stink. Raw, rancid, meaty stink. You can taste the piss, the shit, the cheating, the hurt, the murder. All of it. And then you're sick for days. Puking, diarrhea. It's about the most awful thing in the world."

"So you're gonna eat me?"

"I don't want to. I know what you've done. I remember. I don't want to taste that. I don't want to know what it's like. Not that."

"But you will."

The Superintendent nods. "I have to."

"So why haven't you done it yet?"

"I've been alone here a long time. Alone in general even longer than that. It's been a while since—"

"Since you've had a friend."

"Yeah."

"But now you have to kill me."

"Yes."

"And then you're going to eat me."

"Yes."

"And you don't think that's a little fucked up? You don't think that they might be lying to you? Maybe they didn't choose you because you were born special. Maybe they chose you because they knew you might believe them, that you might do all of these fucked-up things without asking questions. Like Iraq."

The Superintendent shakes his head. "No, I—"

"How do you know we escaped? How do you know we weren't let go—maybe we did our penance and got lost somewhere along the way. Maybe you're the bad guy. Maybe you're the one doing all the awful things. Just think about what you're saying, what you're doing. This ain't right. This shit ain't right. They're playing you for a sap."

"That's not what's happening."

"Then just fucking do it! Get it over with. Eat me and send me back to the great beyond. You're right. All of this is real. Every last bit of it. Hell. Demons. Mirrors that can scare spirits. Hallways that move and change to keep us lost. All of it."

The Superintendent narrows his eyes. "I didn't say anything about the hallways."

Burke smiles, his shit-eating grin crawling all the way up to the wrinkles around his eyes. "You didn't?"

The Superintendent stands up, his hand on the pistol. "No, I didn't."

"Well, shit." Burke sighs. "So this is it, then."

"Afraid so."

"Not like this, though."

"There's no other way."

"Not sitting down. Not shot in the face like that. Don't let this be an execution. Let me stand."

"I can't."

"I won't struggle. I won't fight. Let me die on my feet, that's all I ask. Pay me that kindness. Let me die like a man."

"No," says the Superintendent firmly.

"I thought we were friends."

"I was friends with Burke. You aren't him. You're something . . . else."

Burke smiles. "You're right. I am."

The walls quiver, mirrors vibrating. Burke's eyes become a solid, glassy black, and his smile shifts into something sinister without his muscles moving at all. The entire building buckles under the strain, groaning against the evil taking hold of it. Everything shakes. Everything except the Superintendent. He stands firm, raises the revolver, points it right at Burke's heart.

"I've seen this show already. And it didn't turn out so well for her."

Burke struggles against the restraints. They stretch, threatening to burst. Still, he smiles. "Sure. But was there an extra chair last time?"

"What?"

201. THE KNOTTY ALDER DOOR

He awakens facedown on the floor, head splitting, ears ringing, covered in the battered remnants of the dining room chair. The Superintendent isn't sure how long he's been out, but the swollen puddle of drool creeping away from his face suggests it has been more than just a few minutes.

He shoots upright, looks around. The door is wide open. All the mirrors are shattered, glass scattered across the floor in wide arcs. Burke is gone. The Superintendent pats himself down. The keys! Gone. He fumbles for his revolver, finding it a few feet away, and says a silent prayer for small miracles. But this is bad. Really bad. There is no telling how long ago Burke escaped, no telling how far he's gotten.

He wipes the splinters of the chair from his suit and cradles the knot on the back of his head. He checks his hand for blood. Not enough to worry him. He shakes off what he can of the blow and races into the hallway.

The elevator is 133 steps away, but he has no idea in which direction. The halls could have moved while he was unconscious and probably have. Time is running out. Burke has the keys and could open the front doors, could get out into the world, never to be seen again. Not by him anyway, not by the Landlord. There won't be any clean white room waiting in his future. All of this for nothing. All of it. He can't let that happen. He can't let Burke out. Burke was a monster in life; there is no telling how bad he could be now that he's brought some of Hell back with him.

He takes a left—as good a choice as any—and starts counting steps. The lights flicker overhead, the ever-present buzz like a swarm of gnats further aggravating his headache. He moves slowly, carefully, gripping the gun tight, unsure if Burke has even managed his way off this floor. Step. Step. Step.

Nothing but the buzz.

Step. Step.

The building groans again, creaking, shifting. No, no, no! If he wasn't entirely lost before, he's lost for sure now. He runs, bolting around one corner, barreling down the hallway beyond. Ahead of him, the hallway twists, rolling over itself, and snaps into place with a slight wobble like waves rippling across the surface of a pond.

He turns the corner, looks down the hall, and sees Burke's knotty alder door, still open. It was on the exact same side of the wall as he'd left it. Somehow he was now on the other side.

No turning back now.

He presses on, sprinting in the same direction as when he had started. He rounds the corner and races down another hall. Another corner. Another. Another. And another.

And then the elevator.

He reaches for his keys before remembering that he doesn't have them. He will have to take the stairs. Fuck. He hates the stairs.

He looks up at the small brass arrow above the elevator doors. It points at 3 and doesn't move. Why the hell would he want to go up? Then the answer hits him hard, and his heart sinks so deep in his chest that he could poke it through his navel. He isn't ready to leave. Not yet. Not alone.

The Superintendent steps to the side, grabs hold of the stairwell door handle, summons all of the courage he has left, and pulls it open, his eyes shut as tight as he can manage.

THE HOUSE WITH THE RED FRONT DOOR

It was a white house, the kind with two pillars out front, a green, well-manicured lawn, and a bright red door dead center like a beacon. Eight Thirty-Seven Briar Street. It had a long driveway and a two-car garage, but there was only one car there, and had been for quite some time.

He was seven years old and this was the first time he had seen them. Not the cars. The things.

Every child hides under the covers from the noises he hears in the dark. And until this night, so too had the Superintendent. It was late, he was thirsty, and now that Mommy had gone to live with Daddy's friend, he had to get up and get his own damned water. That's what Daddy said. Be a fucking man. Be a fucking man. It became a mantra. Be a fucking man and get your own damned water. He always stank when he said it, so the Superintendent became accustomed to sniffing out how angry Daddy would be that night. Some nights he didn't get angry at all. Some nights he just cried. But not tonight. Not at first.

He was angry as all hell that night. He'd punched walls. Screamed about the bike in the driveway. Drank everything in the house. Kept saying *that bitch* and *that literal motherfucker*. The Superintendent went to bed early that night. It was all he could do to not get hit again.

So he crept down the hallway on his tippy-toes, every muscle tense, trying desperately not to squeak the hardwood floor. Some of the boards were loose, but he knew where each one was. He took five steps, counting silently in his head, then turned, took two steps more, and turned again. Seven steps. One step. Two steps.

And then he smelled it. It didn't smell like anger. It smelled like fear. It smelled rotten. It smelled like old death. It was something the Superintendent wouldn't understand for a long, long time.

The therapist would tell him that he imagined it; that it was a memory created after the fact. But he knew better. He knew what it really was. And when he saw it for the very first time he knew nothing would ever be the same. Tall, lithe, impossibly thin. Claws. Glinting teeth. Cold and sickly. Corpse-pale gray. All of it. It slunk from the shadows, swelling large and terrifying out of the dark, hulking over his tiny seven-year-old frame.

It leaned in, growling low and mean, sniffing him up and down, vacuuming up every scent.

Then came the *POP* from Daddy's room. It was like fireworks, but sadder. Lonelier.

And the thing grew excited, forgetting the young boy in front of him, darting for Daddy's room like a dog racing for fresh meat. Teeth bared, snorting, leathery wings knocking pictures off the walls of the hall. Daddy's door flew open, the light of a nearby lamp enough to reveal the remaining half of Daddy's head, with just enough light left over to see the rest of it dripping red and viscous from the ceiling.

The thing pounced, reached in through the wide hole atop Daddy's head, and pulled his soul out screaming into the night.

It knew. It knew before it happened. It was waiting for him to do it.

That's what they were. They were the things that knew. Death didn't follow them and they didn't bring it. But you never saw them without death nearby. Seeing them meant death. Seeing them meant Hell.

No. This wasn't some memory he created after the fact. That was therapist bullshit. This happened. He knew it. And it kept happening. Time and again. This was real. It was all real. It had to be.

THE STAIRS

The Superintendent spends a lot of time with his memories. He clings to them like a group of friends he can't quite stand anymore but knows deep down he can't live without. Sometimes they hang in the air like a stench; sometimes they are as real as anything else. But he always knows the difference between a memory and the present.

The stairs don't.

Even with his eyes shut he sees it. Clear as day. Iraq. The dark. The stars a full half of the world. The flashes of the mortars around him. He is halfway between his bunker and the latrine. He tries to remember how many steps he has left. But he can't. He doesn't know where he is.

And then he remembers that he isn't there at all. Not now. This isn't Iraq. These are the stairs. He tries to ignore the screams and the whistling and the explosions. But the stairs will not relent. They keep screaming. They keep whistling. They keep exploding around him.

He has to keep walking. He has to count the steps from the door, not the latrine. This isn't real. This isn't real. This is not real.

One. Two. Three. Four. Only fifty-nine more steps to go. Five. Six.

An explosion. Red mist. Winthrop. This is the night Winthrop died. He never knew Winthrop, but everyone will speak about him in the morning as if they had.

Seventeen. Eighteen. Nineteen.

He hears the soul torn from its mooring, but he can't see the thing. Not tonight. Not that night. He has to remind himself. He isn't there. None of this is real. Not this time.

Thirty-three. Thirty-four. Thirty-five. Turn.

He hopes he is counting right. Hopes Burke won't be waiting for him at the top of the stairs. Hopes that this is the last time he has to take the stairs.

Fifty-eight. Fifty-nine. Another flash, but no mist. No more screams. No more souls being dragged off to Hell. But snarls. He hears the snarls. He hears them waiting. They know death is coming. It might even be his own.

Sixty-three.

He reaches out into the dark. Grasps for a handle he can't see. Prays silently that he hasn't lost count.

302. THE BRAZILIAN ROSEWOOD DOOR

The door opens and Iraq fades away, only the darkness of the unlit stairwell enveloping him now. Concrete stairs and wrought-iron railing trail behind him into the gloom before vanishing entirely in the murk—a distance he doesn't remember traversing. Not for a moment. Just outside, past the door, the third floor beckons—less frightening than the stairs, but no safer. He thinks back to how recently he'd been here, wondering just how long ago that really was. The Superintendent isn't good with time anymore. When he's hungry, he eats; when he is thirsty he drinks; and when he has to piss, he does. Time doesn't otherwise seem to matter in the building, doesn't seem to make much sense. Was it this morning that I was here? Yesterday? Last week?

He honestly can't remember.

And it doesn't really matter.

He steps out into the hallway, scanning for Burke, not seeing a damn thing but tacky wallpaper and shadows from a handful of burnt-out lights. The large brass arrow on the elevator points sternly to 4. Fuck. In the time it took him to make it up the stairs, Burke has moved on. The Superintendent has to move quickly, has to make sure this floor's last remaining occupant is still in his room.

The shadows on the wall flutter just enough to look like a trick of the eyes. His heart skips a beat. But nothing comes of it. Room 302. One hundred forty-five steps. He turns and starts counting, takes a right where there should be a left, walks fifteen paces before another sharp turn.

Down the hall he sees it: apartment 302. The one with the Brazilian rosewood door, the grain of its wood dark and wavy, its finish a deep crimson—almost blood red from his distance. Wide open. A gaping maw having loosed its terrible tenant into the halls. Or has it?

The Superintendent slowly reaches for his gun, drawing it silently as he takes several careful steps down the hall. His training kicks in, heart pounding, adrenaline surging through his veins. He's kicked in a lot of doors in his life. Shot a lot of people on the other side. Of all the things he has to do as superintendent, this comes the most naturally.

He breathes in through his nose, out through his mouth. In through his nose, out through his mouth. In through his nose, out through his mouth. His heart slows, his head clears.

The tenant in 302 is a problem for him. A tough case. The first he'd chosen not to eat. He couldn't bring himself to do it. The creature is foul, to be sure, but it understands the nature of what it is and how it came to appear. And the Superintendent just couldn't eat it. It was the first—the genesis of all this trouble.

And now it has to die.

He spins around the door, gun trained, finger on the trigger.

Nothing. Nothing but a chair in the corner and three shattered mirrors. There is no telling how long it's been in there, how hard it focused to stay quiet, or how powerful it's grown in the subsequent weeks. All that is certain is that it is loose, either prowling these halls or upstairs with Burke. But which?

It only takes three breaths to get his answer.

The hallway grows ice cold, the lights dimming, a sloppy, congealed mess of blood slithering across the walls like creeping moss. The blood has a texture to it as if it's been drying in the sun but is still wet and sticky to the touch. Black masses of curdled blood and tumors form static waves as fresh blood oozes onto every inch of wall.

Then comes a sudden skittering across the ceiling—like a thing with more limbs than it should have, all of them made of claw and bone.

The Superintendent spins around, trains his gun at the sound, breath coming out in pillars of steam.

Nothing.

Then a hellish giggle from behind him.

He spins. And he sees it. Standing on the ceiling.

Four feet tall.

Overalls stained in blood.

Blond bowl cut falling on his face as if he were standing upright.

Little Jamie Osmunt. Eight years old. Fresh from the second grade. Eyes glassy black, mouth wide in a hellish scream, shark's teeth lining his mouth in numerous rows.

He wasn't eight when he died, but he was eight when he damned himself. And that's how Hell spits you back out—the way you looked the first time you dipped your toe into its fires. For a moment the Superintendent recoils at the flood of memories from the first time he killed Jamie. The image of Jamie's five-year-old brother at the bottom of a ravine, skull crushed beneath a large rock, made to look like an accident. That was how the Superintendent had envisioned the girl Burke raped—pieces of skull in pooling blood with a small boulder mashing in a pulp of gray matter.

But the images don't stop there. He remembers Jamie's years of cats and dogs. The first girl Jamie drugged at a bar and left in the woods. The seventeen girls who followed. The feel of the cop's bullet as it tore through Jamie's chest, snuffing him out. All of that races in and out again in the span of a hot, steamy breath.

And he regrets, more than ever, never having eaten the small boy.

He fires and the child leaps out of the way, falling sideways to land flush on the left wall.

Jamie runs, barreling at him, 102 demon teeth bared and snarling.

He fires again, winging it in the shoulder.

The beast flips, bellowing, landing on its feet, still sprinting without missing a step. Clawed hands reach out, grasping, paces away.

He fires once more. The bullet strikes true, tearing a hole between Jamie's eyes, blowing out the back of its skull like smashed melon.

The child falls limp and broken at the Superintendent's feet, still reaching, claws inches away from his toes.

There is no time to drag the body back into the room. He has to get to the fourth floor. Has to stop Burke before he unleashes any more of these monstrosities into the building. But that means he has to take the stairs. Again.

THE STAIRS

The desert. But not like last time. It's still dark and there are howls in the distance. Behind him the Humvee crackles, upturned, tires shredded, bodies hanging out of it just as he remembered. And on the ground, Burke, gurgling his last breaths.

He needs to wait for the choppers. He needs to hide from enemy fire. But he can't. He has to walk. He has to walk sixty-three steps. These are the stairs. The desert is an illusion. It's all in his head. He knows that now. It doesn't make the fear any less real, doesn't make his heart beat any softer, doesn't make the staccato of gunfire any quieter. But it makes it easy to ignore

Burke as he reaches out to him, gasping for him to stay, and it makes it easy knowing the thing bounding out from the dark doesn't want him. Not yet. It's not his time.

One. Two. Three. Four.

401. THE BLACK OAK DOOR

The Superintendent skulks out from behind the door, shaking off the last shivers of his memories. He glances up at the elevator's arrow and sees it still pointing at 4.

Burke is here, somewhere in the halls. Somewhere waiting to ambush him. His fingers squeeze the grip of the gun.

He rounds a corner. Rounds another. Winds through a sharp, abnormal series of twists and turns. Finds himself staring down another long hallway. At the end, Burke.

Unlike any of the other doors that open off the sides of a hallway, the black oak door sits at a dead end.

Burke is fumbling for the right key to open it. But there are too many keys, too little time.

He tries this key, then another. Then he stops. He knows he's being watched. Knows the Superintendent has the drop on him.

"Did you find our friend on the third floor?" Burke asks over his shoulder, not turning around.

"Yep."

"So you brought the gun."

"I did."

"And have you figured it all out?"

"What do you mean?" asks the Superintendent.

Burke turns around slowly, hands held open, up just above his shoulders, key ring dangling from around a single finger.

"This," he says, motioning to the building. "Have you figured it all out? What it means? What is really going on?"

"I know what's going on."

"You think you know what's going on. But do you really? Or are you still accepting everything at face value?" He looks around. "This place isn't what you think it is. It isn't a building atop a crack in the world. Those aren't magical wooden bullets and hallways don't rearrange themselves of their own volition. And you, you're not who you think you are. Do you even remember your name?"

"Yes. Yes I do."

"No you don't. You know how I know?"

"How?"

"You keep calling me Burke."

The Superintendent narrows his eyes. "Because your name is Burke."

"You were right when you said I wasn't Burke. That I was something else. I am something else. A shadow. A reflection. Of you. You're Burke."

"No. Fuck you."

"You said it yourself—you get confused sometimes. Things don't make sense. The logic of this whole place vexes you, twists you around so you can't tell day from night or remember when you last ate. How long has it been since you last saw me? A few minutes? A few hours? Days maybe? Does anything about this place make sense to you? It's all phantoms. This is Hell and you think yourself some punisher of the damned, condemned to consume the sins of others because you refuse to face up to your own sins. Acknowledge that it was you in the desert who died in the dirt. Who raped that girl and caved in her skull with a rock. Who did oh so many terrible things that you don't even want to think that it was you who did them. All that. Have you figured all that out yet?"

The Superintendent stares down the hallway at the shade

glaring at him, gun trained, sights set. His finger twitches on the trigger, confusion and regret setting in. "No," he says.

"What a sad and lonely Hell you've created for yourself."

He thinks back, back to the desert, back to his father in the chair, back to things in the darkness and the Landlord by the fireplace. And he tries to picture the girl, see her face. He can see her breasts, her brown sausage nipples, the sweat on her body as she pushes into him, crying. But he can't see her face. Because none of it is real.

It's conjured. Fragments put together from other memories as told by Burke. He remembers the desert all too well. The smell, the stink, the howls. It is real. All of it. None of what Burke said is true. This is no Hell. He is not Burke. This is something else. He is something else.

"Bullshit," he says. "The dead lie even more often than the living. You only tell enough truth to keep yourselves from being predictable liars. I'm not Burke. I never was. Nice try."

Burke raises his hands a little higher in the air, smirking. "I had to try. You gotta give me that."

The Superintendent pulls the trigger.

Burke's back explodes, showering thick black hellspit over the walls and door. He slumps slowly to the ground, bleeding out.

The Superintendent advances slowly, gun at the ready to fire again. Burke clutches his wound, his smile eroding quickly.

"Fuck you," says Burke, tears welling in his eyes, a bit of black spittle spraying out with every *F*. "Fffffuck you." He coughs. "You don't know what Hell is like."

"No. But I have an idea. And I know you have it coming."

Burke raises his hand from the wound, sees his own rancid ichor clinging to it. "Why'd you go?"

"Why'd I go where?"

"To war, asshole. I know why I went. But you. What? Did

you think you'd find the courage to fight your boogeymen or some shit? Is that what it was?"

The Superintendent nods. "That's exactly what it was."

"Did you find it?"

"Not there." He pulls the trigger, sending Burke back to where he belongs.

He breathes a sigh of relief, says a silent prayer for the part he liked of his friend, then stares at the black oak door. He stares long and hard, thinking about what to do next, thinking about Burke.

Then the Superintendent rears back, kicks the door in with a single vicious blow, firing wantonly. He doesn't hesitate. He doesn't fear what might be waiting. This is what he has to do, and it is best just to get it over with. It is going to be a long day . . . or night—he isn't sure which. But he has two more doors to kick in after this, two more souls that need purging.

And sometimes the old methods work best.

THE SUPERINTENDENT'S QUARTERS

He eats. He hates every moment of it, but he eats.

The bodies are stacked awkwardly in an awful pile, one atop another, flesh and oozing black spilling across the hardwood floor, maggots wriggling out of their wounds. The corpses gaze out, eyes lifeless, seemingly begging for mercy. For freedom. But there's no life left in them. Only sin. Disgusting, filthy, rotten, sour sin.

The Superintendent sits at the table, fork in one hand, carving knife in the other, slicing pieces of them off and jabbing them angrily into his mouth. He chews, his teeth grinding against fatty tissue, the taste getting worse with every bite.

He's lost track of how many times he's thrown up, stopped

bothering trying to make it to the bathroom. Black, fleshy vomit covers the floor beneath his feet, dribbles down his chin and onto his suit. There's almost no gray left to the suit at all—just black. Blood and puke covering almost every square inch of him.

He chews. He tastes the sin. Remembers the details. Sees the horrors. And he grows sicker every passing minute.

He thinks that maybe, if he had more time, he could eat them one by one, taking the time to regain his strength and see out his term as superintendent. Take the time to digest all that sin and seek penance for it. But that ship has sailed. He had that chance. It's exactly what the Landlord offered. And he had to go and fuck the whole thing up.

It is on him now. All his fault. Every bite is killing him. Damning it. All the color draining from flesh. There is no other way around it.

In the corner he can hear it. Scuttling, scurrying, waiting for the right moment to pounce, its pallid skin catching hints of the light, even as deep as it is in the shadow. The Superintendent just waves his knife at it.

"I'm not done yet. You can't have me until I'm done."

The thing waits. The Superintendent is doomed. It knows it. He knows it.

So the Superintendent keeps eating, slicing his way through body after body, doing the job he was hired to do. Whether he likes it or not; whether he understands it or not; whether it means anything to anyone else or not. That's not the point. These things can't come back. Not again. That's all that matters now.

And as he takes his last few bites—hours, days, maybe even weeks after he started—his body failing, eyes bloodshot, arm so weak it can barely lift the fork, he waves his knife at the thing in the corner, the thing waiting for him. He knows what's next. What's coming for him.

He waves at the thing, waving it over, whispering, "All right. It's your turn. Do what you've got to do."

He doesn't scream. Doesn't whimper. Not even a little. There just doesn't seem much point to it anymore.

THE LANDLORD

The oak door swings open and the Landlord slides the key out of the lock. He offers a carnival barker's arm to the room, presenting its space and grandeur to a nervous young man. The young man looks around carefully, taking it all in, unsure what to make of it. The hardwood floors have been recently cleaned, but the walls are still stained from years of smoke.

"So that's it, then?" asks the new superintendent.

"I'd hardly say 'that's it' about the job," says the Landlord. "It's a hard job. An important one. Not a lot of people can do what you do. Most of them, well, they can't serve out their term."

"They leave?"

"Sometimes."

"But if I stay? And fulfill the terms of the deal, I mean."

"Then we'll fulfill our end as well."

"A bed with a roof over it. Three meals a day."

"For the rest of your life."

"And the voices. The . . . things."

"The doctors will have pills for that."

"One year. That's it?" asks the new superintendent.

"One year. That's it," says the Landlord.

"I'm in. Sign me up." He puts out a firm hand.

The Landlord shakes his hand, nodding, mood darkening for a moment as he hands over the jangling ring of keys.

The Soul Thief's Son

Author's note: The following Colby Stevens story both begins a few weeks after the events at the end of Queen of the Dark Things *and takes place in the weeks after Colby and Mandu left Kaycee with the Kutji. A glossary follows for those new to Colby's adventures or for those in need of a refresher.*

Deaths as a Means Rather Than an End

An excerpt by Dr. Thaddeus Ray, Ph.D., from his book *Dreamspeaking, Dreamwalking, and Dreamtime: The World on the Other Side of Down Under*

I died once, as a child. I wouldn't recommend it.

I had been left by my guardian to learn the ways of the dreamspeakers and Clever Men of the Outback, and had already spent some time with the man who would be my principal teacher. We'd just lost a friend to the denizens of dreamtime, and the wounds from her loss were still fresh in my mind.

The events that would follow would lead me to making a terrible mistake, and as with many neophytes first trafficking with spirits, I followed that with an even bigger one in hopes of correcting it. I died so that someone else might live, and neither of us got what we wanted, though both of us, I feel, got exactly what we deserved.

The takeaway is this. The other side is a dark, treacherous place that our souls spend their entire lives trying to both find and understand well enough to navigate. I wasn't ready, and odds are good that neither are you. Death should always be a last resort in spirit trafficking, and even then, it should be avoided. Sometimes it is better to accept the consequences of a mistake than to try to fix it on the other side.

I
..

NOW

Colby Stevens stormed up the path toward Mandu's old house only to see Mandu's successor, Jirra, sitting with a beer, shirtless, sunning his dark Aboriginal skin on the front porch. Jirra waved, shaking his head with a shit-eating grin on his face.

"Jirra," said Colby bitterly, "we have business."

"Too right," said Jirra. "Was there nothing that deadly old bastard wasn't right about?"

Colby looked at him coldly, brushing off his friendliness. "You lied to me."

"'Bout what?"

"About Mandu."

"No I didn't," said Jirra.

"You told me it was his time. When I asked how he died, you said it was his time. But he was murdered."

"And how do you know that?"

"Don't play with me," said Colby. "We both traffic in powerful spirits."

"Too right. I reckon we do."

"So stop playing games."

Jirra nodded knowingly. "Both are true. Mandu was ready to go and he was murdered."

"So why didn't you tell me that?"

"I was honoring the wish of an old friend. And teacher."

Colby narrowed his eyes in disbelief. "Mandu Merijedi told you to lie about how he died?"

"To you, yes. But only to you."

"Why?"

"He said for you to learn what you needed to learn, you had to leave here without hate in your heart. Undistracted. He said you would need the hate for later, but first you were required to get a ring. Did you get the ring?"

Colby looked down at the Ring of Solomon on the ring finger of his right hand. "So all of this? He saw all of this?"

Jirra nodded. "And half a dozen other things affecting the lives of this village. He was . . . he was a true dreamhero. We just didn't know how great a one until he was gone. The ripples of his adventures will affect the waters of my people for a very long time. I'm beginning to doubt that even I'll live to see out all of his prophecies."

"How did it happen?" asked Colby, his eyes both serious and sad.

Jirra killed the last of his beer and tossed the bottle into the brush. It shattered against a pile of a hundred other shattered bottles. Then he motioned inside. "This is a beer story."

"They're all beer stories with you."

"You only ever ask for the beer stories." Jirra walked inside, leaving the door propped open behind him. Colby followed reluctantly into the dark house.

Inside the two sat once again at the cheap kitchen table with the mismatched chairs, each with a beer. Colby stared across the table impatiently, fingering the sweat on his bottle, but Jirra only smiled, taking his time. "The old fella really knew you well, eh?" he asked. "Had you pegged."

"How did he die?"

"Well, you killed him."

"I what? I didn't murder him."

"You didn't murder him. You *killed* him. When you were a kid. You just didn't know it yet."

Colby sat back in his chair, his brow furrowed. He took a swig of his beer, trying to read Jirra. For all his warmth and their shared history, Jirra was still a Clever Man, and Clever Men played games. He wasn't sure what Mandu's protégé was up to, but he needed to figure it out before he walked into some sort of trap. "Is this a lesson?" he asked. "Or are you just fucking with me?"

"Bru, let me tell you something. Mandu comes to me at the end of his life and says, 'Jirra, Colby will be back one day. You'll know it's him because he will be brought on the back of a powerful spirit.'"

"Right. The demon."

"Yeah. Then he says, 'He'll be back a few weeks later. You'll know it is time for him to arrive when you've returned victorious from a long, frustrating journey. Then and only then can you tell him the full story. Until that time, only tell him that I was ready, eh.' So I say to him, 'Ready for what?' And he smiles. Bastard just smiles. A week later he was gone."

"You're not answering the question."

"Bru, this morning I opened the fridge and there wasn't a

beer in it. Not one. It's blasted hot out there and I got me no beer. So I had to go into town, only the truck broke down half-way there. Had to walk the rest just to get someone to come get the truck. But then the fella at the store says, 'Sorry, fella, I'm all outta beer. Just sold me last sixer,' and I'm like, 'What do you mean, you sold your last sixer?' and he's like, 'Bru, did you see how hot it is out there?' So I got to wait around for my truck to get patched up. Then I gotta—"

"Skip to the end. Did you get the beer?" asked Colby.

Jirra pointed at the beers. "I just got home not ten minutes ago, eh, bru. So yeah, I got the beer. And yeah, I'm gonna drink my beer. And yeah, I'm gonna deal with the fact that that mean old bastard was laughing because he knew about all the bullshit I was gonna have to go through today and didn't have the fuck-ing courtesy to give me a heads-up about the goddamned fan belt. *Victorious from a long, frustrating journey.*" He looked off out the window into the brush, as if yelling at Mandu him-self. "It was a beer run, you old asshole!"

Colby smiled. "Okay, okay. So how did I kill him?"

Jirra peered from across the table. "Do you remember the first time you died?"

Colby stared darkly at Jirra, the color slowly draining from his skin. Memories more than a decade old began flooding back to the forefront of his thoughts. He sipped his beer. "Yes. Yes, I do."

2
..

THEN

Every boy needed to learn how to hunt from his father. And every boy needed to make his first kill on his own. Not just any kill—a close kill. The feel of the blade in your hand, the warmth of the blood as it courses over your fingers, the steam wafting from an open wound, the smell of the sweat, and the smell of the fear. Every boy needed to watch the life drain from the eyes of his prey up close; needed death to see him staring back, unafraid. Warra had followed his father hunting for years, watched him stalk his prey in the outback, learned the fine art of a quick kill, and tonight, on this black, moonless abyss of a night, his father was going to let him take the lead.

Nine-year-old Warra Gaari was finally going to kill.

Together they hid in the dark, crouching between the branches of a prickly bush, ignoring the thorns cutting into their bare brown, scarred flesh. Warra, thin and gangly, knelt close beside his father, Koorong, trying to keep his breath silent and still. In his hand, Warra clutched a bone wand, his father's pointing stick, crafted from the leg bone of *his* first kill. If to-night went well, Warra would be carving his own pointing stick by morning.

Firelight flickered in the distance, painting long shadows across the barren desert, the occasional patch of scrub clinging for dear life to the dirt, but otherwise the tiny campsite was alone in the wide-open expanse. There would be nowhere to hide. But the night was dark—a deep, terrifying kind of dark, the stars blazing pinpricks, the Milky Way a glimmering cloud— and the campfire was only large enough to cook a decent meal and chase away the night's chill. They would be able to sneak up unseen until the last moment.

Not two hundred feet away from them sat a portly man in a tattered T-shirt, cross-legged, enjoying a beer by the fire. Nei-ther Warra nor Koorong knew his name. They'd tracked him by fire's light, having chosen him because he was alone. Warra's first kill needed to be easy and clean. There would be time to teach him more elaborate methods of assassination when he was older.

Warra looked up at his father. Koorong looked tired, weaker than normal. His skin had paled, the whites of his eyes were a jaundiced yellow, and wrinkles were slowly spider-webbing across his face. And yet he looked as determined and dangerous as ever, the ravages of time doing little to rob the spring from his step.

Koorong quietly uncoiled a rope, tying a lasso at the end. He motioned down to it with a glance, Warra nodding in return, memorizing every detail. They stood up, each creeping silently in the sand through inky black night. They stayed behind the man, out of his line of sight, worried he might at any point turn around. But the night was dark and the man had drunk his fair share and then some, and the two were upon their prey in no time.

The lasso landed squarely around the man's shoulders, Koorong quickly yanking the rope back to tighten it around his neck. The man jerked backward, Koorong's strong, bear-like arms winding the rope back, dragging the man through the dirt, his screams muffled by the noose choking him to death.

Then Koorong jumped astride the man, pulling out a black flint dagger and plunging it into his victim's chest. The man gurgled, struggling weakly against the giant atop him, Koorong slicing a clean semicircle beneath his heart. Blood spurted, drenching Koorong, who then squeezed the wound just so as to cause blood to stream into a small basket that hung from a cord around his wrist.

Koorong waited, the life draining from the man's fight.

Then the heart stopped.

With the skill of a surgeon, Koorong pinched the rent flesh

together and whispered an incantation as he massaged the torn flesh. And within seconds, the wound was healed, the skin smooth. The man's eyes opened, his breath restarting with a deathly shriek.

Koorong hopped off, once again crouching in the dark as the man staggered to his feet, walking drunkenly back toward the fire. Taking the pointing stick from Warra's hand, Koorong leapt at the man once more. He clubbed him over the back of the head with one hand, then sliced his back twice with the knife in the other.

The man exploded, his soul bursting like a pile of leaves blown apart by a stiff wind, his scream like a strangled animal set on fire. For a moment the man was gone.

Then the leaves set themselves aright and the man re-formed, a leaf at a time, once more staggering toward the fire as if nothing had happened.

Koorong snatched the man's soul out of the air with a single hand and stuffed it into the small basket in which he'd caught the blood. Then he motioned to his son, tossing him the pointing stick with a knowing nod.

It was time.

Warra's heart raced. His mouth went dry. His knees quaked with excitement, his left foot tapping uncontrollably in the dirt.

It.

Was.

Time.

He leapt toward the warm light of the fire, knuckles white around the hilt of the stick.

The point went in one side of the man's throat, coming out the other with a wide spray of crimson.

Warra flicked his wrist and the throat exploded, the voice

box dangling from a few remaining tendons, arterial spray pumping spurt by spurt into the night.

The man dropped to his knees in the dirt, mouth agape, gasping silently for breath. His eyes stared up into the starlight, body paralyzed in fear, fingers curled, grasping painfully at nothing at all. Then he fell face forward with a thump, body limp, dead.

Warra smiled, watching the steam rise into the cold night air. For a moment he daydreamed that it was the man's soul, drifting out into the afterlife. But he knew better than that. The man's soul was safely in his father's basket. This was just the leftover meat, a dinner for worms. Even though his father had captured the lifeblood and the soul, he had let Warra make his first kill.

And it was everything Warra had ever hoped it would be.

Warra turned to smile at his dad, who stared back coldly in return. Koorong never smiled. But he nodded approvingly, which meant the world to Warra. It was as warm and loving a nod as ever he gave, as good as if Koorong had picked him up with a fatherly embrace and swung him around, laughing. Warra's insides tickled with pride. Then Koorong handed his son a machete.

"Hack the leg off at the knee," he said to his son. "We'll clean the meat from the bone and you can carve your own stick. But choose wisely. The left leg is better for spirits, the right leg better against men."

Warra felt the weight of the machete in his hand as he looked down at the man's legs. He raised the blade above his head with both hands and brought it down in one fell swoop. Koorong's son had chosen the right leg, and his father nodded in approval.

Then the two disappeared silently into the night, the man's

body still steaming by the fire, his soul safely tucked away in Koorong's basket.

3.

A Man and His Soul

An excerpt by Dr. Thaddeus Ray, Ph.D., from his book *Dreamspeaking, Dreamwalking, and Dreamtime: The World on the Other Side of Down Under*

Amongst the many powers of the Clever Men, or men of high degree, is the ability of their sorcerers to steal souls from the living, leaving behind conscious, breathing individuals who appear every bit as they were before the theft. Over the course of the following three days, however, these victims die from any number of terrible ailments, all of which can be attributed to the loss of their soul.

At first this process might seem counterintuitive. After all, dreamwalkers away from their bodies leave behind comatose husks, devoid of any sentience. Soul-stealing, on the other hand, leaves behind the human being as he was, though weakened, easily fatigued, prone to memory loss, and on the road to certain death. How is it that these sorcerers can swipe the souls from the body while the body still walks around as it did before?

The answer, it seems, lies in the parsing of terms. These sorcerers aren't so much severing the soul from the body as they are scraping the soulstuff out of a man's system, leaving behind only what is caked into his being like resin. Whereas dreamwalkers use this resin as a sort of "sealant" to hold their soul together, the art of soul-stealing involves puncturing that outer layer, draining the essence, and leaving behind the physical "husk" to buy the time necessary to put distance between the victim and his assassin.

We are, at our core, animals. What separates us from the lower animals is our soul. Without it, we can still function, but only on an instinctive level. Soul-stealing is practiced in many cultures around the world. In some practices, like the voodoo of the Caribbean, soul-stealing is used in zombie creation, leaving mindless yet living servants with no personality or memory. In Australia, the aim is murder, pure and simple. Sorcerers steal the souls of others as a form of cultural warfare, to settle vendettas or as offerings to the spirits.

But in certain cases, people have been known to survive such attacks and live short, hollow lives, eating, sleeping, and otherwise interacting with the world around them thanks to some sort of vestigial memory, but unable to perform any higher level functions. There are tales, however, of sorcerers who have not only survived such attacks but found ways to maintain a certain level of activity through various methods of feeding off dreamstuff.

4

It has been said by many that Koorong Gaari was the only man in all of Arnhem Land to have his soul stolen by another sorcerer and live to tell the tale. His was a heart and countenance so bleak and malicious that there could be no other explanation.

His eyes were pools of hate, his lips always curled into a scowl that could wilt trees in full bloom. The air chilled around him, even on the hottest days, and night grew darker when he was around, even the stars dimmed when he was close.

Koorong had been the only Clever Man within a thirty-mile radius of his home since he'd killed the last one ten years earlier. He'd long since wiped out all the sorcerers along the coast, moving from tribe to tribe, dreaming to dreaming, skulking along the songlines until he cornered and siphoned the souls out of each and every last one. And content that he was no longer in danger of being usurped, convinced that his was the strongest eye in Arnhem Land, he had settled down to a peaceful life, killing now only when necessary to obtain the souls he needed to live.

Warra stood beside him at the riverbank, the dawn light tickling the horizon as Koorong hefted a bottle of freshly drawn water from beneath the surface. "It has to be moving," he said to his son. "Flowing water. Always flowing; never stagnant. Stagnant water will sour the soul. Be like drinking a snakebite, eh. It will burn all the way down and eat you from the inside. Also, take it from the deep, not the surface. The dream is stronger deeper in the water." He lifted the bottle into the coming light, eyed it for impurities. Clean. Not a bit of silt or fish shit.

He reached into the basket at his wrist, plunging his hand in and drawing the soul out by the scruff of its neck. The black writhing mass tried to wiggle out of his grip, flopping around, snapping at the air, but Koorong held tight, having done this hundreds of times before, jamming it quickly against the mouth of the bottle. The soul, trying to escape, squeezed in through the opening, unaware that it was now trapped. Koorong stoppered the bottle with a slap and shook it violently.

The water darkened, swirling with fluorescent bits of violet and soft pink. The soul struggled but couldn't break the glass, couldn't loosen the grip of the rubber stopper. Slowly but surely it faded, softened, until it gave up the fight and became one with the water. And when it was done, Koorong pulled the stopper from the bottle and drank every last drop of the man trapped inside.

Koorong's color darkened from a pale creamy coffee brown to a rich, sun-scorched black, his eyes losing their jaundice, his skin tightening around his mouth, eyes, and forehead. What a moment before had looked like a man of fifty now looked thirty-five. The plundered soul was doing its work and doing it well.

"Now," he said, his youthful vigor returned, "let's get to making you that pointing stick."

IT WAS NIGHT AND THE CAMPFIRE HAD DWINDLED TO A SINGLE dim log belching embers. Koorong sat close, watching the last flickers of flame. It was his favorite time of day. Once the fire was gone, the rest of the outback would be asleep and he could relax. His son lay only a few feet away, deep asleep, hugging his freshly carved pointing stick like a teddy bear. The Clever Man didn't feel much anymore, but when he looked at his son, he felt pride. Warra was the one thing in Koorong's life that made him feel alive, that really reminded him what it was like to live life with a soul of his own. And to see Warra following in his father's footsteps, on the road to being a Clever Man all his own, made Koorong's otherwise hard heart swell.

But as he watched his son dreaming and the log sputtered as it died, the soft crunch of twigs and gravel drifted in on the night air. Someone was watching them.

Koorong had nerves of steel and knew exactly what to do. He didn't look, didn't react at all. He simply stood, taking a large branch from the ground to crush the last remnants of the log. The log came apart like snow, disintegrating into smoke and ash, and Koorong took the opportunity to cast his gaze, as if lazily, out into the dark across the bush. His eyes were sharp, especially at night, and while most people wouldn't be able to make out the shadow of the man creeping in the bushes fifty-some-odd meters away, he saw him clear as day.

The man crouched low, behind a shrub. Whoever he was, he was bad at this.

Koorong knelt down, then used a bit of Clever magic.

A shadow of Koorong appeared sitting beside him, and instantaneously Koorong wrapped the dark night around him like a blanket until he winked out and the shadow seemed more real than he. Then Koorong ducked out into the dark to surprise the intruder. He stalked quietly, hushing his footsteps with a wave of his hand, coming up closer and closer on the interloper. Slowly, silently, he slipped his pointing stick from his belt. Koorong was going to make this quick and quiet.

The man crouched by the shrub, peering at their campsite, entirely unaware that Koorong was five seconds from killing him.

Koorong leapt, jamming his pointing stick into the neck of the . . .

A shadow. A trick. A phantom.

Just like his.

No mere thief was watching them. There was another Clever Man.

Footsteps crunched a hundred paces away, running. Koorong turned, reacted, darting across the outback at an inhuman speed. He clutched his stick, waved his hand, manipulated the very dream that surrounded him, bending space so that he might gain ground on the man running away from him. His feet stopped touching the earth, and in the span of a breath Koorong was running on the very air, six inches above the ground, carried along by a strong wind at his back.

The shadow ahead of him loomed larger as Koorong gained ground; then it stopped dead in its tracks, turning to face Koorong. Koorong waved his hand and pointed the stick at the ground, stopping immediately. He looked around him for a trap; finding none, he scrutinized the figure.

"Ey, Koorong," said the stranger.

"Do I know you, fella?" asked Koorong.

The stranger shook his head. "You knew my friend. Your son made a pointing stick out of his leg bone."

"Tragic."

"Too right."

"So you came here to kill me?"

"No," said the stranger with a broad grin, "I'm here to distract you."

"Distract me from . . ." Koorong's eyes grew wide and his vision went white with rage. Without a thought he turned and ran, using every trick he knew to get back to camp. The bush flew past at a blazing speed. But he was too late. As he approached, he saw two men dart off into the darkness.

He didn't bother to give chase; he cared about only one thing. Warra.

His son lay on his back, coughing. Koorong knelt beside him, cradling his head, looking into his eyes. He was breathing and he was conscious. *They must have gotten scared off before—*

Then Koorong noticed the small cut beneath his son's heart.

The men hadn't come to kill his son—at least not outright. They came to steal his soul.

They could have killed him. That would have been the decent thing to do. Koorong had stolen the other man's soul, not Warra.

Koorong had handed down the death sentence, not his son. All Warra had done was kill him, mercifully, before the three days of sickness set in and he died a miserable, painful death. This wasn't justice, it was cold-blooded revenge—something with which Koorong was far too familiar.

He picked up his son in both arms.

"Dad," Warra whispered weakly, "I don't feel good."

"I know. Dad is goin' to get help. It'll be okay, eh?"

Koorong took off into the night. He wasn't fond of singing the songlines, but tonight he did. Tonight he needed to respect the spirits, needed their attention and aid. And this would be the worst possible time to offend them.

"Spirits!" he called. "Spirits, hear me!"

But no answer came. Sure he was clever, and yes, he had the strongest eye in Arnhem Land. But Koorong was the Soul Thief. He subsisted purely on the spirits of others to stay alive. And there was no spirit in dreamtime that wanted anything to do with him.

Except for one.

The dingo slunk out from the shadow of a rock barely lit by the coming dawn. "What's all the racket?" he asked in a yip.

"Spirit! Are you the dingo?" asked Koorong.

"I am a spirit," he replied.

"But are you the dingo?"

"What is it to you?"

"I have business."

"And what could you possibly have to offer me, dingo or not?"

"I . . ." Koorong stopped. He hadn't thought this through. He was already negotiating with a spirit without knowing the spirit, what it wanted, or coming to the table with anything to bargain with. He was up against the wall, rooted but good. And yet he had no choice. "Spirit, my son."

"I don't want your son. That boy has no soul."

"No, spirit. I know he has no soul."

"And he's far too stringy to eat."

"I'm not offering my son."

"Good, because that would be a terrible deal," said the spirit.

"I have nothing to offer but my service."

"You're the Soul Thief, right?"

"Too right."

"And you have a strong eye?"

"The strongest in Arnhem Land."

"Three services."

"Spirit, I can't promise you—"

"This is not a negotiation."

"This is a negotiation. If it be proper business, then it is always a negotiation."

"Okay, then," said the spirit, "two services."

"No, I—"

"Your son is dying and you want to negotiate further?"

"Spirit." He paused. "I would do anything for my son. I was not thinking. Two services."

"Oh, then three services it is."

"Spirit, we've already agreed!"

The spirit smiled, nodding his head. "Too right. Two services of my choosing at my behest. In exchange, I will help your son. Do you agree?"

"I agree. Now, please, give him his soul back."

"Oh, I can't do that," said the spirit. "Your son's soul is already gone. Those Clever Men knew you would want it back. They're long gone now. And they've released your son's soul. He's dying."

"But you said you could help him."

"I can. You already know what needs to be done to save him."

Koorong looked down with sorrow upon his son, then again at the spirit. "He has to become like me."

"Like father, like son."

"He needs to drink the soul of a Clever Man."

"Yes."

"But I've killed every Clever Man along the shoreline, and every one that I know of in Arnhem Land save one—and he is far too far away for me to get to in time."

"I told you I would help your son, and I will." The spirit smiled. "You spoke of a Clever Man too far to reach."

"Yes."

"But he is here. Close. On walkabout. And he has with him another, younger Clever Man—strong eye, powerful spirit. Enough power between the two of them to reforge your son's soul so he might live. I will tell you where they are. You and your son need but to claim their souls as yours."

Koorong nodded. "And the services I owe?"

"You will continue to owe. I will ask for them later."

"I am at your service."

5

Koorong huddled with Warra in a bush, their breaths short and shallow, bodies low and well hidden, waiting for the sign. They could see the campfire, an eleven-year-old whitefella and a Clever Man relaxing around it, completely unaware. It had taken all day to travel to this spot, and true to the spirit's word, they were there.

Koorong steadied himself. Though he was a soulless man without real fear, this Clever Man was Mandu Merijedi. His eye was strong and he was as clever a fella as Koorong knew. He would have liked to kill him in a way he could have sa-

vored, taken his time and made him suffer. Instead, it needed
to be quick and brutal. There were two of them, and there was
no way to catch them both unaware without Warra. Looking
around, Koorong tried to think of any number of clever ways
to divide them and kill them separately. But there were none—
none at least that Mandu wouldn't see through right away.

Warra turned to his father, his eyes warm with the glaze of
childhood, but his visage growing sicker by the minute. While
he didn't look any older, his skin was growing pale and beginning to sag. "Can I, Dad?" he asked very quietly.

"Can you what?" Koorong whispered back.

"Put my pointing stick in the whitefella? I can do it."

"We have no other choice. You'll have to do it. But first, tell
me now, and tell me the truth: do you remember how to steal a
soul?"

Warra nodded confidently.

"This is no time for pride. You'll only get sicker if we don't
get you these souls. Can you do it?"

"I can do it."

Koorong looked down at his son and put a firm hand on his
shoulder. "This isn't like a dingo," he said. "Stick him quick.
Don't give him a chance to react."

Warra nodded. "Okay."

"When I say."

"We go."

Each held his breath. "Go."

Koorong and Warra tore off together, each clutching his
bone wand.

Ahead of them Mandu and his young pupil stared lazily
into the fire.

The campfire flickered out, then flashed, relighting with a
puff of bright light.

What was he up to? Koorong wondered. Though he knew he had the drop on them, he also knew better than to underestimate another Clever Man, no matter how dim or ignorant of the law he might be.

They bolted without a sound over the desert ground, slipping through the dark, coming in at an angle at which they would not be seen until they struck. The two jumped, diving into the camp, weapons raised.

Warra's wand sunk into Colby's back, Koorong's pointing stick passing right through Mandu's head.

Shit, thought Koorong. They'd been had. Rooted for certain.

The fire winked out, the illusions evaporating, leaving the two exposed in the moonlight.

Warra looked up at his father. "What now?" he asked, both terrified and confused.

Koorong narrowed his eyes, grinning wickedly, digging his bullroarer out of his dilly bag. "We let them know Hell is coming for them." Then he waved at the air, whipping his arm around and letting the bullroarer loose.

6

The night erupted with the sounds of anguished torment, braying, cackling, setting the whole desert on edge. Mandu's run slowed to a walk, his jaw hanging open in shock, his eyes wide with terror. That was the sound of three screaming souls; he knew it well. *Koorong,* he mouthed silently. At once Mandu knew what was at stake. The spirit that had come to him in his dreams was right. They had somehow attracted the attention of the most fearsome sorcerer in Arnhem Land. And whatever it was he wanted, it was important enough to bring him out of the marshes and into the deep desert. These were not Koorong's songlines; he was trespassing. All of which meant he was after something worth killing for, and knowing of his reputation as he did, Mandu assumed it probably involved harvesting a soul. Maybe even his. But most likely, Colby's.

Mandu resumed running even harder than before, the sound of Koorong's bullroarer driving his feet faster than he had ever run.

Colby was right on his heels, pushing himself as hard as he could.

Colby and Mandu exchanged glances.

Mandu pointed a wild, excited finger at a nearby tree. "Colby," he yelled, "the tree!"

"Why are we running and not fighting?"

Mandu looked back over his shoulder into the night. "You don't want to fight him. Powerful sorcerer. Strong eye. No soul."

"No soul? That's malarkey! Everything has a soul."

"Everything you've seen, all of the impossible worlds, and you still question what is true? It can all be true. Why not this?"

"Why would he want us?"

"There are a number of reasons. Because you don't belong here. Because I shouldn't be sharing these secrets with a white-fella. Because we both are powerful enough to keep him alive for quite some time."

"Wait. Did you say that this is because I'm white?"

Mandu shook his head. "Because you're an outsider. You're not Aboriginal."

"Oh. I didn't know you weren't supposed to teach me."

"It was worth the trade. But you turned out to be very clever. You could be a great Clever Man or sorcerer. If you survive."

"So who is he?"

"Koorong."

"Koorong?"

"Yeah."

The two darted into the tree, sinking into the wood, letting it wash over them and carry them miles away.

They emerged in a crowded oasis, two trees to choose from. Mandu pointed at one halfway into the thicket and they leapt into that, vanishing again.

This time they emerged in the desert, no other trees visible for a hundred meters. So they ran, hoping if Koorong could walk through the trees, he wouldn't choose the right ones for a good while.

AFTER AN HOUR OF TREE HOPPING, THE TWO FOUND THEM-selves deep in the bush of Arnhem Land, panting, worn out.

"If he finds us," said Colby, clutching his side, "I hope he kills us quick." Despite being in good physical shape, he had never sprinted so hard for so long in all his life, and the exertion was taking its toll.

Mandu smiled, catching his breath. Colby's sense of humor was very much in line with his own. "If they do, I'll let them kill you first," he said.

"Good. I don't like the sight of blood." Colby took a deep breath, trying to control his breathing. "Who is Koorong?"

Mandu nodded. "Once," he said, "there was a young sorcerer hunting along a river who spied a beautiful girl gathering fruit from a tree. He had never seen a girl her equal. And since he didn't know her, he knew she must be from another tribe. Knowing that many nearby tribes didn't care much for his people, he thought it best to hide in the bush and follow her home to see if her tribe was friendly or not before approaching her.

"He followed her the whole path home, over open ground with little bush, without being seen. As he suspected, she belonged to a rival tribe. Worse still, she had a young suitor with whom he had quarreled in the past. The love he felt for this girl was strong, but he knew that very first day that she would never consent to love him back. He needed to get her another way.

"So he went out to the same spot by the river the next day and waited for her to come back. Sure enough, she did. This time, though, the Clever Man disguised himself as the girl's suitor and approached her, pretending to be him. There he tried to seduce her, but she was chaste and would not sleep with him. Then the sorcerer, much larger and stronger than the girl, took her anyway."

"Oh," said Colby, "I don't think I'm old enough for this story."

"No one is old enough for this story. It's not a very happy one."

"Okay. Go on."

"Once he was done, he left, disappearing back into the bush, leaving the girl to run home to tell her father—her village's Clever Man—what her suitor had done. But her father did not believe her, for he had spent the entire day out hunting with her suitor and knew that he could not have done this. Immediately her father knew what had happened. She had been deceived by a sorcerer, one powerful enough to mask his true identity from her.

"The Clever Man decided to set a trap for the sorcerer, telling his daughter's suitor to bring two of his closest friends to help. Then he commanded his daughter to go out to the river the next day and pick fruit again as if nothing had happened. There, he and the three young men hid in the bush, waiting for the sorcerer to reappear.

"Just as he had suspected, the sorcerer again approached his daughter, disguised as the suitor. He again tried to seduce the girl, and when she rebuked his advances, he again tried to take her. That was when the Clever Man and the three young men sprung their trap. They pounced on him, tying a rope to each arm and each leg. The three men and the daughter each held a rope, holding the sorcerer spread-eagled. Then the father took two things from the Clever Man. First he took his manhood with a knife, sealing the wound with magic to ensure that he could never take another girl again. Then he took his soul, infused it into the manhood, and fed the parts to the river crocodiles. With their vengeance complete, they left the Clever Man by the river to die a slow, agonizing three-day-long death.

"But this was no ordinary Clever Man. His will to live was great and his eye stronger than any other Clever Man alive. He knew what he had to do to survive. So he waited until nightfall and snuck into the girl's camp. First he stole the soul of the father in his sleep, mixed it with the river water from the spot where his soul had been taken, and drank it. Then he snuck into the homes of the three other men, one at a time, and stole their souls—all of which he put in his bullroarer.

"Finally he went to take the soul of the girl, but when he did, he sensed that she was not alone, but with child. His child. So he left her there to grow pregnant. Over the next three days the father and his accomplices all grew sick and died, leaving the village without a Clever Man to protect them. But the sorcerer stayed near, kept a watch on the girl, and once she was close to giving birth, he crept back into her camp at night once again. He gave her a choice: marry him and raise their child or die. She refused him one last time.

"Then he killed her, cutting his unborn son out of her belly, never to know the touch of his mother. It was the last piece of him left in the world, the last thing that bore any bit of his soul, so he carried the child away and raised him to be a powerful sorcerer just like him. The two still walk, to this day, hunting for souls to keep the sorcerer alive."

"Koorong wants to drink our souls?"

"To live, yes."

"We can't let him do that."

"No, we certainly cannot."

"And that baby. Is that his—"

"His son, Warra."

"Is he clever?"

"Very."

"What do we do now?"

"You get some sleep. There's something I have to do."

7

Koorong and Warra sat around the fire, warming themselves against the steadily dropping desert temperatures. Despite the scorching heat of the day, it was getting colder by the second, approaching near freezing. The fire Mandu had made was a good and hot one. It would serve well until dawn.

Warra curled up against a rock, head bobbing on his neck, already passing out, the day's excitement and his failing health having exhausted him. Koorong, on the other hand, never slept, having lost the ability to do so long before. He simply sat, watching his son drift off to sleep, one of the few remaining pleasures he had left in life. And as Warra finally relaxed, every muscle in his body giving itself over to the sandman, Koorong turned to the spirit peering over his shoulder.

"What makes you think I won't kill you where you stand?" he asked, his voice grumbling like the deep bass of the groaning earth.

"Because you can't," said Mandu.

"I most certainly can."

"You can kill my soul, but then you can't harvest it. And that's what this is really all about, isn't it?"

"You've disrespected your dreaming. You're taking a white-fella into Arnhem Land. Teaching him our secrets. Letting him into degrees of circles you have no right to initiate him into."

Mandu waved away the withering critique with a single hand, as if swatting away flies. "You talk. Words come out. But they mean nothing. You don't care about that. Laws and traditions mean nothing to you." The two stared at each other in silence, Mandu taking a seat on the other side of the fire. "You have no idea who the boy is or why he's here."

"I know all I need to know," said Koorong.

"The only people who say that are those who are both igno-rant of what they are talking about and too obstinate to bother changing their mind when they aren't."

"I'm not going to stop coming for you."

"I know," said Mandu. "You are no longer human enough to see reason. You know only what your instincts allow."

"Careful, Mandu, you presume much that you cannot see."

"We both do. Which is why you thought you could trust whatever spirit told you where to find me."

Koorong nodded, narrowing his gaze. Mandu knew more than he was letting on. "They've not lied to me so far."

"So far as you can tell, you mean."

"They told me you were teaching the whitefella things you ought not to be sharing."

"His name is Colby. And they didn't tell you anything about him."

"And how do you know that?"

"Because," said Mandu with the flicker of a smile, "if they

had, you'd not be so keen to be near him. I've been with him for days and I barely know what he's capable of."

"Capable?"

"Very strong eye. Dangerous, though. His are the old ways of his people. Scorched earth magic. Ruinous stuff. Takes the dream right out of the air and makes awful things with it. Given time, he will drain the world of every last drop of dreaming. But I can train that out of him."

"Given time," said Koorong ominously.

"But I don't think we have much time, do we?"

"No. We are sadly out of time, all of us. You can't scare me off with your lies."

"No lies," said Mandu. "No need for them."

"No?"

"People believe that when you find someone you can share all of your secrets with, someone you can be completely honest with, then you have found the love of your life. That just isn't true. There will always be things you have to keep from them, things you yourself are ashamed of. Things you want to keep even from yourself. No, the one person you can really trust, the one you are free to be completely honest with, is the man who hates you enough to try to kill you. That's a man who cannot judge you any worse than he does now, and whose opinion simply won't change."

"I might hate you, Mandu, but that's not why I have to kill you. One thing has nothing to do with the other."

"Run out of powerful souls?"

"Yes."

"Keep that up and you will one day be left with only your son to feed off of. And where will you be then?"

"Starving." He looked down at his sleeping son. For the first time, so did Mandu. At once Mandu saw the wound below the heart and the paleness of his flesh.

"What did you do?" asked Mandu.

"I didn't do this. Other Clever Men did."

"In retaliation for something you did."

"It doesn't matter why," said Koorong, a twinge of guilt stabbing him in the gut.

"How long does he have?"

"Quite some time. He'll live long off two souls as powerful as you and your student."

"I wouldn't count on that," said Mandu, shaking his head. "The boy has a powerful destiny."

"No destiny is written in stone. Those dreams that fill you with all your hope and dread are nothing but idle speculation of the spirits. Don't let them fill your head with more lies. Speaking of which, which version of the story are you telling these days?"

"About you?" asked Mandu.

"Yeah."

"The one that's close enough to the truth to keep people frightened, but far enough away from knowing how you do it."

Koorong grinned broadly. "Good. Good. And you've edited yourself out?"

"Of course."

"You were never that interesting a character in it, anyway."

"Not yet."

"Not ever."

"What did the spirits ask for?"

"It doesn't matter," said Koorong. "The spirits will get what the spirits want."

"Of course it matters. Spirits don't trade for nothing. You're doing their will, even when you think they are doing yours. Do they have what they want? From you?"

Koorong peered closely at Mandu. "Are you asking me if I've fulfilled my part of the bargain?"

Mandu nodded. "Too right."

"No."

"Then you have no choice."

"I don't."

"I thought as much."

"So why come?" asked Koorong.

"Truth?"

Koorong nodded hesitantly. "Of course. Why bother with a lie at this point?"

"For my conscience. I've seen this. The spirits told me my past was coming, showed me all the signs. I know what paths of destiny look like after this. This was the last choice I really get to make. Everything else from here on out, through the end of your sad, miserable life, will stem from what *you* decide to do. Tomorrow morning that little boy will wake up, he'll look out at the rising sun, and he'll ask you, 'Dad, what now?' And your answer will determine the direction of all our lives."

"You put too much stock in your dreams. I remember when I used to have them. They showed me only lies."

"Well, very soon I'll get to find out if they've treated me any better. Before this is done, it will rain terribly. Twice. It has to. For justice."

Koorong pulled out his dagger with one hand and picked up a smooth stone with the other. Then he casually, deliberately, sharpened the blade, making sure to stroke it after each slowly spoken sentence. "Have they shown you your own beating heart ripped out of your chest? Your soul being drained into a catch? My son sticking your whitefella with his wand? Carving out his femur to turn into a pointing bone? All while you both bleed out together?"

"No," said Mandu.

"Then they've lied. Get running. We'll catch up to you soon enough."

Mandu smiled, nodded, and bid Koorong adieu, his spirit vanishing, embers popping off him like the fire, turning to ash as he faded away.

Koorong stood up and stared out into the darkness. Mandu and the whitefella would be too far away now. They would keep moving, stay on the run. The clock was ticking. Two days. One day left before his son was too sick to move; two until he was gone for good.

"I told you I would help your son," said the spirit from behind him.

Koorong turned to meet his gaze. But he wasn't a dog anymore. He was a man. Copper skin, deep wrinkles, and a wide, untrustworthy grin, he was unlike any man Koorong had ever seen. "He was warned."

"Yes."

"By a spirit."

"Yes."

"By you," said Koorong accusingly.

Though it seemed impossible at the time, the spirit smiled even wider. "Yes."

"Why?"

"I told you, I'm going to help your son. You would not have taken their souls. Not there. Not like that. They needed to be scared. They needed to know what they were up against so they could go to the one place they felt strong enough to make a stand."

Koorong stared off into the distance, deep in thought, trying to work the whole thing out. Then it dawned on him. *Hammer Rock.*

8
· ·

The forest was still, dead quiet despite the life teeming through-out. No insects chirped, no cane toads croaked, everything dug well into holes and hollows. It was as if the swamps had been cleared of every living thing, the eerie calm unsettling, dream-like. Mist rose off the billabongs like a ghostly militia setting the charge, the forest beginning to take on the night's chill.

Koorong knew exactly what this meant. He was walking into a trap.

With a gesture he motioned for Warra to ease his pace and keep his footfalls silent. But in the thick mud, even as small and light as Warra was, it was nearly impossible not to snap twigs or make the occasional sucking sound of a foot being pulled from the muck.

Mandu had chosen well. He knew this land. He knew the perils of the wet season. And he had something up his sleeve that was keeping everything else in the forest from piping up. Whatever it was, Koorong preferred caution over bravado. There was no time to be foolish—one mistake and he would lose his son forever.

"They know we're coming," said Koorong.

"I know," said Warra. He coughed weakly. "We'll just have to be stronger."

Koorong nodded. Even in death, his son was stoic. If ever he needed proof that Warra was in fact his son, it was this. He placed a firm hand on Warra's shoulder and they pressed on through the forest.

They came upon a large stone plateau, rising like a giant mushroom out of the sea of mangrove trees, its faces sheer, wider at the top than at the middle, reds and browns dripping down the sides, jagged rocks climbing the western face like chiseled stone steps. It looked like an abandoned Aztec temple, overgrown and swallowed by time, overlooking a wide billabong. *Hammer Rock.*

As they drew closer, they could see the ten-thousand-year-old rock art, ancient but bright, unmolested by time. Reds, ochers, blues, blacks. Smears and stains, depictions of stick men covering it top to bottom, colors often inverted with negative space, detailing the magic aura of dreamtime with pigments, leaving the stick men colored by the rock, dotted here and there with little dabs of paint.

The fire was visible, glowing atop Hammer Rock, flickering like a giant torch rising out of the marsh. The trees around the rock danced, their shadows long, strobing in the firelight; the magic in the air the only thing thicker than the mud. This was about the worst place in the world to sneak up and steal a man's soul.

This was not to be an ambush, but an all-out brawl.

Mandu had warned him. All Koorong could do now was hope his visions were lies.

They crept closer, using the shadows of trees to mask them from the firelight for as long as possible. Warra stuck close, Koorong painfully aware of how dangerous this raid had become. They were thirty yards out from the rock, but Koorong couldn't even be sure that Mandu and the whitefella were really there. Mandu was clever enough to paint the night with an illusion; he was also clever enough to know that Koorong would expect that. Though Koorong was looking right at Mandu, there was no way of knowing which trap he might be walking into—the one in which Mandu ambushed him from hiding, or the one in which he did it from plain sight.

Mandu and the whitefella sat quietly next to the fire, neither of them moving very much at all, both of them bristling and tense. Koorong's anxiety grew. The closer he got to Hammer Rock, the more it dawned upon him that he might never step away from it; Warra might never step away from it.

This spirit who was so eager to help had set him up. And he had walked proudly into its trap, thinking himself its master all along. He'd been a fool.

But now was not the time for self-pity. Now was the time for savagery. If he was going to survive this, if Warra was going to survive this, they would have to be vicious, merciless, and cruel.

Koorong raised his arm and whipped his bullroarer around in the air, filling the night with the echoes of Hell. The very trees seemed to cower, the darkness creeping in on the fire.

"Mandu!" Koorong shouted at the rock. "I've come as I promised."

But the figures around the fire did not move.

"Mandu! Don't think I can't see through your trickery at this point!"

Still, they did not move, Mandu's eyes not even flickering at the sound of his name.

Warra looked nervously up at his father. "Dad?" he asked. "Is that them?"

Koorong looked around, then peered closer, trying to discern what trick this was. "No," said Koorong, "it's them. It has to be them. This is no illusion."

"But . . . they're not moving."

"That's because they're clever."

"Cleverer than us?"

Koorong grimaced. "That remains to seen."

Warra's hand clutched his pointing stick while his father still spun his bullroarer.

The night was none but noise and chaos. And still the figures did not move.

Koorong nodded and the two raced in, blitzing toward the fire. The bullroarer howled. The figures remained solid and unwavering until the very last second.

And then they shot to their feet, both of them leaping off the rock at once, each in a different direction.

Colby leapt into a tree, vanishing.

Mandu did the same on the other side of Hammer Rock.

At once Koorong realized what was happening. He and Warra were alone. In the dark. Surrounded by nothing but trees.

"Warra, keep your—"

A staff emerged from a tree, clobbering him midsentence, knocking him to the ground; the bullroarer falling silent, toppling with him to his side.

Warra looked up in time to see Mandu appear from out of a trunk, as if he were popping up out of a pool of water, before dunking quickly back into it. Distracted, he didn't notice Colby, who appeared and elbowed Warra in the nose, breaking it.

Colby grunted as he struck Warra, and jumped back into the nearest tree before Warra could retaliate.

Warra dropped to the ground next to his father, grabbing his nose as blood spouted from it. His eyes welled with tears, face flushed numb with pain, brain ringing. He was out of sorts with the world, completely off-balance. For a moment he forgot where he was. Then he let free the anger and rage brewing in his belly and jumped to his feet, screaming bitterly.

"Where are you, whitefella?" he bellowed. "Coward!"

"Right here," said Colby, appearing behind him, rabbit punching him in the base of the skull. "No fair fights for soul thieves." The whitefella fled again through another tree.

Warra flailed, swinging his pointing stick wildly, hitting nothing but air. "I'll kill you!"

"Nope." Colby materialized again, this time clocking Warra in the jaw.

Gone. Nothing but the night air. Night air and trees. Trees like doors. A thousand open doors.

Koorong scrambled to his feet, his hand massaging the growing knot on his skull. "Relax," he said. "Try to feel the trees. You can sense our opponents coming through. Point your stick at the tree when you do and you'll stick yourself one of them."

Warra nodded, trying not to show how terrified he was.

"Stay close to me. We have a better chance working together."

Koorong grunted, falling to his knees, struck again on the back of the head by a walking stick. Mandu winked at Warra before blending back into bark.

Warra kicked the tree with all his might, but only hurt his foot. "Which trees are they in?" he asked, his voice more frightened than angry. "We should cut them down and trap them there."

"They aren't *in* the trees," said Koorong. "There is no space inside of the tree. They're just doors, the spirits of each tree connected to the ancestors that birthed it. Mandu and the whitefella are in the forest, just like us, waiting for the right moment." He looked down at Warra with pride. "But you have the right idea." Then he smiled cruelly, began singing and stamping his feet in the mud, drawing upon the most powerful magic he knew.

The earth shook. The ground grumbled. Trees quivered. And the entire swamp filled with the sound of slowly snapping timber. The forest moaned, creaking, trunks falling away from the pair, ancient trees trying to hold firm to the ground, but failing, falling, dying in the mud. Koorong and Warra stood in the middle of a circle of uprooted timber.

"That," he said, "is the end of that."

The air of the forest was thick and heavy, but once again eerily silent.

Koorong held his hand out, palm up, swearing in an ancient tongue. Fire erupted, a sphere of burning blue dancing on his fingertips. "Mandu!" he yelled. "You don't have your trees now. Let's do this proper." He lobbed the flame into the dark, the orb lighting a small radius as it passed before detonating bright orange against a tree.

The blaze licked the bark, climbing the branches, setting the whole tree alight.

"I can play this game too," he said. "I can set your whole sacred wood on fire. Scrape the painting off the rocks. Burn the very dream out of the air."

"And it will all grow back," said Mandu, walking out into the light of the burning tree, bullroarer in one hand, walking stick in the other. "And the rocks will be repainted. And the dream will be dreamt again. But you will never again have a soul of your own. It will never grow back. You will always be an animal, feeding off the imagination of the souls you drink. But your son, he'll be spared that fate. He'll be dead by morning."

Koorong cursed again, another ball of fire appearing in the palm of his hand.

"Kill him, Dad," said Warra.

"Quiet," said Koorong softly. "Not until we know where the boy is."

"I'm over here," said Colby, flanking them from behind.

Koorong smiled wickedly over his shoulder, eyeing Colby. "Not so clever standing so far from your teacher."

"The time for cleverness is past," said Mandu. "Now is the

time for strength. And in that respect, my student is much stronger than I am."

Koorong spun, flinging the orb at Colby like a hundred-mile-an-hour fastball.

Colby held out his hand, and the orb stopped. It sizzled away, disintegrating into embers before fizzling out a few feet in front of him. He cocked his head, unimpressed.

Koorong took a step back toward his son, understanding now the folly of this raid. Fear welled within his gut, tightening his muscles, roiling into a frothing anger. His bullroarer burst into flames and he flung it about, lighting the forest around them with a hellish green glow, the sounds tortured, anguished, the swamp itself moaning with the voices of the dead.

Then the blaze loosed itself from the bullroarer, spiraling out and away, a fiery corkscrew drilling into the darkness. Koorong raised his spinning arm above his head, slowed its spin, then snapped it like a whip, cracking a fifty-foot length of flame at Mandu, scalding him across the chest, broiling his exposed flesh.

It. Was. On.

Lightning flashed and the swamp lit up, thunder grumbling with the patter of a wall of rain sweeping in. Koorong grinned, the flaming whip writhing at his side. Finally a break, a turn in the tide. There was great power to storms, and he had spent years learning how to harness it. Then he remembered what Mandu had said. *Before this is done, it will rain terribly. Twice. It has to. For justice.*

Winds gusted past, blowing the tree fire long, flames whirling like a flowing cape. At once everyone braced themselves against the gales, Koorong grabbing Warra, Mandu steadying himself with his staff. Only Colby stood unwavering, having spent so much time in the elements that he'd long ago learned how to stand against a storm. His feet became one with the earth, his center of gravity constantly shifting against the strong bursts. He stood there, showing off, acting every bit the eleven-year-old he was.

Koorong closed his eyes, reaching out to the storm, its tendrils twitching rhythmically, rippling like waves through the dream. He could feel the lightning coming, feel it building pressure within the cloud. This was the moment he was waiting for. "Warra," he said, "kill the boy."

Lightning flashed immediately overhead, bright and furious, the thunder quaking everything the instant the bolt struck home. A tree exploded with the strike, raining timber and fire in a twenty-foot radius.

Koorong ran straight for Mandu, and Warra in turn charged Colby. The lightning bought them precious seconds, blinding everyone for an instant, letting them cover the ground they needed to get in for the kill. Colby and Mandu weren't expecting the sudden charge, their eyes stinging from the rain, ears ringing from the thunder. By the time each noticed, it was too late.

Koorong pounced, teeth bared, growling, a ball of fire boiling up in his hand. He swung wildly at Mandu with his flaming whip, Mandu blocking it with his walking stick, embers and sparks exploding as the blow glanced away. Mandu darted back, sweeping his stick in front of him to keep Koorong at bay as Koorong flung another flaming sphere at him.

Mandu ducked, letting it explode against another tree behind him.

Koorong jumped again, arms out wide to grapple Mandu, flaming whip trailing.

Mandu stepped back into a tree, sinking into it, Koorong following, slamming chest first.

Koorong howled, pushing himself off the tree with both hands, then kicking it repeatedly out of frustration. "I. Will. Gut. You!" he shouted with each kick. Then he whipped it with his bullroarer, the fiery lash embracing it, setting the whole tree immediately ablaze.

Across the field his son gritted his teeth, growling low and mean, a bone wand clutched tightly in his hand. He slashed at Colby, who jumped back in time for the stick to miss him with a wide berth.

"I don't want to hurt you," said Colby.

Warra ran the point of his stick across his own tongue, slicing it. "You won't," he said. He let the blood pool in his mouth, swished it around, concentrating. The he leaned his head back, gargling incoherently through the blood. Steam billowed from his mouth and he turned, hocking a pinch of sizzling spit at Colby.

Colby ducked, the spit soaring past his cheek, hitting a fallen tree beside him instead. The gob ate through the wood, burning a hole the size of a nickel all the way through to the other side. Warra smirked at the look of horror registering on Colby's face. The boy was clever; had been taught tricks of his own. He wouldn't disrespect any longer, finally knowing what was at stake.

Now it was a fight.

The boy spit again, the battery acid wad toppling end over end. Colby slipped aside, hands up and back like he was being held up, the spit missing him by only half an inch. Warra swished more blood around in his mouth, lips puckered, eyes smiling.

Colby had had enough.

He reached out with a single hand and unleashed a pent-up reserve of kinetic energy, slamming into Warra's chest like the fist of an angry giant, lifting his feet off the ground, throwing him head over heels over head. Warra crashed to the ground, ass up, folded over like a soft taco, his toes touching the ground six inches past his head.

Warra scrambled, hurt but not injured, pawing blindly for his wand. Tears blurred his vision. He trembled, frightened— really, truly scared. No one had ever hit him like that before, not even his father. And it looked as if the whitefella wasn't even trying. His hand found the sharp end of the stick, slid his fingers up to the handle, took a deep breath, pushing the fear down into the pit of his gut like his father had taught him.

Time to use it.

Behind him, a hundred feet away, his father furiously kicked over trees, upending them, exposing their roots, dirt clods exploding around him. "Get out here!" he screamed. "Get out here and face me!"

Mandu laughed from the darkness, the sound of it echoing through woods.

Fists balled, knuckles white, Koorong screamed again. "Get out here!"

Mandu stepped out of the tree, directly behind Koorong, calm, patient, as if he'd peered into the heart of the universe, seen its collapse, and was no longer afraid. "Last chance, Koorong. This is where you get to decide your future. And what you really care about."

"You," said Koorong over his shoulder, hesitating to move, waiting for the right moment. "I care about killing you. Taking your soul. Putting everything back where it belongs."

"But you can't. Some things can never be put back together, no matter how many of the pieces you have. Even with a whole thing laid out in front of you."

"You took it. You should know better than to keep it."

Mandu shook his head sadly. "That's what you never understood. I never took anything. What you want, it isn't mine to give. You are two different creatures now. The animal and the remorseful spirit."

"I don't believe you."

"You don't have to. In fact, this all ends for the best if you don't."

Koorong spun about, swearing, cracking his whip, unleashing a gout of flame at Mandu. Mandu arched his back, the flame searing his chest from inches above him, missing the trunk of his body. He grunted, flesh blistering instantly.

Losing his balance, Mandu's legs caved beneath him, hurling him to the ground. Koorong reared back, his flaming whip dangling behind him, coiling and twisting in the wind. Mandu scuttled backward through the rain and mud, his body now spattered head to toe. Then he nodded.

"Remember," Mandu said, "that you made your choice already. You made it. No one else."

It was still raining as Warra ran his pointing stick down along the flat of his arm, carving a long, thin cut, blood pouring out, mixing with the raindrops. He flung the blood into the growing puddles, singing dark notes with broken harmonies. The water began to ripple and shift, growing, rising up off the ground, a mix of swirling blood and rainwater standing as tall and wide and willowy as a nine-year-old boy.

The waterbeast rushed Colby, its liquid hands out to strangle him, the blood rushing to the fingers—red hands on a muddy brown body.

Colby unleashed a wild blast of energy, creating giant claws out of thin air. The claws grabbed the waterbeast from both sides, dug in, ripping through the chest, and tore the thing apart. The water hung suspended for a split second, then dropped all at once as if dumped from a bucket.

It was all the time that Warra needed. As the water splashed to the ground he tackled Colby, throwing his body weight against him, crumpling him into the mud, wand pressed to his neck. Colby struggled, but Warra, despite being two years his younger, was stronger, more able. He was a feral kid living off the land, tough, as weathered as a mesa, and he held his ground, immovable.

Colby was not getting up.

"Get off me," said Colby, struggling to keep the sharpened point of the leg bone away from his neck.

Warra shook his head. "I'm gonna carve your soul out. It'll be my first."

"No! Stop!"

"Then I'm gonna carve your leg bone out of your leg and make me a bone wand with it. Your bones will point good. Lots of magic in them. Lots more than this one."

"No!" shouted Colby, the knife creeping deeper into his neck. "Please don't!"

Then Warra spoke in a deep, grumbly voice, mimicking his father. "Don't worry, it'll all be over soon."

The rain stopped. Colby could see the sky clearing over Warra's shoulder. Warra loomed over him large and unyielding. His eyes seething, his skin tight, his breath heavy and hollow, whistling through gritted teeth. He reared back, raised the dagger behind his head, and swung it down on Colby's chest.

Colby squinched his eyes tight, praying for it all to be over.

Then the world exploded.

The sound of the blast echoed for miles.

Koorong tumbled to the ground, blown over.

Mandu cowered still, covering his ears.

The whole of the forest shook and then fell silent.

Koorong jumped to his feet, looking over at Colby, who lay on his back, staring up at the sky, alone.

"Warra?" Koorong asked quietly. "WARRA?" he called louder. He looked down at Mandu. "Where is he?"

Colby crawled to his feet, staggered. "I'm sorry," he said, tears beginning to choke his words. "I didn't . . . I didn't mean to."

"Where is he?"

"I'm sorry!"

Mandu shook his head with knowing sorrow. "I told you. You made your choice."

A drop hit the ground. Then another. The soft patter of rain. Koorong looked up and saw that there were no clouds. But the drops pattered faster, now interspersed with meaty chunks, thumping lightly. Blood. The sky was raining blood.

Koorong stared down at his hands as the downpour subsided, his son's blood covering him, dripping into his cupped hands. His eyes welled up, his jaw clenched tight. "Warra?" he asked. "WARRA?"

But Warra Gaari was no more, nothing but a crimson smear across the swamp, dripping from the leaves, soaking into the grass.

Mandu climbed to one knee, also covered head to toe in blood, supporting himself on his walking stick, his chest raw and burning. "I tried to tell you. But you—"

"No!" shouted Koorong. "I'll kill you."

Koorong lunged. Then a force unlike any he'd ever felt hit him like a truck. Ribs cracked, his insides compressed, the wind was knocked out of him.

Colby shook his head, arm extended, energy receding back into his hand. "I'm sorry. But your son made me do it. Don't make me do it again."

Koorong doubled over, gasping in the dirt, and sobbed. Hate bubbled up inside, but he didn't dare release it. Colby would kill him where he stood. He knew that now. This had all been a terrible mistake. The spirit had betrayed him, sacrificed his son.

They would pay. They would all pay. But not now, not today. Today he would run. So run he did.

He jumped to his feet and vanished into the night on foot, taking with him what little of his son that he could.

Colby helped Mandu to his feet and the two exchanged troubled looks. "I didn't . . ."

"I know."

"He wouldn't stop. I tried to make him stop, but he just—"

"I know. But we can't trouble ourselves with that now. There are other things. More important things."

Tears ran down Colby's cheeks and he too began to sob. "He wouldn't stop!"

Mandu put his hands on his shoulders. "It's okay. You had to."

"But I've never killed anyone before!"

Mandu leaned in closer, his gaze incredulous. "Fella, I've heard the stories about you. I've spoken with spirits. You've killed before."

"Not people. Only bad things. Only spirits."

"People and spirits are one and the same, just different sides of the same coin."

"No," said Colby, wiping hot tears from his blood-soaked cheeks. "It's not the same. People are different."

"People are no different. That's the whole point."

Colby continued to sob, eyes closed, refusing to believe it.

"Colby, that boy, he didn't have a soul."

"What?" Colby asked, looking up.

"He was like his father. Someone had taken his soul."

"Where is it now?" he asked excitedly.

"What do you mean?"

"His soul. Where is it?"

Mandu pointed up. "He's with the campfires on the other side of the sky."

Colby smiled, wiping away the rest of his tears with a single open palm. "I know what to do," he said.

"What?"

"I know how to save him. I can bring him back."

"No, Colby. You can't bring him back."

"Yes I can! I took him apart. I can put him back together. All I need is his soul!"

Colby ran off, darting into a nearby tree. For a moment Mandu pretended to be worried, to follow Colby toward the tree, but he had no intention of chasing the boy. The spirit had shown him this too, and he knew that if he stopped this part from happening, nothing of Colby's destiny would come to pass.

9

Colby hopped from tree to tree, thinking all the while about how to die.

He knew he needed to reach the campfires on the other side of the sky, and had mostly worked out how to put a body back together for Warra's soul, but couldn't think of just how an eleven-year-old boy could reach the land of the dead and still come back. He thought about sinking a knife into his own chest, dying in the mud to cross over. But that seemed like a one-way trip. Then he thought about waking up Yashar, asking him for a third wish, a wish strong enough to get him across. But Yashar was so far away, and there was no telling whether or not he would even wake up. And then, as he stared into the deep dark of the night sky, a shooting star blazed across it. It was bright, parts of it bursting in the atmosphere, breaking up on its way to Earth, sprinkling sparkles in its wake.

It was a rock thrown from one side of the sky to the other.

Colby wondered what made him think of that. Then he remembered the story of the woman who jumped from the rock into the sky. *Remember the stories,* Mandu had said. *Remember the stories.* He thought for a moment, remembering the details of the legend. He thought of the djang he felt within the rock she leapt from. And it all came together.

"I know how to get there," he said to himself.

Then he turned and ran headlong into a tree, sinking in, emerging from another, miles away. And then he ran into another, emerging miles farther. And another. And another . . . until he was in the desert once more, running as fast as he could, racing the sunrise over cooling sands, to find the rock from which he would leap to his death, to find the campfires on the other side of the sky.

He ran faster and faster, his feet no longer touching the ground. He sought trees that stood alone, using them as bridges to their siblings dozens of miles away. And soon, before he knew it, he found himself standing before an all-too-familiar boulder.

He scaled it quickly, time working against him, and crouched low, palming the stone.

Colby could feel the djang churning deep within it. It was powerful. Immensely powerful. While the dreamstuff was thick in the air around him, there was something far more potent, refined, within the rock itself. And as he tapped into it, taking that power into him, he let go of this world, leaping into the sky with all the force of the Saturn V rocket.

And Colby Stevens crossed, for the first time, from our world into the next.

10
.....

The Deeper Dreaming

An excerpt by Dr. Thaddeus Ray, Ph.D., from his book *Dreamspeaking, Dreamwalking, and Dreamtime: The World on the Other Side of Down Under*

There are three states of being either reachable or conceivable by man. There is our world, the waking world, which is entirely made up of physical vessels, some of which contain dreamstuff. There is the world beyond the veil that some call dreamtime, which is equal parts physical and ephemeral, a world in which both dream and real can touch. And then there is the deep dreaming, a place entirely of soul and dream, where the physical has no bearing.

The deep dreaming is where all the worlds of the beyond exist. Heaven. Hell. Asgard. Yomi. Skyworld. And ten thousand others we don't have names for. Some are vast, seemingly endless realms of energy, joy, or torment. Others are small pocket worlds, the constructs of a short-lived people or a single powerful being. The dreamings most commonly discussed are the ones to which people travel after their death. These worlds lack physicality, and only a select few possess both the power and the knowledge to find their way back to their bodies, if their bodies still exist at all. But for most, it is a one-way trip, and even the most powerful spirits rarely find their way back.

I'm certain there is some rhyme or reason to their assembly and distribution, some fourth-dimensional structure that binds them together like an atom or a snowflake; we simply lack the potential to understand the intricate ways the deep dreaming comes together. Instead, it appears like a randomly moving and shifting assemblage of worlds, drifting aimlessly on an empty black sea, without so much as a center point to orbit, the smaller, forgotten worlds breaking away, drifting into nothingness.

Energy cannot be destroyed, only consumed, transformed, or redirected. All things in the beyond are made of energy, and thus all things are relatively eternal. Time holds no sway over them; only other energy. Thus belief has a profound effect on the structure of these dreamings, resulting in constantly shifting landscapes, timeflows, even consciousnesses. Most beings in these realms exist out of time, in a perpetual state of "living in the now," unaware of there being either a past or a future.

While this keeps beings from intentionally altering the world around them, it also can lead to widespread simultaneous shifts as everyone reacts to environmental changes as if they are as it always was and as it was always meant to be. Unlike the physical world, in which properties are concrete, or dreamtime, where even fluid mechanics are held in place by steady belief, punctuated only by slow change, the deeper dreaming is pure dynamism, with entire realms able to go from stasis to chaos in the course of a few brief moments.

Odds are, if you're reading this, your only trip to such a place will be after your death. However, if you somehow manage to loose your soul from your body and are offered the chance to make a trip to one of these realms, it is highly encouraged that you decline. These realms are dangerous beyond words, placing your very existence at risk every second you spend inside one. Avoid them at all costs.

11

It's always night in the land of the dead. Campfires roaring, twilight fading, hope flickering in the distance like a far-off thunderstorm in a drought. It is not a place for the living; even light and hope come here to die.

The campfires on the other side of the sky burn a cold blue, flickering like buzzing streetlamps. They give no warmth to the world, no comfort. From across the gulf between life and death, they twinkle like sterling jewels, but here, in the land of the dead, they serve only to draw in the weak like moths. Spirits swarm, too lost or confused to see the land around them for what it is, thinking the lights beacons. They mutter, tell stories, recount lives long gone, hoping for heroes to find them and lead them on to their greater rewards. Waiting for day to break.

For most, the heroes never come.

At some point Colby had stopped flying and begun falling; his guts shifted, innards wrenching and dipping as he fell. He rocketed toward one of the fires, burning cold white melancholy twenty feet high. The spirits around it stared into the glow, ignoring him as he slammed into the ground behind them. Colby stood and approached; he listened close, hearing fragments of tales, some bold and terrifying, others mundane. One woman recounted a recipe for seared fish. Another talked about her son chasing toads.

"Don't pay too much attention," said a spirit to Colby from

over his shoulder. "Listen too long and you'll spend eternity like them, muttering about lives that ended aeons ago, lost in stories about nothing in particular, all with the same ending."

Colby turned and faced the spirit: a large, pale white crocodile, low to the ground, its flesh scarred and leathery, its eyes the milky white of death. It spoke through its large flapping jaw, teeth dull and chipped. "Are you Mandu's friend?" Colby asked of the crocodile.

"Of sorts," said the croc. "I show him things. And we have a history."

"What kind of history?"

"A long and tangled one. Come, I'll tell you on the way."

"The way to where?" asked Colby.

"You came for the boy, yeah?"

"Yes! How did you know that?"

"Mandu and I have friends in common, friends who walk in both worlds."

Colby smiled. "So you'll show me where the boy is?"

"Yes, I have a pretty good idea where he's hiding. But it's a dangerous walk. We have to leave now." The croc turned, its stubby little legs awkwardly swinging its body around, tail slinging after. Then it ran, a brisk, surging bolt out into the darkness beyond the fires.

Colby followed. Moving was effortless. The air around him felt fluid, as if the world were flowing around him rather than he trying to push through it. He thought forward and he went forward.

"Only the strongest spirits can do that," said the croc.

Colby giggled slightly, overwhelmed. "I don't know how I'm doing it."

"You're changing the Skyworld around you. Be mindful,

though. Too much change and the entire world can go sideways. You can crumple the whole thing up, fold it in on itself."

"Where are we going?"

"There was once a man named Djarapa," said the croc.

"Is this going to be a story?"

"Yes."

"You guys sure tell a lot of stories."

"History is everything. A place isn't where something is. It is what happened there. It is what it means to be there. Look around you. What do you see?"

"Nothing," said Colby.

"Nothing?"

"Well, I see campfires." Colby looked up at the sky for the first time since he arrived. It was deep and black, spotted with stars. But the stars were orange and flickered more than they twinkled.

"Are those . . . ?"

"Campfires? Yes. So you know where you are?"

"Yes."

"But you can't see anything around you, yeah?"

"Yeah."

The croc stopped walking and swung its large head to look up at Colby. "That's because this is the land where the dead walk. The dead are the history. This land is their history. And you don't know it. So you can't see it for what it is. And if you remain ignorant, you never will."

Colby nodded. "Tell me the story."

"There was once a man named Djarapa," the croc said again. "Who though clever, was very lazy. There was much work to be done, but he never wanted to do it. He used to con others into doing his work, and when they got wise to his antics, he began tricking children into doing it, pretending the chores were games. Soon everyone in the village knew what Djarapa was up to, so he had to find another way to get his work done.

"One day he decided that if no one else would help him do his work, he would have to build himself someone that would. So he collected up all manner of strange stones, wood, shells, and straw, and fashioned them together into something tall and manlike. It had the trunk of a fallen tree for a body, pebbles for eyes, straw for hair, stones for teeth, and shells all over it for decoration. Then Djarapa waited, trying to lure spirits into it. But as clever as he was, no spirit would enter such an ugly thing. So he cast rituals and spells, trying to awaken the wood itself, but it would not come to life.

"After three days and nights of trickery, singing, and rituals, Djarapa grew very angry and yelled and screamed at the wooden golem to come alive. But it would not. Finally, fed up with the whole thing, he kicked the golem and swore. Then he walked away, into the bush.

"Just then he heard a great scraping coming from behind him. He turned and listened, hearing crunching and cracking and the sound of wood and stone warring with each other. Then the bushes parted and the great wooden man, Wulgaru, stepped out, chasing Djarapa. Djarapa ran as fast as he could, but no matter how fast he ran, Wulgaru kept pace. Djarapa ran for miles, growing tired from the effort. But Wulgaru, made of wood and stone and straw, never tired, and gained ground on him.

"Djarapa knew there was only one way to lose the golem. He ran to the river, making deep, noticeable tracks in the mud, leading right to the water's edge. Then he crept lightly away, leaving no tracks at all, and he hid in some bushes. Just then Wulgaru appeared, storming after the trail and plunging into the river.

"Djarapa let out a sigh of relief until a moment later when Wulgaru emerged from the other side, still searching for Djarapa, rampaging into the outback. From then on, the golem attacked and devoured anyone and everything evil it came across, but left alone those of pure heart and good intention. For hundreds of years it did this, roaming the deserts and swamps and rivers and mountains, looking for Djarapa, who was long dead.

"But over time the stones that were its teeth fell out and the straw blew away and the wood finally rotted and cracked. Then one day Wulgaru sat down on a riverbank and was no more, falling apart and crumbling into dust."

"Did it come here?" asked Colby.

"You are wise," said the croc. "It did come here. And immediately it set about devouring the evil souls around him. Those that were here saw the danger in this. Skyworld is not a place of either good or evil. It is a place for history of all kind. So the souls here banded together and dug a giant pit ten men deep. Then they lured the golem with evil souls who ran as fast as they could and leapt over the giant hole. Wulgaru chased them, falling in, unable to climb out.

"Now, whenever someone has something they need to hide, to keep out of the reach of evil men, they toss it into the hole, where Wulgaru sits and awaits its chance to devour another evil soul."

Colby nodded, keeping pace with the white crocodile. "And we're going to that pit," he said knowingly.

"Yes we are."

"Because that's where the boy's soul is hidden."

"Or at least," said the croc, "that's where it should be."

They ran as fast as they could, speeding through the hills and plains of Skyworld. The farther they pressed, the brighter and lighter it became. Soon they found themselves walking through the swamps of Arnhem Land.

"Hey," said Colby, "I'm starting to be able to see better. Why is it getting light all of a sudden?"

"I told you. It's always been light. The darkness is your ignorance of the history around you. If this place is lit, then you know where we are."

"It looks like the outback. We're near Hammer Rock."

"Yes," said the croc. "Imagine that."

"Croc, who are you?"

"Someone who learned the same lessons as you, but not the way you learned them." The croc looked around, waving with a single stubby leg. "What do you know of this place?"

They stood at the bank of a river, its water flowing slowly, trickles of blood marbling the surface.

"Nothing. Just that it's near the rock."

"That is where I was born," said the croc. "Across the river, just there. A second time. Third, maybe. Depending on how many lives you think I have."

"I don't understand."

"Once there was a young Clever Man whose tribe asked him to solve a problem. You see, I'd lived along this part of the river for a very long time and had never given his village much trouble. But one day I started acting strange, too strange for them. I had only eaten one person before then, and that had been someone who had gotten too close to my wallow. The villagers had no problem with that. They understood. It was my nature, after all. But when I started running up on land, snatching children from their huts at night, eating men hunting in the bush—well, they decided it was time to put me down.

"Animals like me aren't supposed to house powerful spirits.

We're not supposed to be that cunning. But I was, so they assumed I must have been possessed, taken by an evil spirit."

"Were you?" asked Colby, peering across the river to the croc's birthplace.

The croc nodded. "It was the thing I'd eaten. A man's soul infused in a piece of meat."

"A soul infused in . . ." At once Colby understood. "You . . . you're Koorong."

The croc nodded its large, bulbous head, smiling with a wicked row of chipped teeth. "I am the Koorong who loved a girl and made a terrible mistake, the Koorong who was justly punished. I am the Koorong who awakened a crocodile that hunted the waters of Mandu's village. I am the Koorong that sired the boy you murdered and came to find."

"Warra," said Colby. "I didn't mean to—"

"Doesn't matter what you meant," interrupted the croc. "All that matters here is what you did. He's dead."

"Are you taking care of him now?"

"He doesn't know I'm his dad."

"Why not?"

The croc looked up sadly at Colby. "Because he thinks the soulless shell I left behind is his father. And in a way, he's right. More of a dad than I could be. But that's also how he ended up here so soon. The dad he's waiting for will never show up. He doesn't exist over here. He's meat. Instinct. Living hate running on an engine that cannot be sustained. Nothing more."

"What does that make you?" asked Colby.

"The Koorong that is trying to set things right."

"How did you die?"

"The young Clever Man. He tracked me to my lair, found where I was fermenting my kills. He covered himself in muck and guts and waited for me to return. He lay in wait, watched as I devoured the corpse of his friend, let me fill my belly until I was slow and sleepy. Then he pounced, driving a spear right into my skull. He carved me up, took me home, but first ate a piece of me raw. Claimed my soul right there. From then on, I was bound to him."

"So you've been haunting Mandu?"

"Helping him set this right. Preparing him for the role he is to play in your life."

"My life?" asked Colby. "What does this have to do with me?"

"Everything," it said. "You share a powerful friend in common. Come on, we still have a way to go."

12
....

Moments later they stood along a ridge overlooking a dark valley pockmarked with fires. In the center of it was a towering gray-green flint plateau, from which lightning bolts shot into the sky, exploding among the flickering orange stars above. Thunder cracked and echoed through the valley, a steady rumbling shaking it from one side to the other.

"What is that?" asked Colby over the dull roar.

"That's where we have to stop to ask directions."

"Directions? I thought you knew where you were going."

"I do," said the croc, speaking louder over thunder. "I've just never been there."

"Why not?"

"Because Wulgaru eats the souls of the evil."

"Yeah, but you're not evil," said Colby.

The croc looked up at him, speechless. Colby opened his mouth to speak again, but closed it as understanding set in. It hadn't dawned on him that Wulgaru might try to eat Koorong, but then again, he hadn't known this was Koorong when he first had heard of it. But then an even more terrible thought occurred to him.

"Croc?" asked Colby. "Is Wulgaru going to try and eat me?"

"Why would he try to eat you?"

"Because I murdered a boy."

"That's a good question. We'll see," said the croc. "We'll see. Come. There's someone you should meet."

Atop the plateau stood two men. Their soot-black skin was charred and crispy, painted head to toe in long unbroken chalky lines. One man's skin was painted entirely in white, the other's in ocher. Both wore enormous feather headdresses and nothing else. And in their hands they wielded mighty hammers, the hafts the length of a grown man, the heads the size of their torsos. They swung their hammers down on the flint in alternating blows, sparking massive bolts of lightning that flew up and away, into the sky.

"These," said Croc, "are the Lightning Brothers." He pointed to the one in red. "This one is Yagjabula. And that is his younger brother Yabiringi."

"Are they making lightning?"

"Yes," said Yabiringi, interjecting, his eyes still on his hammer. "For the storms back home."

"Why?" asked Colby.

"Because someone has to. Why not us?"

"Everyone needs a purpose," said Yagjabula. "Back home we had a different purpose. Here we do much more good."

"Lightning isn't good," said Colby. "It's dangerous."

Yagjabula shook his head and swung his hammer. Thunder left the plateau shuddering. "All things have a purpose. Even the things that seem bad at first. Even you."

Colby narrowed his eyes, grimacing. "I'm not bad."

"You're a murderer," said Yabiringi. "Like my brother." The earth quaked from another hammer swing.

"You should have kept your hands off my wife," said Yagjabula. "She was *my* wife."

"But I saw her first. And she was beautiful."

"But she *married* me."

THUNDER.

"Only because you were older," said Yabiringi.

"And better looking."

"So you're a murderer *and* a liar."

"Keep it up. I'll take your head off again."

THUNDER.

"You wouldn't. You have work to do."

"I'll do it on break. Swing so hard your head will pop off."

THUNDER.

"Sorry to interrupt," said the croc. "But we need directions."

"To where?" asked Yagjabula.

"Wulgaru."

"Oh," said Yabiringi, "you don't want to go there. He'll eat you both."

"He will not," said Yagjabula.

"He will too. Can't you see the evil on them? Look at the whitefella's hands. They're both murderers."

Colby looked down at his hands. Bloodstains running almost to his elbow. He felt nauseated, guilty.

"But they're remorseful. You can tell by their eyes."

"Wulgaru only looks at your hands, not your eyes. And remorse doesn't keep you from being evil."

"It most certainly does. That's the definition."

Yabiringi put his hammer down for a second, propping himself up on the haft. "You're only saying that because you think feeling bad about killing me makes you less of a bad guy."

Yagjabula smiled and swung his hammer, the flint cracking loudly, the bolt splintering eighty different ways in the sky. "Who said I felt bad?"

"You feel terrible."

"I don't think that I do."

"You're a bastard."

"I mean, it was *my* wife."

"I hate you."

"And you had it coming."

"You can shut up now."

"It felt so good taking your head clean off like that in one swing. Just *POP*—and it was off."

"Shut up."

"Kicked it around a little. Made a game of it."

"You can stop," said Yabiringi. "I get it."

"Didn't feel bad at all."

"But now you feel terrible."

"Not so much."

"But this kid feels awful."

"He looks it. I don't think Wulgaru's gonna eat him."

"I think he will."

Yagjabula stopped swinging and smiled at his brother. "Fancy a wager, yeah?"

"Yeah, that sounds good. A proper wager."

"What do we bet?"

"Loser has to swing twice as much for a whole day so the other can drink."

"That sounds fair. I'm going to get proper drunk."

"Don't count your drink yet. We haven't even told him where to find it. He might chicken out and change his mind."

"The bet's off if he's a coward."

"Oh yeah, the bet's off if he is."

"Although," said Yagjabula, "whether or not he's too scared to go in would make for an interesting side wager."

"Oooh, it would."

"Fancy a side wager?"

Yabiringi smiled and nodded, his headdress bobbing on his head. "I do fancy a side wager."

"Then it's agreed?"

"Agreed."

The two swung their hammers at the same time, sealing their bet with a sky full of lightning and a low-magnitude earthquake.

"We'll tell you where he is," said Yagjabula. "But you gotta promise not to chicken out."

"Oy! Not fair. No cheating on the wager."

"We didn't agree to that."

"That's it! Bet's off!"

"I will take your head off again, I swear."

"Do it! Give me an excuse to hit you back."

The two began swinging again, lightning flashing upward, the sound near deafening.

"Where's the pit?" asked Colby.

"What?" asked the two, simultaneously lowering their hammers.

"The pit. Wulgaru. Where is it?"

Yagjabula smiled broadly, his teeth a bright white against the ocher paint and charred black of his skin. "Just follow your fear. You'll feel it try to keep you away from the valley he's in. Fight it. Go in. And you'll find it easy enough. Just look out at the horizon and walk the way you're most scared to go." He swung his hammer again. The plateau lit up brighter than ever, resounded with thunder louder than ever. The storm they were feeding was brewing stronger.

"Thank you," said Croc.

"Anytime," said the brothers in unison.

Colby looked out and scanned the horizon, unsure of what to think, and then felt his gut sink like he'd eaten a lead sandwich. His throat tightened and he began to sweat. That was it, out to the west. The darkest valley, the one with no fires of its own. That was where he felt the fear.

"Why aren't there any fires?" asked Colby, climbing down the face of the plateau.

The croc followed swiftly after, scaling down the rock with a fretful scurry. "Because no one is there to light a fire."

"Why not?"

"That's where we keep the things we fear most. Few people go there. Even fewer return. Those that do, come back changed. Sometimes for the better, sometimes not. The rest learn first-hand why we fear it."

"Have you ever been in there?"

"No," said the croc. "And I never will."

Colby at once was very scared. "You're not going with me?"

"I can't risk not coming back. There are things in that valley that have no tolerance for things like me. My sins are too great and I still have to absolve myself of them. So I'll stay here."

"But what about me?"

"You?" asked the croc. "Anything out there that isn't more afraid of you than you are of them deserves what they get."

Colby shook his head. "I don't go places alone. Not yet. I'm not old enough. Please?"

"No one is old enough to go into the valley alone. But you've actually got an advantage."

"What is that?"

"You're not old enough to know all the things you should fear. Now go. Warra doesn't have much time."

"What do you mean, he doesn't have much time?"

"Do you know how Warra's soul came to be here?"

"Someone stole it."

"Right," said Croc. "In revenge for a friend Warra murdered. The spirit that told the Clever Men where to find Warra traded them the information in exchange for Warra's spirit, which the spirit brought here. And left near Wulgaru."

"Why did he do that?"

"The spirit has its reasons."

"But if Warra murdered someone . . ." Colby trailed off, putting it together. "Wulgaru is going to eat him."

"He very well might, if he hasn't already."

Colby took a deep breath, clenched his fists, and nodded stoically. "Thanks, Koorong," he said. "I hope you can make things right." He took a step toward the fear, his gut tightening. Colby closed his eyes, took one last deep breath, and propelled himself forward, moving the very darkness around him.

13
....

Colby ran, the sound of thunder fading, its whine trailing behind him into the never-ending night. The darkness grew blacker, deeper, lonelier, like a second death. Here the winds became stronger, howling across the desolate nothing. Dust kicked up, turbulent little desert devils called willy-willies moaning past him—none caring enough to stop to pick a fight. And as he pressed farther he found that this fear wasn't so much deadly as it was empty. Hollow. Unpopulated.

He began to believe that there was nothing worth fearing in this valley at all. And yet, that didn't help.

He pressed on again toward the fear, the foreboding dread now a crippling weight on his back. It became harder and harder to focus, each step met with doubt. His mind fought against him, throwing what-if after what-if his way. But he held strong, refused to give in. Made every step measured, valiant.

At last he could see it. The hole must have been a mile wide, dug deep, its sides too steep to climb. And just on the edge stood a familiar shadow as still as a stone.

Warra. His dark skin was now colored a pale bluish-white, the life and the sun drained from his very being. Scars ran over every inch of his body, as if he were a jigsaw puzzle that had been hastily put back together. His eyes were black orbs, his teeth stained with plum sauce, pulp dug deep in the recesses. "Why are you following me?" he asked. "Stop following me."

"I came looking for you," said Colby. "To bring you back."

"Who are you?"

"A friend of your father's."

"My father has no friends."

"He does. You just don't know it."

"I don't want to go back. That body isn't mine anymore. That life isn't mine anymore."

Colby shook his head. "There isn't a body. I'll make you a new one."

"Why isn't there a body?"

Colby swallowed hard. He didn't know quite how to say this. "I didn't have a choice."

"A choice about what?" Warra looked at him suspiciously. Then it dawned on him. He reached instinctively for his bone wand, but it was gone, still in the land of the living.

"It wasn't my fault."

"Of course it was your fault," said Warra, his voice raspy, reverberating, out of sync with his own mouth. "You killed me."

"The thing you left behind, your body, it was trying to kill me. I didn't have a choice."

"Yes, you did. You could have let me kill you."

"That was not an option."

"Yes it was," said Warra, sneering a little. "You just didn't like it. Be a man. Accept what you did."

Colby swallowed hard. "Can you forgive me?" he asked, eyes downcast.

"Get rooted. You'll have to forgive yourself, because I sure won't."

Nodding, Colby looked at Warra. "Please, I have to make this right. I have to take you back. Come with me."

"Why should I?"

"Because I can't let you die again."

"Well, since you asked nicely." Warra stepped to the side.

"Thank you." Colby took a step forward.

Warra stepped backward and went over the side, plummeting into the pit.

"No!" screamed Colby. He looked down into the abyss, a tumultuous sea of black filled with uncertainty and a history Colby didn't fully understand. Colby steadied himself, took a deep breath, and jumped in after Warra.

The fall was quick and painful, the drop slamming him through an accumulation of junk. He hit the ground with a hard, dull thud, the force dazing him. Colby hopped to his feet, bolting through a narrow alleyway flanked on both sides by piles of refuse, looking for the boy he'd murdered.

Around him were the discarded dreams, wishes, nightmares, and relics of thousands of souls. Items of power and importance, tokens of sentimentality. The pit was a thrift store of found treasures, tossed away to be kept out of the wrong hands. Towers sprung from walls, tenuously stacked, precariously placed, teetering in the wind.

Colby slammed his fist hard against a stone wall and it

burst like a flare, lighting the area enough to see. He scanned the walls as he ran, looking for Warra. There were swords and stopwatches, stuffed bears and headdresses. Spears. Boomerangs. Vases, baskets, and kangaroo bags. Knickknacks with a thousand different purposes. But not a soul to be seen.

Then there came a deep, grating grumble, followed by a terrible, hollow rumble, and the sound of stone scraping against wood. Heavy, dense footfalls thumped the earth, echoing through ramshackle halls. Wulgaru had awoken. And he was headed Colby's way.

Colby turned and heard Warra scrambling through the pit. He had little time left. He needed to find the boy.

Colby closed his eyes, reached out into the tendrils of energy around him, tickling the webs, trying to find something that vibrated the same way a soul did.

Something clamored behind him, knocking over a stack of miscellany. Colby ignored it, reaching out farther, scanning the whole of the pit now. Footfalls, light but swift. Warra. He reached out farther still, up the stacks. And there he was.

But it had taken too long to find him.

Colby braced himself for the hit.

Warra charged, hunched over, throwing a stiff shoulder into the small of Colby's back as he grasped his waist with both arms. Both went facedown into the dirt.

The screech of stone grinding against stone was getting louder. Wulgaru was coming. Seconds away.

"Warra! Get off! Get off or we're done for!"

Warra responded by punching Colby in the back of the head with his fist, pounding his face deeper into the dirt. Colby bucked but couldn't shake the boy off.

"Warra!" he screamed.

"You're done for now, fella." Warra stood, put out a stern

elbow, clenching it tight, ready to drop it dead center into Colby's back. He let his legs go limp, dropping, the sound of stone and splintering wood suddenly overwhelming behind him.

A large hand held him in midair several feet above the ground. Warra stared and saw the massive golem, eight feet tall, solid wood trunk for a torso. It gnashed its stone teeth, held its gaping maw as wide as it could, hoisting a struggling Warra into the air.

Colby scrambled to his feet and ran off down the cobbled-together corridor between the walls of junk.

Warra sneered at Wulgaru, the golem snapping its teeth together, flint sparking. "Do it," said Warra. "If you're gonna do it, just do it."

Wulgaru crammed him into its mouth, the teeth shredding the boy's soul as it did. Warra screamed—a blood-curdling wail punctuated with sobs—but it didn't last long. First the golem chewed off his legs, snapping bones, tearing flesh. Then in quick succession Wulgaru finished off the rest, bit by bit.

Colby rounded a pile of trash, pulling down pieces of junk to scatter in his wake.

But the sound of stone grinding against wood continued to follow him. Colby looked down at his hands, still stained as red as before. He crouched low to the ground, summoning all the belief and might he could into his knees.

Wulgaru appeared, plowing through stray objects, flint teeth chattering, sparkling in the dark like a windup toy monster. It stepped forward, pawing at Colby, preparing to grab him, to swallow him whole.

Colby sighed deeply, guilt weighing heavy on his heart.

Wulgaru stared down at him, giant palms hovering over him.

Then it turned around and wandered back the way it had come, looking for other souls to devour.

Wulgaru had judged him.

He was no murderer.

Colby sat on the ground, thunderstruck, crying. He'd failed. Warra was gone, gone for good now. But he'd tried to save him, tried to make things right. There was nothing left for him to do here—no child to return to his body, no family to reunite. It was time to go home.

Colby sprung into the air with a force even greater than before, rocketing out of the pit and into the sky. Below him were thousands of campfires, flickering, lonely, beckoning him to stay.

But this wasn't his time.

So Colby Stevens continued to soar toward the earth, away from the cold grip of death, the air buzzing louder with the tingle of life the closer he got to the world of the living.

14

Colby landed squarely atop the rock from which he'd first launched himself, to find Mandu sitting beneath it by a fire, waiting for him. Mandu smiled.

"It's about time," he said.

"Oh, quit it. I was gone maybe an hour."

Mandu grimaced. "You were gone for two months. I would have given you up for dead if not for the visions I had of you in my dreams."

"No, that wasn't . . ." He thought back on his many lessons, remembered what it was like to be in Fairy Time. And he knew that Mandu's words were true. Colby Stevens had been dead and gone for two months and had only now returned.

"Did you find him?"

"Yes," said Colby sadly, hopping off the rock.

"And?"

"He wouldn't come back."

"Understandable."

"And he tried to kill me."

"Oh."

"And Wulgaru ate him."

"I see."

"It's all my fault."

"No, it isn't," said Mandu. "That child was evil. Pure evil. He was born of evil. He was raised by evil."

"Then why did you let me go?"

"Let you?" said Mandu, cocking a curious eyebrow.

"You could have stopped me."

"If there's anything I've learned, it is that there is no stopping the destiny of Colby Stevens."

"Well then, why did I go?"

"That boy was born of evil. He was destined for it. But he was never given the chance to choose it for himself. His father, Koorong, wanted him to have a chance at redemption. He made a pact with a powerful spirit. That spirit arranged for you to give him that chance."

"So some spirit used me?"

"Of course it did, Colby. And it won't be the last time it happens either."

Colby sat on the ground, defeated, frustrated, feeling used.

"Don't worry," said Mandu. "It was also a powerful lesson."

"Yeah? How?"

"Did you meet Wulgaru?"

Colby looked up. He nodded. "I did."

"And were you judged?"

"I was."

"And are you still here?"

Colby stared up at Mandu. He thought for a second. "I need to learn more songlines."

"Why?"

"It was all dark up there. I didn't know the history. I need to learn. I need to hear all of the stories."

"I know some stories."

"I know," said Colby. "And I'd like you to tell them to me."

15
....

Koorong stood in the desert of the outback, screaming into wasteland. "Spirit, show yourself!"

There was no answer.

"Damn you, spirit! You promised!"

"I promised to help your son," said the spirit from behind him. "And I did."

"You did no such thing!"

"I did. I sent you a dreamhero. You thought I was giving you souls, but I was doing you one better. I sent a dreamhero to bring your son's soul back."

"Well, where is he?"

"I said I would help your son, not save him. I gave him the chance to save himself. But he did not want to be saved. He did not want to come back. I cannot help those who do not want my help."

"You deadly bastard. You rooted me."

"I gave you what you asked for. I fulfilled my end of the deal. Now it's your turn."

Koorong shook his head. "No, you failed me."

"*You* failed you. I sent Mandu to warn you and you did not heed him. I gave you every opportunity to make things right.

Now you owe me two services or what little there is left to you is mine." The spirit grinned viciously.

"What do you ask of me?"

"Only two things. One, you are not to step into Arnhem Land for a hundred and eight moons. Not to collect your possessions, not to chase down a soul. You are exiled until then."

"And the second?"

"No harm may come to Mandu Merijedi until your exile is ended."

"That's it? That's all you ask of me?"

"I think it is more than fair a trade."

Koorong nodded. "When my service is done, we'll have business again, spirit."

"Please," said the spirit, "call me Coyote."

16
....

NOW

Colby and Jirra stared at each other across beers. Then Jirra told his story.

"Mandu came to me one afternoon, just as a storm was brewing. Handed me a mason jar filled with dirt. Told me to dig a hole behind the house and bury it before the rains came. He looked sick. His eyes were heavy and weak. His hair had almost overnight gone completely white. He walked with a hunch and the color was draining from his skin. I said, 'Are you okay, fella?' He smiled at me, shook his head weakly, and said, 'It is my time. Go, bury the jar. Don't forget where. I'll explain later.'

"So I did. I came back and that's when he told me I was the new Clever Man now, and that you would turn up one day asking about him. He said I could tell you anything up until that point right there, but anything after that would have to wait until you came back. And here you are."

The two looked at each other over the old cheap table, Jirra absentmindedly picking at the chipped lacquer.

"So," said Colby, "are you going to tell me?"

Jirra shook his head. "Follow me. This part I have to sing."

JIRRA AND COLBY STOOD ATOP THE HILL WHERE MANDU WAS buried, the stones still perfectly outlining the grave. Colby walked over to the ornately carved tree trunk that served as a headstone and began recognizing even more stories than before. He saw the jar. He recognized Koorong and the Kutji. And he saw himself, standing with Jirra.

Then he took a long swig from his beer. It was all coming together.

And that's when Jirra began to sing.

17
....

THEN—108 MOONS LATER

It was past midnight and Mandu Merijedi sat in the rain before a tree stump, carving the last of his visions into the wood. Thunder cracked, roaring through the land, a torrential monsoon kicking into full gear. Dark clouds rolled above, blacking out the sky, belching torrents of rain. He looked around, saw that all the dirt had turned to mud beneath widening puddles, and smiled.

Lightning struck close, lighting the land a bright purple noon. And that's when Mandu saw him standing on the hill, fifteen feet away, soaked to the bone—Koorong Gaari. Koorong stood tall, angry, growling, pointing stick in his hand.

"Mandu Merijedi!" he shouted over the downpour. "It's time."

Mandu nodded, still smiling. "Yes," he yelled back. "But perhaps you should come closer so we don't have to yell so loud."

Koorong shook his head. "Under the circumstances, I don't think that's wise."

"That hardly seems fair, *especially* under the circumstances." Then Mandu patted the ground beside him, offering a seat to Koorong. Koorong shook his head, declining. Mandu continued. "You're here about your son. Do I have time for one more story?"

"I don't think so," said Koorong bitterly.

"I'll tell it anyway. It's a short one. Crocodile was far from home and dying of both hunger and thirst. He wanted to eat Tortoise, but Tortoise was very clever. 'Tortoise,' said Crocodile, 'I'm very thirsty.' 'Drink this water,' said Tortoise. 'It is good enough for me, it will be good enough for you.' But Crocodile said, 'No, I don't like salt water. I drink only freshwater.' 'So dig a well,' said Tortoise, not wanting to hear Crocodile's whining."

"I know this story," said Koorong, walking toward Mandu. "This is the one where Crocodile digs a hole and Tortoise convinces Bandicoot to hide in it."

Mandu nodded, pointing a wise finger at Koorong. "And hungry Crocodile grabbed onto Bandicoot's tail and wouldn't let go. Tortoise told him that if he didn't let go, he would die. But Crocodile was so hungry that he couldn't bring himself to give up the meal."

"Yes, yes, yes. And Crocodile died, Bandicoot's tail still in his hand."

"You're very thirsty, Koorong. Very hungry. Perhaps you should dig a hole." He patted the ground once more, offering a seat. "Come, you look tired."

Koorong leapt, slamming Mandu's back into the mud. Pin-ning him to the ground. Jamming his dagger in between Mandu's ribs, just beneath the heart. There he cut a perfect semicircle, blood spurting into Koorong's wrist basket. But there was no soul. Only black, sickly blood.

Mandu still smiled, big and broad, ever the cat that ate the canary, thick drops of rain spattering across his face. "Looking for something?" he asked with a musical lilt.

Koorong flew into a rage, pounding the mud with his fist, shouting. "Where is it? Where the fuck is it? Your soul? Where?"

"Oh, that? I put that in a jar this morning."

Koorong punched Mandu hard across the jaw, failing once more to remove the smile. "Where's the jar?"

"I had my student bury it in the backyard this afternoon. I'm sure if you look, you might find it. It's somewhere around here. Though with all the rain, it might be hard to see any signs of digging. You could always ask my student, but he's on walkabout. By the time you find him, well—how much time do you have before you need to drink another soul? A day? Two? You spent a lot of spirit getting here. And there are so few Clever Men in Arnhem Land this season. You haven't had a soul in weeks, have you? You were waiting for mine."

"I will take a soul from here."

Mandu nodded. "Oh, good idea. But the whole town went on walkabout to visit relatives. I stayed behind. Too tired to walk without a soul. It really isn't very pleasant. I don't know how you do it. Will you stay here? Grasping Bandicoot's tail?"

Koorong reared back and punched Mandu, breaking his nose. Then he punched him again, knocking out his front teeth. And again. And again. And again.

And still Mandu kept smiling, blood pouring back into his throat.

"Stop smiling! Why are you still smiling?"

"Because I've seen how this ends. All of it. I die here. You die in the bush looking for a soul. Both of us dead before it stops raining." Mandu stared up into the storm. "Not much longer now."

Koorong gritted his teeth and drove the pointing stick deep into Mandu's heart, their foreheads pressed together, Koorong watching as the light faded from Mandu's eyes.

"I hope you haven't put much stock in seeing your son in the afterlife," said Mandu, rasping, wheezing his last few breaths, staring unblinking back into Koorong's eyes. "First of all, without a soul, you don't get one. Second, your son isn't there. Colby. He killed him twice."

Koorong pulled out the dagger and stabbed him again. And again. And again.

And with that, Mandu Merijedi was gone.

Then, with Mandu finally dead, Koorong rose to his feet, swearing loudly, and wandered off into the rain, searching for a soul he would never find.

18
....

NOW

"So where was it?" asked Colby.

"What?"

"The jar? Where did you bury it?"

Jirra looked at the ground, in both sadness and wonder. "I didn't want to dig up the backyard, so I buried it up here—figured that it wouldn't be that big a deal. I mean, I didn't know what was in it. Mandu was sitting next to it the whole time, patting it each time he taunted Koorong."

Colby smiled weakly at Mandu's final joke. "So you buried him with the jar?"

"In the dirt with his soul."

"Together again." Colby looked off into the distance wistfully.

"Colby, Mandu never told a story that didn't have a second, secret meaning. Whether warning or prophecy."

"You think I'm Bandicoot," Colby said, nodding.

"Let's say 'hoping' and leave it at that."

"So I did kill him, in a way."

"Yeah, bru. You did. *In a way*. But in a way, that deadly bastard is still here, still working his way through our lives. It'll be decades before his story has run its course."

"I guess it's up to us now to finish Mandu's story."

"It is," said Jirra. "But we better make it a good one, okay? You know how he always loved a good story."

glossary

ARNHEM LAND: A region in the Northern Territory of Australia populated almost entirely by Aboriginal peoples.

BULLROARER: An ancient ritual musical instrument and a device historically used for communicating over vast distances. It is a wood slat at the end of a cord, spun over the head to create a loud whistling sound.

DJANG: The energy of a place that can be used to connect with the powers of a place.

DREAMSTUFF: The raw energy of creation that is around us at all times. All spirit and magic is formed by manipulating it.

FAIRY TIME: A realm beyond our own, inhabited by spirits and fairies, in which time flows erratically, sometimes faster, sometimes slower than our own world.

KUTJI: Australian shadow spirits formed from the souls of the dead who have not yet fulfilled their life's desires.

ROOTED: (*slang*) Fucked.

STRONG/STRONGEST EYE: Powerful/most powerful magic. Used to describe an Aboriginal magician.

YASHAR: A Djinn bound to Colby by a wish. During this part of Colby's story, he is deep asleep and has left him with Mandu for safekeeping and training.

about the author

···

C. Robert Cargill is the author of *Sea of Rust*, *Dreams and Shadows*, and *Queen of the Dark Things*. He has written for *Ain't It Cool News* for nearly a decade under the pseudonym Massawyrm, served as a staff writer for Film.com and Hollywood.com, and appeared as the animated character Carlyle on Spill.com. He is the screenwriter of Marvel's *Doctor Strange*, starring Benedict Cumberbatch, and cowriter of the horror films *Sinister* and *Sinister 2*. He lives with his wife in Austin, Texas.